THE Counterfeit BILLIONAIRE

SCANDALS OF THE BAD BOY BILLIONAIRES

IVY LAYNE

GINGER QUILL PRESS, LLC

The Counterfeit Billionaire

This book is a work of fiction. Names, characters, places, and incidents either are products of the author's imagination or are used fictitiously. Any resemblance to actual persons, living or dead, events, or locales is entirely coincidental.

Cover by Jacqueline Sweet

Find out more about the author and upcoming books online at www.ivylayne.com

CONTENTS

THE UNTANGLED SERIES

Unraveled (October 2018)

Undone (Winter 2019)

Uncovered (Spring 2019)

SCANDALS OF THE BAD BOY BILLIONAIRES

The Billionaire's Secret Heart (Novella)

The Billionaire's Secret Love (Novella)

The Billionaire's Pet

The Billionaire's Promise

The Rebel Billionaire

The Billionaire's Secret Kiss (Novella)

The Billionaire's Angel

Engaging the Billionaire

Compromising the Billionaire

The Counterfeit Billionaire

Series Extras: ivylayne.com/extras

THE ALPHA BILLIONAIRE CLUB

The Wedding Rescue

The Courtship Maneuver

The Temptation Trap

ABOUT

THE COUNTERFEIT BILLIONAIRE

CHASE

I've been on my own since my parents kicked me out. I
made my first million at twenty and never looked back.
Then I found out I was the long, lost son of the wealthy and
powerful Winters family.
Their name means fame, fortune, power.
F**k that.
Blood doesn't make a bond
The Winters might be glad they've found me, but they need
to understand one thing:
I was never lost.
Until now.
When a mix-up leaves me homeless, I find myself living in
Winters House.
It's too close. Too much. Too in my face.
The little café down the street is the perfect escape.
Perfect coffee. Amazing brownies.
And Annabelle.

She has a smile like sunlight, enough energy to fuel an army, and I can't get her out of my head.

I want everything from her.

Her heart.

Her body.

My life is upside down, and Annabelle is the only thing that makes sense.

ANNABELLE

My divorce shattered my bank account and my confidence in equal measure.

But my café is thriving and I've almost saved enough to buy my own place.

I finally have my life on track.

The last thing I need is a distraction.

Especially one as gorgeous, confident, and charming as Chase Westbrook.

I know men like him. They're sweet and seductive, right up until they rip out your heart.

Our flirtation started off innocent enough, but as each day passes I'm afraid I'll do the one thing I know will destroy me.

Fall in love with Chase.

CHAPTER ONE

CHASE

„**W**e have a problem."

We have a problem. Those were the last words I wanted to hear from Charlie Winters.

I didn't need a problem. I already had enough of those as it was.

I leaned back in my chair, crossing my arms over my chest. "What kind of problem?"

I didn't have to ask. There were only a few possibilities.

It could be about the family. This was the least likely. Charlie is my half-siblings' cousin, and while that made us sort-of related, Charlie was never the chosen emissary of family news. She left that to her older brother Aiden.

It could have to do with my sister, Violet, who was dating Aiden and, if my guess was right, would be his fiancée any day now.

I know what you're thinking, but my sister dating my half-siblings' cousin isn't as weird as it sounds.

Okay, it *is* as weird as it sounds.

Maybe I should explain.

Here's the short version: Violet and I grew up not knowing we'd been adopted. The Winters grew up not knowing one of their own had been given up for adoption as an infant.

I'd discovered the truth at eighteen, but I told no one, not even Violet.

You're probably thinking that's weird, too. Why didn't I go straight to the Winters and claim my birthright? They're disgustingly rich, obscenely powerful, and a piece of that should have been mine.

I didn't want it.

I have my reasons. And I've made my way pretty damn well without their influence.

But now, because I'd been careless, the Winters had discovered me and Violet had fallen in love with the head of the entire clan, Aiden Winters.

So here I was, smack in the middle of the family I'd been avoiding since I'd discovered they existed. And now Charlie Winters had a problem.

I fought the urge to sigh.

Charlie is a spitfire. Younger than me, she's the princess of the Winters clan, a workaholic vice president at Winters, Inc. until Aiden fired her.

Once she'd gotten past her anger, she'd realized she hated working for the company and had gone into business renovating houses with her husband Lucas.

Which brought us to option number three. The problem was my house. I did not want the problem to be my house.

I hadn't meant to buy a house.

I definitely hadn't meant to buy a ramshackle pseudo-Victorian cottage in the Virginia Highlands neighborhood of Atlanta. I had a perfectly nice condo in Midtown, thank you very much.

But I liked to hang out with Charlie's husband Lucas, who worked with her on their renovations when he wasn't running his division of scary hackers at Sinclair Security.

I'd taken to stopping by their latest project and chipping in when I was tired of staring at a computer screen. I'm a coder and a serial start-up addict. I can fall into my laptop for hours on end, but when I surface, I like to get my hands dirty.

Lucas and Charlie were always glad for the help. One afternoon in early July I'd gone along with Lucas to see a foreclosure.

Mistake.

I never thought the first time I fell in love it would be with a house. I'd wanted it. I'd needed it. It was made for me. Well, except for the part where it was falling down around our ears.

But I'd loved the tiny lot, walking distance to Highland Avenue and shaded with old growth trees. I'd loved the peaked gables of the roof and the detached garage with a studio above that would make the perfect home office.

I'd been instantly at home in the wide-open kitchen, bathed from the light streaming in through the tall windows.

The idea of owning it had gone straight to my head. Before I knew it, I was buying the place, hiring Charlie and Lucas to fix it up, and putting my condo on the market.

I did not have time for a problem. The condo was in a hot location and I'd sold it for above my asking price after an insane bidding war. We closed in two weeks.

The plumbing fixtures were supposed to be installed in the studio today, and Violet and I planned to camp out there until the woodwork and other finish carpentry was done in the main house.

Our bags were packed, stacks of boxes waiting for the moving van. A problem was not on the schedule.

Charlie tucked one of her auburn curls behind her ear and gave me the same grin she used on Aiden when she wanted to get out of trouble. I didn't envy him raising this one.

I liked Charlie. She was fun, a smart-ass, and one of my favorite Winters. According to her brothers, she'd also been a handful as a teenager.

At least my Vivi had been a sweetheart. She didn't start giving me older brother heart attacks until...well, right about the time she met Aiden Winters.

"Don't try the cute grin on me, Charlie. Just don't tell me it's the house."

Charlie's grin dissolved, and she adjusted the papers on her clipboard, rearranging them and tapping them neatly on the edge before re-fastening them in place, avoiding my eyes.

"Well, see, the thing is... Remember that quarter-sawn oak that we special ordered for the living room and the entry?"

I nodded. When she'd shown me the difference in the grains between regular and quarter-sawn oak I'd had to have the quarter-sawn, though I'd balked a little at the difference in cost. I could guess what Charlie was getting at.

"There's a delay."

"There was a mix-up with the shipments and the one that was supposed to go to us ended up going to another project. It's going to be at least three to four weeks."

Before I could say anything, Charlie held up a finger. "Unfortunately, that's not the only problem. We had a delay on the appliances for your kitchen, and the fixtures for the bathroom in the studio. I know you and Violet were planning on staying there while the woodwork was finished, but we're not going to be able to get a C.O. by the time you close on the condo."

"And we can't live there without the Certificate of Occupancy? Even if we don't tell anyone?"

"Chase, you won't want to. There's no bathroom. Maybe you're okay peeing in the yard, but do you think Vivi's going to like that?"

She wasn't wrong. My sister was tough, but she liked her creature comforts. She would not be happy with a sleeping bag on an unfinished floor and no bathroom.

"Charlie, you're killing me here. Violet and I are all packed up. We've got to be out of the condo by the beginning of next week," I said, trying to work out the logistics in my head while I glared at Charlie, who managed to look sheepish.

"I can't believe the first time a job really goes sideways and it's yours," Charlie said, shaking her head.

A suspicion tugged at me, and I couldn't stop myself from asking, "Does Aiden have anything to do with this?"

Charlie burst out laughing, the sound light and irreverent.

"I wouldn't put it past him. You know how he's been scheming to get Violet to move in with him, but I swear this is ordinary bad luck. I'm really sorry. At least you have a place to go. There's plenty of room at Winters House for both of you. You can stay there until your place is ready. I promise it won't be that long."

I wasn't sure I believed her about Aiden. I'd learned he was honest to a fault, but he was also determined to talk

Vivi into living with him. She was equally determined to take things slow.

Heads of state folded in the face of Aiden Winters' hard glare, but my Vivi put her hands on her hips and glared right back.

Usually, I'd be on her side. I was, mostly. But I also knew she loved Aiden to the depths of her heart. She belonged with him. She was just scared.

All she needed was a nudge. Maybe this was it.

Still, I hated the idea of moving into Winters House. My relationship with the Winters family was a hell of a lot more complicated than my sister's, and the idea of packing up my suitcases and installing myself in one of their lavish guest suites didn't sit right.

Ever since they'd discovered Anna Winters had given up her child at birth, they'd been looking for me. The Winters children had lost too much family in their short lives.

First Anna and James Winters in what the police had called a murder/suicide. Then Hugh and Olivia Winters had died in a nearly identical crime years later.

So much loss. So much death.

The remaining Winters were eager to hold on to any scrap of family they could find. Even the bastard son who'd been tossed aside the moment he'd been born.

They'd been looking for me, but I hadn't wanted anything to do with them.

I'll admit, I might have been wrong about that.

I'd imagined Anna as a desperate social climber who'd gotten rid of me so I wouldn't interfere with her pursuit of James Winters and the wealth he could give her.

In my mind, my half-siblings and their cousins had been

spoiled, entitled brats who would sneer at the idea I had any claim on such a lofty family.

Instead, they weren't that different than anyone else. Private jet and mansion aside, they were honest, loyal, and not the least bit superficial.

They'd suffered the worst losses imaginable at a young age, and every one of them knew what was important in life.

Love and family.

Not money.

Not power.

Love. Family.

They were good people. I was glad as hell my sister had found a man like Aiden to watch out for her, glad she'd been welcomed into the family with open arms.

I just wasn't sure I wanted to be welcomed along with her.

They all wanted to pretend the past was as simple as Anna giving me up and them finding me years later. Everyone wanted to talk about my mother. About Anna.

No one wanted to talk about my father. Anna might have been beloved, but the man whose seed created me had destroyed all of their lives.

Evil.

There was no other word for William Davis. He'd been responsible for Anna and James' deaths. He'd killed Hugh and Olivia himself. And he'd come so close to killing my half-sister, Annalise, it was a miracle she'd survived.

That man, that monster, was my biological father.

The Winters family thought we could brush that aside.

I knew they were wrong.

Now I'd have to move in with them, to pretend we were the fucking Brady Bunch when we all knew my father was a lot less Mike Brady and a lot more Hannibal Lecter.

It wasn't my worst nightmare, but it was close.

If I didn't think it would hurt my sister's feelings, I'd get a hotel. Charlie must have seen what I was thinking because she said quietly, "Chase, it'll be okay. I know it's weird, but it's only for a few weeks. I swear. And if you hate it, you can come crash at our place."

She and Lucas lived in an arts and crafts house Charlie had restored. It was only a few blocks from my new place and I'd hung out there more than a few times.

I didn't answer, just shook my head. Still, in that quiet, soothing tone, Charlie ventured, "Maybe this is a good thing. I know you see Gage at the office, but that's work. We've all noticed you dodging the family. And I get it. I do. But there's no harm in getting to know us better, is there?"

Talk about loaded questions. Whether I liked it or not, Charlie's aunt was my mother. Her cousins were my half-siblings. There was nothing I could do to change that, so I might as well embrace it and take advantage of the opportunity to hang out with my family.

The logical side of my mind laid all that out while the rest of me wanted to take off running and never look back. Our history was complicated and dark and ugly.

Maybe they wanted to forget the past, but I didn't see how we could.

CHAPTER TWO

CHASE

"**C**harlie!"

A woman's voice called out across the café, and Charlie smiled at the interruption with a hint of relief. She stood, shoving back her chair, and launched herself at the tall, rangy woman with long cinnamon hair and warm brown eyes who approached our table with a wide, engaging grin.

The woman pulled Charlie into her arms and squeezed her tight. "Where have you been? I haven't seen you in weeks. Aunt Amelia and Sophie are in every other day, but you? You've been a ghost. Not even for a hot chocolate."

Charlie returned the enthusiastic hug and stepped back, winding her arm around the woman's waist and turning her to face me.

"Chase, this is Annabelle Woods of Annabelle's Café. Annabelle, this is Chase Westbrook. He's Violet's brother."

I appreciated that she didn't try to add the rest of the family connection to the introduction. I stood and held out my hand, surprised by the firm grip of her long fingers.

"You've got a great place here," I said.

It was. With exposed brick walls, overstuffed velvet couches, and plenty of seating, the café was welcoming and fun.

Charlie pulled out the third seat at our table and gestured to it. "Can you sit with us for a few minutes? It's not too busy right now."

Annabelle looked around the café, then made a gesture at the barista behind the counter before she said, "Sure, I can take a few minutes. Have you two had lunch?"

Charlie shook her head. "I haven't, did you eat, Chase?"

"Not yet," I said, my stomach making itself heard with a rumble. "Do you do lunch?"

"We don't have a big menu, but we do have sandwiches and chips."

"Can you eat with us?" Charlie asked.

Annabelle looked to the back of the café, her eyes fixed on the narrow hallway that I guessed led to the restrooms and her office. After thinking for a few seconds, she shrugged a shoulder. "I have to eat sometime. Sure."

"Good, then you can save me from getting yelled at by Chase," Charlie said with a wink in my direction.

See what I mean? Charlie was great, but she could be trouble.

Annabelle narrowed her brown eyes on me and raised an eyebrow. "Why would you be yelling at Charlie?"

She seemed ready to jump in and defend her friend. I could appreciate that, but not as much as I appreciated the way it felt to have those warm eyes fixed on mine.

I waited until she took a seat before I answered, using the time to take a good, long look at Annabelle Woods.

Long, straight, shining cinnamon-colored hair. Brown eyes surrounded by thick, dark lashes. A tall, lean frame.

Not much in the way of curves, but she had a tight, heart-shaped ass and pert, teacup breasts.

I didn't imagine every woman I met naked, but with this one, it didn't take long for my brain to slide right between the sheets.

I hadn't been dating much lately. Too much shit going down in my personal life to add a woman into the mix. But Annabelle... There was something interesting about Annabelle.

It wasn't her ass or her breasts that drew me in. It was that smile, wide and bright. At least until she'd thought I was giving Charlie a hard time. For now, the smile had faded, but it would be back. I'd make sure of it.

If her smile was that good, I needed to hear her laugh.

I settled into my chair and stretched out, crossing my legs at the ankle and my arms over my chest. Giving Charlie an exaggerated and knowing glance, I said, "Charlie and I are meeting so she can explain to me why my house is going to be four to six weeks behind schedule when my condo closes well before that."

Charlie pretended to study the papers on her clipboard again, and Annabelle nodded knowingly. "Oh, one of those meetings. Well, I can understand wanting to yell. Carry on."

At Charlie's outraged, "Annabelle!" I laughed.

Annabelle joined in and I discovered I'd been right. Her laugh was as appealing as her smile, bright and loud and clear as a bell. Now that I'd heard it once, I had to hear it again.

Annabelle got up to grab two menus, and we ordered sandwiches with chips. She disappeared through the door behind the counter and came back a few minutes later with a tray of food, including two brownies and a slice of cake.

Deftly, she set the tray on the table and served, leaving

for a moment to return the tray to the kitchen. Eyeing the brownie and piece of cake, I asked, "Do you make all the food in-house?"

Annabelle munched on a chip and swallowed before she said, "Most of it. I try to keep it simple. Oatmeal, muffins, and biscuit sandwiches for breakfast. Sandwiches and soup for lunch. Occasionally a salad if I'm feeling crazy. I don't like cooking so much as baking. I love baking."

"She gets up at four in the morning to come in and start baking for the day," Charlie said, shaking her head. "Four AM. I like brownies, but not that much."

"It's worth it for my brownies," Annalise said, a smile curling her lips.

Setting down my sandwich, I broke off a chunk of the brownie and popped it in my mouth. Rich dark chocolate exploded across my tongue, a hint of bitter to offset the sweet, and underneath something I couldn't quite identify. Chewing slowly, I tried to tease out the flavor. Espresso? And... Cinnamon?

"Good, right?" Annabelle asked, taking a generous bite of her sandwich. It was two-thirty in the afternoon, she'd been up since four, and was only now eating lunch. I didn't have to guess how she carried that lean frame.

She fairly bristled with energy. I imagined any stray calorie that got close enough to Annabelle Woods was sucked up and put to use in an instant.

"Amazing," I agreed. "I can't miss the chocolate, but is there espresso? And cinnamon?"

She swallowed before she answered, with an amused shake of her head, "Espresso, yes. But not cinnamon. Nutmeg."

"Wait till you taste the cake," Charlie said through her own mouthful of sandwich. She'd teased Annabelle about getting up early, but I knew Charlie didn't exactly sleep in. I'd caught her on site more than once before seven AM when I'd stopped by for a quick look on the way to work.

With a glance at the slice of cake, thick with frosting, I said truthfully, "I can't wait."

We ate in silence for a few minutes, all of us too hungry to bother with conversation. Just as Charlie was setting down her sandwich, her phone beeped. She glanced at her screen, eyebrows knitting together as she swiped open the message and read. A moment later her phone came to life, ringing, then beeping, then ringing again.

Under her breath, she muttered, "Oh, shit," before answering with a brusque, "Yeah? Don't tell me what I don't want to hear." A long pause during which I could see the muscles in Charlie's cheek tightening as she ground her teeth together.

Abruptly she stood, murmured, "Be right back," and walked out the front door. Annabelle and I watched her through the plate glass windows as she paced on the sidewalk, eyes spitting blue fire.

"She's something, isn't she?" Annabelle said, watching Charlie with an affectionate smile.

"She is. How long have you known the family?" I asked.

From the way they talked about her, I already knew they considered Annabelle an honorary Winters. I'd never been into the café before, but the rest of them were regulars. Even Violet was here a few times a week, addicted to Annabelle's mochas since Charlie had first dragged her in.

"Since preschool. Annalise and I were in the same preschool class. We bonded over being the two Annas. We were tight right up until she left—" Annabelle looked away, picking up her sandwich and taking a bite, clearly uncomfortable.

I didn't have to ask why. Annalise Winters had been driven from home by a stalker. The creepy, psychotic stalker who had finally died in a fire after trying to kill her only a few months before. The creepy psychotic stalker who happened to be my biological father.

I knew what Annalise had been through, knew what he'd intended for her, and the thought of sharing blood with a man like that turned my stomach.

I didn't want to talk about it any more than Annabelle, so I settled for, "Everyone's relieved that she doesn't have to worry anymore. Are you two still friends?"

That smile again. Fuck, that smile. Wide and bright, brimming with life. When Annabelle smiled, she sparkled with it. I knew before she spoke that the answer was yes.

"It's been so good to have her home. Good knowing that she's happy, and safe, and back with Riley. I always loved them together. And it's nice to have my friend back. She's changed a lot, we all have, but in her heart, she's still Lise and she always will be."

"So you pretty much grew up with them then?" I asked.

"Pretty much." Annabelle looked at me out of the corner of her eye, maybe sensing my discomfort. She started to speak, then stopped as Charlie approached the table, flopped into her seat and reached under the table for her bag, dragging it into her lap and shoving her clipboard, phone, and tablet inside. "Sorry to bail on you guys, but we're having an inspection crisis with the new property Lucas and I bought."

"Bad?" I asked, curious. I didn't know that much about rehabbing houses, but I'd been around Charlie and Lucas, pitched in often enough, that I'd picked up a little here and there.

"I don't know," Charlie said with an edge of sarcasm,

"how bad is it when your inspector missed the termite infestation in all of the floor joists?"

Shaking her head, she muttered under her breath something about kicking someone's ass.

"Pretty bad then," I agreed.

"You want me to wrap up your sandwich?" Annabelle asked, already getting up. She went to the counter, said something to the barista, and came back with a cardboard food container. Charlie set the remains of her sandwich inside before breaking off half of the brownie and dropping that in as well. "I'm going to need the chocolate."

Annabelle opened the takeout container and put the rest of the brownie inside. "Take it all. I'll get another one."

"You're the best." Charlie leaned over and hooked an arm around Annabelle's neck, smacking a kiss on her cheek. "I'll be back soon, I promise. Things have been crazy lately, but we need to get together."

To me, she said, "I'll nail down a definite timeline. And I'll call Aiden and Mrs. W and let them know you and Vivi are moving in." Just the thought of it had me gritting my teeth and Charlie shook her head. "It's going to be fine, I promise."

With that, she was gone, leaving me alone with Annabelle.

CHAPTER THREE
CHASE

Annabelle looked at me curiously. "You don't want to stay at Winters House? Do you have something against staying in a mansion with a theater, gym, private chef, maid service, and swimming pool? It's a lot better than a hotel."

I took another bite of my sandwich and chewed slowly. I wasn't ready to explain why I didn't want to stay at Winters House. Annabelle might be their family friend, but I'd only just met her.

I hadn't known her long enough to share my dirty laundry. Not even close. I'd always thought being Anna Winters' mistake of a love child was bad enough. Now that I knew about my biological father and the destruction he'd brought on the Winters family, I wanted to run in the other direction.

I would have been perfectly happy to marry my sister off to Aiden and never see any of them again.

Not content with my silence, Annabelle pushed. "You don't like them? Or is it about Aiden and Violet?"

"Nosy, aren't you?" I asked, trying to deflect.

Annabelle shrugged a shoulder. "Look, I've known them all my life. They're great people. Really solid. Good friends, close to each other. But their whole deal is overwhelming. The money, the house, the scandal. It's a lot. I get it."

I'd assumed Annabelle came from the same background, but the way she talked about them, maybe I'd been wrong. "You didn't grow up in a walled compound with your own personal chef?" I asked.

Annabelle laughed again, the rich, full sound hitting me in my chest and my cock at the same time. It was a heady combination. I watched her lips, stretched wide with her smile, and wondered what it would be like to kiss her.

"Oh, no. No, not hardly. I did grow up in Buckhead, but we lived in a tiny cottage that used to be the gardener's quarters of an old estate that got chopped up. It's a sweet little house, perfect for my mom and dad and me, but it was not what you think of when you think Buckhead. It was probably around the size of Mrs. W's cottage."

"So how did you grow up with them, then?" I asked.

"You know we all went to the same school." She raised her eyebrows, and I nodded in assent. I didn't know, but I could have guessed. She went on, "My father was a math teacher there, and my mother worked in the office, so they got free tuition for me. It was a great opportunity. I got a top-notch education, and my parents made sure I busted my butt so my grades were good enough for scholarships when it came time for college. It's funny, though, you think I'd be jealous, growing up surrounded by all that wealth, when we didn't have much extra."

"But you weren't?" I probed.

Now I was being nosy, but Annabelle seemed happy.

The affection in her voice when she spoke of her parents was real.

I didn't know a lot about that. I hadn't spoken to my parents in years. Not since they kicked me out, and then Vivi a few years later.

Annabelle picked at the corner of the brownie closest to her, her eyes thoughtful. "When we were all little, maybe. I spent a lot of time with Lise's mom and dad. We were in and out of each other's houses so much we might as well have been related. But after they died..."

She fell silent, studying the shiny, bumpy surface of the brownie. "After her parents died, I didn't envy them anything. It was horrible. The attention and their grief. Any of them would have traded every material thing they had to bring back their mom and dad."

Annabelle didn't know it, but she was talking about my mother.

I didn't usually think of Anna Winters as my mother. It's not like she'd raised me. She'd gotten rid of me the moment after I'd been born and never looked back. Suzanne Westbrook was my mother.

Still, I'd spent a lot of time avoiding the thought of Anna Winters' death. Seeing Annabelle's grief, still strong after so many years, made me wonder about the woman who'd given birth to me.

It made me wonder, but it didn't mean I wanted to think about it. Changing the subject, I said, "You're tight with your parents?"

Her lips curved, barely a smile, yet as magnetic as her laugh. Her eyes warm with affection, she said, "Oh, yeah. Always have been. I mean, we butt heads. We can argue politics, movies, food. We can debate anything. It's the

Woods family tradition. But we're tight. They still live here. Dad's still teaching, mom's still working in the office at school. It's nice to have family close."

"I guess," I said before I thought about it. "I really only had Vivi. And now she's marrying Aiden."

"You sound like you're not sure about him yet," she commented. Perceptive.

I shrugged a shoulder. "It's not that. He's okay. But she's my baby sister."

"Is this one of those, 'no man will ever be good enough for my baby sister' things? You do know she has to grow up sometime, right? Isn't she almost 30?"

"Not the point," I said dryly, knowing it was exactly the point. And if Violet was going to find a man to fall in love with, she couldn't do much better than Aiden Winters.

The man was absurdly devoted to her. I was sure he would have tried to talk her into a wedding already if he hadn't known that would scare her off.

Vivi was cautious. Deliberate. She'd been impetuous and reckless a handful of times in her life, but at the core, she was too careful to jump into marriage, even when she was head over heels in love.

That wasn't a problem. Aiden would wait a lifetime if he had to.

I was betting it wouldn't take a lifetime to wear her down, especially if we were moving into Winters House.

"Aiden's a really good guy," Annabelle said. "I've only seen him with your sister once, but he's never been like that before. He's always distant with the women he dates. Aloof. But with your sister..."

Annabelle grinned, and I rolled my eyes.

"Spare me the details. She *is* my baby sister."

"I get it. But really, you don't have to worry. Aiden is solid. He's the one who lent me the money to start this place."

At the obvious affection in her voice, an unexpected stab of jealousy hit me. Stupid, when she'd known Aiden most of her life. Of course she'd feel affection for him.

Still, an unfamiliar part of me wanted the warmth in her voice and the smile on her lips to be for me. Stupid. I'd just met this girl.

"He *gave* you the money?" I asked, skeptical. I worked with Aiden. He was not a soft touch. Not long ago, Winters, Inc. had ended up buying my company through a twisted series of events.

In short, I'd been scammed out of my company, CB4 Analytics, and booted to the curb by a guy who turned around and sold it to Aiden less than a week later after scraping off me and all the lead programmers.

Aiden had dismantled the company and absorbed what was left into Winters, Inc. only to find that without me the most valuable tech they'd purchased wouldn't work. It had been a mess on all sides, and once Aiden and I had worked it out, he'd offered me a job until I'd sorted out the problems.

He did *not* offer to give me my company back. Mostly because it no longer existed. The team of programmers I'd assembled had scattered to the winds after the sale. All that was left of CB4 Analytics was my tech. Aiden brought me on to fix it, and he cut me a deal for a percentage of the profits from the project, but that was it.

Aiden was a businessman first and last. We might be family, but not even for family would he make a bad business decision.

In the end, it turned out I didn't care about losing CB4. The truth is, Vivi took the loss a lot harder than I did. I'd stay on at Winters, Inc. until I was done fixing the mess they'd made of my former company. But, in my spare time, I was working on something new. With every day that passed, I was more ready to ditch the corporate gig and go back out on my own.

Knowing Aiden as I did, I couldn't quite imagine him writing a blank check to an old friend, no matter how he might have adored her.

Proving me right, Annabelle laughed that full, rich laugh and shook her head, her shining hair swinging around her shoulders.

"Aiden Winters just give somebody money? No way in hell. But remember, I've known him my entire life. I did not go asking for money. He heard me talking about wanting to buy this place. I worked here as a barista through college. I did a double major in art history and business. Aiden told me to put a plan together."

"And he liked your business plan?"

Another laugh. "No. He took a red pen to that thing and slashed it to pieces. I thought I was going to cry. I'd already shown it to my professor and I thought it was as good as it could be. But not good enough. Aiden sent me back to the drawing board, and I did it again. And again. I think on the fifth presentation, he shocked the hell out of me and wrote me a check. For a while, he was my business partner, but I bought him out a few years after I opened. And I paid back every penny of the loan ahead of schedule."

"Five times? He made you do your presentation five times?" I knew Aiden was a hard ass, but that was over the top.

Affection was clear in her voice when she said, "Aiden taught me more over those five presentations then I think I learned in every business class in college combined. He was relentless. And it didn't stop once he gave me the check. I don't know where he found the time, but he was here constantly that first year, riding my ass about every penny I spent.

"At the time I had fantasies of murdering him and leaving him in the alley behind the café, but I don't know that I would have made it that first year if it hadn't been for him. I thought I knew what I was doing with my shiny business degree and a few years of working as a barista. I had no freaking clue. Aiden didn't know a lot about food service, but he understands business backward and forward. I know he didn't have the time to take on an extra burden, but he did. I wouldn't be here without him. So when I say you can trust your sister with him? I really mean it."

"I do trust him with her, I guess. It's a lot to get used to, that's all."

Annabelle stood and started collecting our plates and silverware, stacking them neatly and efficiently, just as I'd expect from someone who did this all day. Looking at me through her thick, dark lashes, I saw speculation in her eyes.

I knew I looked so much like Vance Winters, Annalise's twin, that we were almost interchangeable. His hair was longer, and he had more visible tattoos, but the resemblance was too close to miss, especially for someone who'd grown up with Vance.

Annabelle had to have noticed it, but she was polite enough not to ask. Good, because I wasn't sure I wanted to explain. Not yet. Not until I knew her better.

"What do I owe you for lunch?" I asked.

Annabelle shook her head. "Nothing. Consider this one on the house. A welcome to the family kind of thing."

Shoving my hands in my pockets I studied her and decided I had to ask. "Then let me take you out to dinner as a thank you."

Like a door closing, all that warmth, all that vibrant energy, vanished. Annabelle wouldn't meet my eyes, but she gave a sharp shake of her head and said, "I appreciate being asked, but no. I don't date customers."

"Why? Is that like a barista code? Don't date the customers?"

"Yes, exactly. Don't date the customers. It's bad for business."

She lifted the stack of plates, turning to go. I tapped her shoulder before she could escape.

"You welcomed me to the family," I said, "so you know I'm not just a customer. You really won't let me take you to dinner?"

Annabelle gave another shake of her head, her shining silky hair tumbling around her shoulders. A faint blush colored her cheeks and her teeth cut into her bottom lip for a second before she said again, "I do appreciate you asking. But, no. It was nice to meet you, Chase. I'll see you around."

Before I could think of another approach, she was gone. I gathered my things slowly, thinking. Annabelle Woods was an unexpected surprise. I should probably leave her alone. Maybe she didn't like me, but we'd had too much fun talking at lunch for me to completely buy that.

No, there was another reason she'd shut me down. My life was complicated enough as it was. I didn't need to make it more complicated with a woman. And Annabelle was right, given her lifelong connection to my half-siblings and their cousins, she was family, too.

If I was interested, it couldn't be for a one-night stand.

As I watched her emerge from the kitchen, hands empty, and disappear down the hall to her office, jeans clinging to her tight ass, that shining cinnamon hair swinging with each step, I knew I'd be back.

And eventually, I'd convince her to say yes.

CHAPTER FOUR
CHASE

The light was fading, the sticky summer heat lifting only a bit as I pushed open the door to Annabelle's Café. As always, customers lingered though it was close to closing time. I lifted a hand to wave at Annabelle behind the counter, and she graced me with one of her wide, bright smiles.

I headed back to the armchair in the corner I'd claimed as my own, if only in my mind. Fortunately for me, it was empty. Over the past few weeks, I'd taken to showing up at Annabelle's Café at random times. Sometimes to eat, sometimes for a jolt of caffeine or sugar—I'd quickly become addicted to her brownies—or simply for a place to be away from the office. Away from Winters House.

Violet and I had moved into Winters House a few days after Charlie delivered the news about the delay. Our belongings, piles of cardboard boxes and stacks of furniture, filled one of the garage bays.

Violet had taken up residence in Aiden's suite, and I'd moved into what had originally been Vance's room, then

Sophie's. Sophie had moved out when she'd married Gage, and since their wedding it had stood empty.

Most of the rooms in Winters House stood empty. I imagined Gage and Sophie and Aiden and Violet all planned to fill it with children. They should. Winters House might have been grand and elegant and enormous, but it was a house meant for a family.

For better or worse, the Winters were mine. I was trying to see it as better, but lately it felt like it might be worse.

I thought the presence of staff in the house would make me feel even more like an interloper. I'd grown up in a nice home, and my mother had help with the housework, but a once-a-week day maid was not the same as live-in staff.

Mrs. W, the housekeeper, served as a buffer. If I needed something, I didn't need to bother Aiden or Gage. I didn't have to wander around, trying to figure things out. I just hunted up Mrs. W and asked. She was, in a word, amazing.

Mrs. W kept Winters House running smoothly, and she seemed to know everything about everyone—what they were doing, where they were—but she never asked personal questions. She had, according to Vivi, a very strict line between personal and family. She never gossiped, and she never pried.

She and Vivi hit it off from their first meeting. According to Aiden, Mrs. W couldn't wait for Violet to become mistress of the house.

Mrs. W kept her emotions tucked away, but I could see her affection for my sister in the little things. The flowers at the table were Vivi's favorite. Mrs. W had reorganized Aiden's closet for her before we'd moved in, and always consulted with Vivi on meals and schedules.

I'd wondered, for someone who put so much emphasis on proper behavior and professional reserve, someone who I assumed would hate scandal and gossip—how would a woman like that accept my presence in the household? The abandoned bastard child of one of her former employers.

Employers to whom, from everything I'd heard, she'd been deeply devoted. But Mrs. W had greeted me with as much warmth as she'd ever shown in the short time I'd known her, and when I hunted her down with one question or another she always had a smile for me.

Mrs. W was a lot easier to deal with than the rest of the Winters.

There was nothing wrong with them. They were all nice. They were great. Aiden was the perfect match for my strong-willed sister, and I couldn't have been happier they'd found each other.

Seriously. I could do without walking in to see his hands on her ass, but I could live with it if it meant she was happy.

Gage, my half-brother, lived in the house, and the two of us got along fairly well. We worked together at Winters, Inc. temporarily while I salvaged the mess they'd made of my company.

I didn't blame them for what happened. Not anymore. Not once I'd learned the truth. We'd both been screwed by the same guy and, if anything, the mess was my fault. If only I'd double-checked the contracts...

The crazy thing was, I was almost glad it had happened. For one, if I hadn't lost my company, Violet never would have met Aiden. But more than that, I didn't really want it back.

I'm not an executive. I love designing software. Solving problems. I love the rush of a start-up. The adrenaline and anxiety. The risk.

Running a functioning, profitable company? Not so much. I wasn't ready to leave Winters, Inc. My algorithm wasn't finished, and until it was ready for the market, I wouldn't walk out on them.

But I'd been working on something in my spare time that was a hell of a lot more interesting, and I found myself counting the days until I could get out of Winters, Inc. and out of Winters House.

I'd planned to establish a relationship with the Winters on my own terms. Kind of hard to do that when I was living in their house and eating at their table. They meant well, and it was cool they'd welcomed me with open arms. They didn't have to.

It had to sting to find out their mother had gotten pregnant and given up a child they'd never known. They'd lost her so young, and they could have taken it as a slight on her memory.

That wasn't who they were, and they were eager for any piece of Anna Winters, even her discarded bastard.

Violet aside, my own family was a mess. I should have been happy to have a replacement.

It's just that, all together, the Winters clan was a lot to take in. I'd been a loner for the past twenty years. Having four half-siblings and four cousins all at once left me feeling a little crowded.

Enter Annabelle's Café.

When I was overwhelmed and needed some space, I found myself here. An Americano, a brownie, a comfortable armchair, and my laptop, and I could work in peace. It was hard to get anything done in the house.

I had privacy, but there were so many people coming and going I found it hard to focus. You'd think a café would make it worse, but the constant murmur of conversation turned into white noise. Sitting there, focused on my screen, my fingers flying across the keyboard, I found myself making real progress on my side project for the first time in weeks.

Annabelle had been cautious with me the first time I'd showed up. Waiting for me to ask her out again. Wondering if I was going to take no for an answer.

I would.

I had.

But she was smart enough to guess that I was biding my time. I hadn't given up on the idea of taking Annabelle Woods out to dinner. And more. So much more.

Hanging out at her café didn't just give me the opportunity to get work done, it gave me the excuse to watch her.

Watch her, hell, I couldn't take my eyes off her.

That bristling energy. That bright, cheerful smile and those warm brown eyes. The stride of her long legs as she moved around her café, gathering empties and chatting with regulars.

She loved this place, and she'd made it home away from home for more people than me.

I wanted to take her out.

I wanted to take her to bed.

With each conversation, I'd come to realize I wanted so much more than that. When I was feeling overwhelmed at Winters House or restless in the office it wasn't only the coffee and brownie I thought of.

It was Annabelle's smile of welcome.

A few minutes after I'd settled into my armchair, she was at my side, carrying a small tray she'd loaded down with a cup of soup, a sandwich, a coffee I already knew would be decaf—for a woman who owned a café she had very strict ideas about the proper time for caffeine—and the brownie she knew I'd be craving.

"Thank you," I said.

Scowling down at me she replied, "Eat it all."

"Yes ma'am," I said, giving her my most charming grin. It widened into a full-fledged smile when she rolled her eyes to the ceiling and left without another word.

She'd be back. Annabelle pretended she found me exasperating. And she did, a little. But she also liked me. I knew she liked me because instead of trying to kick me out, she fed me every time I showed up, even when it was close to closing time. Like tonight.

I wouldn't get much work done, but sometimes Annabelle let me hang out while she shut down the café. Occasionally, she even let me help. I wasn't above pitching in if I thought it would soften her up.

That, and she worked so fucking hard. I knew she was up at four in the morning and she closed the café every night at eight. It didn't leave much time for a life. Or rest.

Annabelle was driven and ambitious. She was determined that her café would be a success, and even though it was, she had no plans to slow down. I could respect that.

I knew what it was to bust your ass to make your dreams happen. That didn't mean I couldn't give her a hand every now and then. Especially if it gave her an incentive to put up with me.

The sandwich was gone, coffee mostly empty, soup bowl scraped clean, and the brownie decimated when Annabelle dropped into the chair beside mine and propped her feet up on the coffee table.

I raised my head and looked around, surprised to see the café was empty. The sign on the door was turned to CLOSED and the front lights were off.

I blinked a few times to clear my head. Sometimes when I was working, I lost all awareness of what was going on around me.

"What time is it?" I asked.

Annabelle closed her eyes and dropped her head back to rest on the couch, rolling it from side to side to loosen her neck. "Eight-fifteen. Why don't you eat at Winters House? Don't tell me you don't like Abel's cooking."

"It's not that," I said. You'd have to hate food if you didn't like Abel's cooking. "I'm not used to that much company."

She lifted her head and looked around the empty café that had been half-filled when I'd shown up. "So you come to a crowded café?"

"Not the same. This place is filled with strangers. Except for you. Winters House is...not."

"And you don't like them?" Annabelle asked guardedly.

I shook my head. "It's not that. They're great. It's just..." I trailed off. I didn't know how to explain, and I didn't know how much she knew. "I'm not used to having so many people around," I said finally. "I like my space. And this is a good place to get work done."

"As opposed to the office?" Annabelle asked, with a raised eyebrow.

"What I'm working on isn't for Winters, Inc.," I admitted. I saw immediately that she understood.

"And anything you work on on company property, using a company computer—"

"Belongs to the company," I finished for her.

"You think Aiden would take whatever it is you're doing?" Annabelle asked carefully.

I shrugged a shoulder. I didn't. Aiden could be ruthless, but there were so many reasons he wouldn't steal from me, even if he had the right to. Starting with his innate honesty and sense of fair play.

I trusted him, but I'd learned the hard way how much carelessness could cost.

In answer, I said, "No, not exactly. But I also don't want them to know what I'm doing."

"Why not? Is it illegal?" Annabelle leaned forward and braced her elbows on her knees, her eyes alight with curiosity. "Are you hacking into something?"

"Troublemaker," I accused, shaking my head. "It's not illegal. It's new and I don't know what I want to do with it yet. If Aiden and Gage find out I'm developing new software—"

"They'll be all over it," Annabelle finished.

"Exactly. And until I figure out what I want, it's easier if I don't have to deal with them."

"I get it. Do you want anything else to eat?" she asked, rising to organize my dishes on the tray. I reached out a hand and closed my fingers around her wrist, stopping her before she could get away.

CHAPTER FIVE

C hase's fingers closed around my wrist, sending a warm flutter straight to my belly. I wanted to be immune to him. I was trying. Trying hard, but it wasn't working.

How could anyone be immune to a man like Chase Westbrook? Handsome as sin, with messy blonde hair and piercing blue eyes, a tall frame, and corded forearms that told me no matter how much time he spent staring at his laptop, he took his workouts seriously.

Chase looked so much like Vance Winters it should have put me off. Vance was like a brother. I could appreciate, objectively, that Vance was hot, but I didn't go there.

Looking like Vance should have signaled my brain and my body that he was off-limits, but they weren't getting the message.

I needed to get over it. Chase seemed like a good guy, but my instincts with men sucked.

I couldn't afford another mistake.

Literally.

My bank account had only just recovered from the last one.

Squeezing for a second before dropping my wrist, he said, "I'll get that, what do I owe you?"

"I'll put it on your tab," I said as I always did.

"And when are you going to let me pay my tab?" he asked.

I'd never let him see his mysterious tab that didn't exist. I wasn't keeping track of what he owed me. I should have been. I didn't feed people for free, even friends.

Not if I wanted to keep a roof over my head.

I wasn't quite sure why I kept doing it with Chase. I shrugged a shoulder and didn't say anything when he picked up his tray of dishes and followed me back to the kitchen.

"Don't worry, I'll bill you eventually," I said over my shoulder. Lies. All lies.

"As long as you do. I'm not a moocher."

Proving his point, he put the tray down next to my commercial stainless-steel sink and dishwasher and started to rinse and load.

"Chase!" I protested. "I've told you, you don't have to do that."

As usual, he ignored me. He'd told me before that he'd put himself through college waiting tables. I could tell he knew his way around the inside of a restaurant kitchen.

Not looking at me, he said, "I've got this. Go do your thing in the front and you can come help me finish when you're done."

I propped a hand on my hip and scowled at him.

See? This is why I didn't charge him. What kind of guy was he that he'd work all day, come in here and work some more, and then take on my dirty dishes?

I couldn't figure out what to do with Chase Westbrook. He was too good to be true. I knew all about how that usually worked out.

"What happened to the guy who usually closes with you?" Chase asked.

I sighed at the thought of Grover, the hipster, man-bunned college student who usually worked the second shift and closed with me. He was dating Penny, my barista on the early shift.

The two of them had started out fine and were sliding downhill fast. I leaned against the prep counter and glared at the dirty dishes.

"I think I'm going to have to fire him. He begged me to put him on days with Penny, his girlfriend. If I didn't let them work together they said they'd quit. The last thing I need right now is to lose half my staff."

"You've got me for tonight," Chase offered.

For a second I forgot he wasn't talking about helping with the dishes.

My eyes lingered on the collar of his T-shirt where the narrow black lines of a tattoo peeked out. That tattoo was becoming an obsession. I wanted to see it, but to see it, Chase would have to take off his shirt.

A shirtless Chase was dangerous to my well-being. I didn't date. I wasn't looking for a guy. And if I were, the last thing I needed was a hot, rich, workaholic. Been there, done that, and had the empty bank account, shattered heart, and divorce decree to show for it.

I left Chase in the kitchen and went out front to attack the counters, the espresso machine, and the pastry cases. I didn't stop until every surface gleamed. When the area behind the counter was done, I started wiping down tables, then stacking the chairs upside down so I could do the floor.

Usually, the mindless rhythm of closing the café was relaxing, despite the hard work involved. There were no customers in line and the place was quiet except for the faint rattle of glass and silverware coming from the kitchen. Sometimes I played music, but sometimes I liked to be alone in the quiet.

When I closed by myself it took a lot longer, and I knew when I was done I'd head upstairs to my tiny studio, crawl into bed, and a heartbeat later my alarm would go off at four AM. I needed these brief pockets of quiet to recharge before the day to come.

Movement from the kitchen caught my eye. I looked over to see Chase walking out.

"Did you sweep the back already?" he asked.

"I've got it," I said, straightening and tucking the handle of the broom against my chest. "Chase, you don't have to help."

"I know I don't have to help," he said, shrugging his shoulder and shoving one hand in the back pocket of his jeans. "I don't mind. If I save you some time you can get another hour of sleep tonight."

"Are you saying I look tired?" I asked, teasing, but not.

Who wants to be told they look tired? Not me, even when I knew it was true. I didn't need to look in the mirror to see dark smudges under my eyes. I could feel my energy flagging.

I'm one of those annoying people who pops awake early in the morning pre-caffeinated and ready to go. I run on high speed right up until I drop into bed at night. I've always been like this. I'm not a napper and I'm not a big fan of sitting still.

But lately, with Grover skipping out on second shift and

Penny no-showing to open a few times, I was stretching myself too thin, and I knew it showed.

"I would never tell a beautiful woman she looks tired," Chase said, "I assumed purple smudges under the eyes was a new trend."

"Hardy-har. You think you're funny, but you're really not," I said.

He *was* pretty funny, but this conversation was sliding perilously close to flirting. I didn't flirt. I'd put a ban on flirting, friendly smiles to customers aside.

Flirting led to dating, and dating did not go well for me. I did not need to start building castles in the clouds about Chase Westbrook. He seemed like a great guy, but he was bad news.

He grinned at me, his blue eyes flashing with humor. "No, I know I'm not funny. Hasn't stopped me yet."

He said the last over his shoulder as he headed down the hall to the utility closet where he knew he'd find the mop bucket and industrial strength cleanser for the floor.

I thought about telling him to stop, but there was still so much to do. If he wanted to help I might as well let him. I'd send him home with an extra brownie to soothe my conscience.

My phone rang, the buzz from my back pocket startling me. I didn't get many calls at this time of day. Most people who knew me knew I'd be busy closing down the café. Pulling it from my pocket, I glanced at the screen.

The name I saw stabbed into my heart. TM. Tommy Mosler. The last person I wanted to talk to. Today, or any day. I hit the button to decline the call and shoved the phone back in my pocket.

I knew what he wanted. That he should ask me for anything after all he'd put me through was beyond my comprehension. And that he wouldn't let it go—that he kept calling and stopping by—was making me a little crazy.

Things had been hectic enough with Grover and Penny shifting their schedules. I didn't need crap from Tommy on top of it. I tried to push him from my mind as I went back to sweeping, but, as always, he made it impossible.

My phone began to ring again. Chase was in the back, thank God, and couldn't hear. If I didn't answer, didn't let him have his say—again—he'd keep calling. I didn't want to explain the non-stop ringing phone to Chase.

With a glance over my shoulder at the kitchen, I pulled my phone from my pocket and stabbed my finger at the answer button.

"What do you want?"

"I want to know why you have to be so rude," Tommy said. "It wouldn't kill you to answer my call."

Thinking that it might, I said grudgingly, "I don't have anything to say to you. I want you to stop calling me."

"Do what I'm asking, and I will," he said, trying for charm but unable to hide his irritation.

"I want you to listen to me very carefully, Tommy," I said. "I cannot get you an invitation to Jacob and Abigail's wedding."

"Don't bullshit me. You're always so fucking selfish. After everything you've done to me, I'm asking you for a small favor. Insignificant. You've been friends with Jacob Winters practically since the cradle. If you asked him to add me to the guest list—"

"Stop," I interrupted.

It was always like this with him. He turned everything upside down. *I* was selfish? What *I'd* done to *him*? Was he nuts?

Three years and he could still twist my head around

until I felt guilty because I didn't jump to do everything he wanted. It would be a lot easier to move past him if he didn't keep shoving himself back into my life.

Squeezing my eyes shut and taking a long breath that was supposed to be calming but wasn't, I said, "The guest list was finalized months ago. They can't add anyone else at this point. And even if they could—"

"Of course, they can. When you have that much money you can do anything you want. Two more people won't make that much of a difference. They won't even know we're there."

"Why do you care? You don't even like Jacob and you don't know Abigail."

"Because anyone who's anyone in Atlanta will be at that wedding and it looks bad that I'm not invited. You're making me look bad."

The aggression drained from his voice and he tried charm again. "Annabelle, sweetheart, we've been through so much together. You used to support my career. Can't you help me now? This one time?"

But it wouldn't be this one time. Today it was the wedding. Later it would be something else. Being connected to the rich and powerful, however peripherally, wasn't all it was cracked up to be.

I stared at the floor between my feet and tried to remind myself of all the reasons this man had no part of my life anymore.

I didn't owe him anything. Not even the time I was taking on this phone call.

"This isn't my problem," I said. "And if I called Jacob right now and asked him to add you to the guest list you know what he would say."

"Not if you convince him you really want me there."

"Do you think he'd believe that? Do you think there's a chance in hell Jacob would believe that I want you anywhere near me? The first thing he'd ask is how you're twisting my arm. Because he knows you. And, in case you missed it, he hates you. He doesn't want you at his wedding. He didn't invite you because he can't stand the sight of you. I am not going to ruin his day by asking him to give you access to the most important moment of his life."

"Of course," Tommy said sarcastically. "Of course, because it's all about you, right? You and your deep friend-ship with the Winters family. You have them wrapped around your finger—they'll do anything their precious Annabelle wants—but the second a real person, someone you owe, asks you to help them out—"

I dropped the phone from my ear and hung up. Pressing the power button and holding it down I cut off Tommy's redial, already lighting up the screen. I'd only swiped the broom across the floor twice when the café phone started to ring.

Leaning the broom against the table, I walked behind the counter, picked up the receiver, said, "Stop calling," and, ignoring the bluster on the other end of the phone, hung up to disconnect the call. Then I unplugged the phone from the wall.

CHAPTER SIX
ANNABELLE

I went back to sweeping, trying to clear my head. Tommy was the past, no matter how often he tried to play a role in my present. He couldn't stand the thought that I'd moved on.

Never mind that he'd done the same well before I had. So far before, we'd still been married when he'd moved on from me. If only he'd let me do the same.

Talking to Tommy was like looking in a fun house mirror. Everything I believed of him, he threw in my face.

I was selfish.

I was thoughtless.

I was dishonest and demanding and unreasonable.

It was always me in the wrong. When I accused him of the same, he flipped it back.

If I'd been kinder, if I'd loved him more, then he would have been nicer to me.

If he pushed too hard, it was my fault for not giving in fast enough.

I tried to clear my head and focus on sweeping.

Thinking about Tommy would only ruin the rest of my night. The day had been long enough as it was. I didn't need to spend the rest of it mulling over a past I couldn't change.

I tried to focus on the menu for the next day. I'd rather think about food than Tommy any day.

By the time I finished sweeping the front, Chase had the bathroom, hallway, kitchen, and behind the counter mopped to a shine. The acrid scent of cleaning fluid displaced the warmth of coffee and baked goods.

It would be faded by morning, the café filled with the tempting scents of fresh biscuits and muffins. Just the thought of baking for the day to come lifted my spirits.

"What's the special tomorrow?" Chase asked.

Today I'd made cinnamon buns with raisins and thick cream cheese frosting. They were one of my favorites, but they hadn't tempted Chase. Chase, I'd learned, was all about the chocolate.

"I'll tell you if you give me the mop," I said, picking up the broom and full dustpan, tilting it back carefully to keep the mess inside.

"I'm not giving you the mop," he said, "but tell me anyway."

"Fine, but only because you're bigger than me and I can't take it forcibly. I'm making salted caramel brownies. Do you like salted caramel?"

"Do I like salted caramel? Does anyone *not* like salted caramel? Salted caramel brownies... Man, in the right mood I'd probably kill someone for one of those. Promise you're going to save me one," he said.

"Give me the mop and I'll give you two of them," I promised.

Chase hesitated for just a second and I couldn't help the

smile that curled my lips. I don't know why I found his weakness for chocolate so cute.

Maybe because he looked like the kind of guy who lived on chicken breasts and wheatgrass shots. There wasn't an ounce of fat on his body and yet when I waved chocolate in front of him he couldn't resist.

With a wince, he shook his head slowly. "Can't do it. It kills me to say it. The idea of an Annabelle brownie with salted caramel... I'm going to dream about that tonight. But you've been up since four AM, busting your ass and on your feet all day. No fucking way am I handing you this mop so I can lounge around and watch you work."

"Chase, this is my job. This is my place. I like my work. I don't expect you to clean up."

"Just let it go. I'm almost done. You can send me home with some extra day-old baked goods to make it up to me."

"That I can do," I murmured, giving up and carrying the broom and dustpan to the back where I emptied it and put it away.

From behind me, Chase said in an overly casual tone, "So, did you ever date Aiden or Gage? Or Vance? You were best friends with Lise, so you must have spent a lot of time with them."

I laughed. I couldn't help it. At the thought of dating any of them, I started to giggle, one of those giggles that grows until you can't catch a breath and your whole body is shaking with it.

Through my laughter, Chase said, "What? It's not an unreasonable thing to ask. They're all good guys. You're a beautiful woman. I can guess you were a pretty teenager. Unless you were one of those ugly ducklings with zits and a hunchback until you hit eighteen and woke up looking like this."

He gestured to me in my sweaty T-shirt and coffee-stained jeans, hair in a messy bun—and not the kind you spend half an hour on to make it look messy—an actual mess of hair I'd shoved back in a ponytail holder so I could clean without it getting in my face.

"I wasn't quite an ugly duckling," I said, "but I wasn't a beauty queen either. Mostly, I was plain."

I hadn't been unattractive, but I hadn't been particularly pretty either. I'd had some zits, but not a lot. I'd developed right on time, but sadly ended up with modest breasts and almost no hips.

I never had to struggle with my weight, which I knew made me lucky, but on the other hand, I'd never fill out a bra the way my pre-adolescent self had hoped.

All in all, I was used to my body and my face. I figured I was lucky in some things and less so in others. Pretty much like every other woman I knew.

Sometimes, when I caught Chase looking at me, I had the feeling he saw something I didn't.

He interrupted my thoughts to press, "So that's a no?"

"Why are you asking?"

"Because I'm nosy," he said.

I laughed again and distracted myself, rearranging the napkins and stirrers at the end of the counter. "I never dated any of them. Never wanted to. We were friends, but Lise was my best friend growing up. Dating one of her brothers or cousins... It would have been weird. Plus, their world is not my world. We may have gone to school together, but I didn't really fit in over there. You know what I mean?"

I had a feeling Chase knew exactly what I meant.

"Yeah. Yeah, I get you," he said, and for a moment his charm was stripped away and I saw everything in his eyes. His frustration and hesitancy, his sadness and his anger.

Quietly, I said, "I bet you do."

Surprising me, he explained, "Violet and I grew up with parents who were well-off. We didn't need to worry about money. My mom didn't work, and they're both obsessed with social climbing. But all of that—nice house, nice cars, nice vacations—doesn't mean our lives came anywhere close to the world the Winters live in. That house alone..."

A gust of a laugh burst out. "I know what you mean. I was so little, but I still remember the first time I saw it when my mom dropped me off for a play date. She kept reminding me not to touch anything. Looking back, I think she was very aware of her position in the office at school versus the power the Winters family held.

"She liked Anna and Olivia, and they liked her. But our families didn't socialize. I was always welcome in Winters House and Lise's mom treated me like one of her own when I was there. Later, so did Olivia. They're good people. All of them. Still, I know what you mean. It's a totally different world. And it's not easy to be dumped in the middle of it, is it?"

Under his breath, he muttered, "You don't know the half of it."

I finished with the napkins and straws and started straightening the sugar packets, giving Chase a second to compose himself. He hadn't told me directly and neither had any of the Winters, but I had eyes.

Chase looked so much like Vance I might have thought he was Vance's twin instead of Annalise if I hadn't known better. He had Anna's eyes. His connection to the Winters family was not only his sister's relationship with Aiden.

I knew they'd been looking for a missing child for months, and I was willing to bet all the coffee in my storage room that Chase was that child.

I could also guess that finding the Winters family was overwhelming. Confusing. He was here because he didn't want to face what waited for him at home. The last thing I wanted to do was drag it all out and make him talk about it.

I looked up from the cream and sugar station to find his eyes on me, hot and assessing.

Shit.

I braced, ready to turn him down if he asked me out again. A little voice in the back of my head was screaming, *Stop being an idiot and say yes.*

I wasn't listening to that voice.

The last time I had, she'd destroyed my life.

I had bad taste in men.

Chase was going through a lot right now. He could get a woman anywhere, but what he really needed was a friend.

I wasn't going to go out with him. I couldn't take that risk. But that didn't mean I couldn't be there for him. Friendship lasted a lot longer than love anyway.

Love is a risk. Love is destructive and dangerous. Friendship is safe. Friendship was all I could offer.

Chase dropped his gaze and the moment broke, leaving me with a rush of relief underlain with a hint of bitter disappointment.

CHAPTER SEVEN

CHASE

Life in Winters House was a little too crowded for my taste, but I couldn't deny the meals were worth the inconvenience. Abel, the Winters' full-time chef, was a taciturn, burly man. I hadn't been surprised to find out he'd served his time in the Navy in a kitchen.

He might have been a man of few words, but he said all he needed to with his cooking. Breakfast on weekdays was fairly standard. Eggs, bacon, sausage, biscuits, coffee, and juice.

On a Saturday morning, breakfast was a completely different meal.

All of the usual full-time residents of Winters House were there: Aiden, Gage, his wife Sophie, and their great-aunt Amelia. Added to them were Violet, myself, and Annalise—who had come looking for food after seeing her husband Riley off for some top-secret project that demanded his attendance at the crack of dawn on a weekend.

In any other dining room, we would have been a crowd.

In the dining room of Winters House, we barely filled half the table. The room was spectacular, more suited for a state dinner than a family breakfast.

None of the Winters seemed to notice. I'd been eating there for over two weeks and I still couldn't stop staring.

The long, polished table stretched the length of the room, surrounded by heavy, ornately carved wooden chairs with dark velvet seats. At one end was an enormous stone fireplace, left cold this time of year.

The beamed ceiling rose two full stories above, and along the end opposite the fireplace, an iron-railed gallery framed a library filled with books.

Usually, the majesty of the dining room was a distraction, but after an early morning run, my stomach took precedence over my surroundings.

I wasn't usually a huge breakfast guy, but my sweet tooth and ten miles on the road collided in a plate stacked high with fluffy waffles, butter melting in the crispy indentations, fragrant real maple syrup sinking in. Bacon piled high. Round, crisp links of sausage. A fluffy biscuit slathered in homemade blackberry jam.

It was a good thing the Winters had the gym downstairs. I was going to need it to burn off Abel's cooking.

I looked across the table at my sister, and my heart eased at the relaxed happiness in her lavender eyes. She'd spent too much of her life on her own. Our parents had focused entirely on her after they'd kicked me out and spent most of those years telling her she wasn't good enough. She wasn't worth their time. Their investment. As if she'd been their portfolio and not their child.

I'd tried to make up for the damage they'd caused, but an older brother can only do so much. Aiden Winters was good for her. Violet was as strong-willed as they came, and she needed a man who could stand up to her. A man who appreciated her strength. She'd found that man in Aiden.

I let the sounds of conversation flow around me as I focused on my waffles. I didn't look up until I heard someone say my name. Aunt Amelia was looking at me, a sparkle in her clear blue eyes and a mischievous grin wrinkling her lips.

The Winters' great-aunt Amelia was eighty years old, and technically Sophie was her nurse, charged with managing her diabetes and generally keeping Amelia out of trouble.

The first part of her job was simple enough, but the second was apparently a significant challenge.

I'd heard a few stories about Amelia's pranks, and I'd been careful to stay on her good side. Unlike my sister, I didn't want to come home to a snake under my pillow.

Realizing she'd been trying to get my attention, I said, "What's up?"

"I hear you've been going to Annabelle's a lot," she said.

"Huh, you did? Who'd you hear that from?"

"From Annabelle," she said as if it were obvious. "Are you pestering that girl?"

"Depends on what you mean by pestering," I hedged.

"Are you sniffing around her? Have you asked her out yet?"

"Amelia," Annalise cut in. "Leave Chase alone."

She looked at me and rolled her eyes mouthing, *Sorry*. I shook my head, so she knew I wasn't bothered. Amelia was full of piss and vinegar, and I liked it.

"I wouldn't say I'm pestering her, but I did ask her out. She turned me down."

"You give up too easy then," Amelia said, raising an eyebrow.

"Chase never gives up on anything," Violet cut in.

My sister knew me inside and out. I wasn't a quitter, and I never walked away from something I wanted.

I wasn't giving up on Annabelle. Not that my feelings for Annabelle were any of their business. But I wanted to dig for information and the best way to get information was to give a little. To prime the pump, as it were.

"I asked her out, she turned me down, and I decided the best thing to do was spend a little time with her. Let her get to know me. That way when I ask her out again, she'll say yes."

Aunt Amelia laughed, the sound more a cackle than anything else. "Good luck with that one," she said through her amusement.

"What does that mean?" I asked, looking at Annalise. If anyone knew what Amelia was getting at, it would be Lise. Annalise looked at the table, rearranging her knife and fork beside one another with precision, avoiding my eyes.

It was Aiden who filled in the gaps. "This is Annabelle's business, but she was married, and it didn't end well."

"He was a jackass," Gage cut in, "and if it hadn't been for—"

"Gage. Enough." Aiden said and Gage, who loved nothing more than to bicker with his older cousin, fell silent.

Aiden gave me a measuring look that stretched almost uncomfortably long before he said, "It's Annabelle's story to tell. I won't go behind her back. She doesn't need a one-night stand."

Locking eyes with Aiden, I said honestly, "A one-night stand is the last thing I'm interested in with Annabelle."

"Then you're going to need patience. And you need to understand that she has good reason to be wary. Maybe you don't deserve it, but she doesn't know that yet."

I was digesting Aiden's revelations when, from the other side of the table, Lise said, "I wish I'd been here for her. I was halfway across the country and I didn't know. I'm a shitty friend."

Violet, who was sitting next to her, reached out a hand and wrapped it around Lise's fingers, giving her a comforting squeeze.

Quietly, she said, "Lise, Annabelle understands. Everybody understands. Don't feel guilty. You kept yourself safe. That's what she wanted for you."

"I know," Annalise said in a near whisper. "I'm still sorry I wasn't here for her."

Looking to lighten the mood, Aunt Amelia clapped her hands together with a sharp crack saying, "I can feel it in my bones, today is the day. We're going to find what we're looking for."

I had no idea what she was talking about, but I was more than happy to change the subject. "What are you looking for?"

Before she answered, Amelia cocked her head to the side, her bright eyes locked on mine and said, "What are your plans for the day? Do you want to help?"

Having no idea what I was agreeing to, I decided I was game for an adventure. "Sure. What's the plan? Are we robbing a bank? Hiding a body?"

Aunt Amelia winked at Violet and said, "I like your brother, Vivi." The Winters family had adopted my childhood nickname for Violet, and by the gentle smile on her face, it seemed she liked it.

"So?" I probed.

"It seems there are secret hiding places in the library," Aiden said. "We found one of them when William Davis broke in to retrieve a box of letters he'd written to your mother. My father mentioned them a few times. There are supposed to be three, but he died before he told us where they were, and Mrs. W doesn't know. We've been looking for six months, but we haven't found a thing."

"*We've* been looking," Amelia corrected pointing at Sophie across the table. "The rest of you lot have mostly been getting in the way."

"Which library?" I asked, looking up to the polished railing and narrow walkway above Aiden's head on the far side of the room. It was a library in miniature, tucked into the second level on the dining room, apparently inaccessible.

The secret library was one of the many unique features of Winters House, but the whimsical pointlessness of it in the elegant, stately home made it my favorite. I'd wanted to poke around up there, but I hadn't found the time to ask.

As one, the group shifted in their seats to look at the library above us. Sophie's eyes widened, and she and Amelia stared at each other in shocked surprise.

"How is it we've never looked up there?" Sophie asked.

Amelia grunted and poked her in the shoulder with a bony finger. "You should have thought of it. I'm an old woman. I'm practically senile."

"Right," Sophie said with a roll of her eyes.

Before anyone else could get there before me, I called out, "Dibs on the secret library!"

"Unfair!" Amelia called back "We've been looking for months. We get dibs on everything."

Sophie opened her mouth to speak, but Aiden got there first. "If you wanted dibs, you should have thought of it first. Chase thought of it. Chase gets to look."

"We can all look," Amelia tried.

"No, you can't. Not enough room," Aiden said, firmly

cutting her off. To me, the side of his mouth lifted in a grin, he said, "Mrs. W has the key. I'd ask her about the secret compartments. She didn't remember anything about the main library, but maybe taking a look at the library upstairs will shake something loose."

"Thanks," I said, rising from the table. "Anyone want to tell me what I'm looking for?"

Gage shrugged a shoulder. "We would if we knew. The compartment holding the box with the letters was about eighteen inches square, hidden behind a row of books. The others could be bigger, smaller—"

"Or they might not exist at all," Aiden said.

"You don't think there are more secret compartments?" I asked.

"Maybe there are, maybe there aren't," he said. "So far, the fun seems to be in the looking."

"Got it," I said, pushing my chair in and heading for the door to the butler's pantry on the far side of the dining room. I hadn't gotten used to leaving my dirty dishes on the table, but I'd quickly learned that neither Mrs. W nor Abel appreciated my attempts to do their jobs for them.

I didn't hear the voices until the door separating the butler's pantry from the dining room swung shut behind me.

Alone in the small room lined with glass-covered cabinets filled with dishes, wine glasses, and other dining implements, I stood frozen as the argument taking place in the kitchen leaked through the second swinging door.

I should have left. Eavesdropping was rude, and whatever the two in the kitchen were arguing about, it was none of my business. I stayed anyway. I recognized the voices.

Mrs. W's normally smooth, clear tones were jagged with frustration and a note of something I thought might be fear.

Or pain. Maybe both. Abel rarely spoke, but I recognized his gruff, low voice immediately. Like Mrs. W, he was frustrated. Angry.

"Helen, how long are we going to keep doing this? There's no point to it. None of those kids mind. They love you. They like my cooking well enough that they're not kicking me out."

"That's not the point," Mrs. W replied, her voice tight, the clink of dishes in the sink chopping up her words. "There's so much going on with the family right now. I just think we should keep it quiet. Wait a little longer."

A thump, like a fist pounding the counter. "There's always something going on with the family. There's never going to be a good time. Now is the time. I love you. I love you, and I'm tired of sneaking around."

"Abel. Abel." Her voice softened the second time she said his name, gentle and anguished.

"Why is that so hard to hear, Helen?"

A long, still, silence, during which I seriously thought about sneaking away. I shouldn't be listening to this conversation. It was private and deeply personal.

But the kitchen was so quiet I was afraid that if I opened the door back to the dining room, they'd know I'd been in here listening.

I stayed where I was, silent and still, and waited.

CHAPTER EIGHT

CHASE

Finally, Mrs. W let out a long sigh. So quietly I could barely hear her through the thick door, she said, "I love you, too, Abel. I have for so long. I just... It's so much change."

"A good change, love. Not all change is bad. Look at the last year." Abel's words were so gentle I could barely imagine them coming from the gruff, taciturn man.

"I know. I'm not ready. I love you, but I'm not ready."

"Helen, we've been sneaking around for too long. If you're not ready, you need to get ready. This is ridiculous."

"I'm too old for this. Why do we have to make more of it?"

Another thump on the counter. Abel's frustration was palpable, even from another room. "Because you're not too old for this, Helen. Neither of us are. You act like you're ancient, but you're still young. You have so much of your life left and I want you to spend it with me. I'm tired of you treating me like a dirty secret. If you're not prepared to take the next step, then we're not doing this at all."

"Abel!"

Heavy footsteps. The door slammed. Barely audible, Mrs. W said to the empty room, "Abel, no."

I stayed there, frozen for a few minutes, listening to the murmur of voices from the dining room, the clink of silverware, the scrape of chairs being pushed back from the table.

When I thought enough time had passed, I pushed open the door to the kitchen to find Mrs. W washing dishes, her cheeks flushed and her eyes shining with moisture.

"Hey, sorry to bother you—"

Mrs. W cleared her throat. "It's never a bother, Chase. What can I do for you?"

If I hadn't heard the argument, I would never have known anything was wrong. "I guess you know the search is on for another day?"

Mrs. W smiled fondly. "I supposed it would be. It's become something of a Saturday tradition around here."

"I asked, and they said no one has searched the library above the dining room."

Just as the family had earlier, Mrs. W's dark eyes went wide in surprise. "No. No, they haven't."

"Aiden said you didn't remember where any of the secret compartments are," I probed.

"I don't. It's not that I don't recall. It's that I was never told in the first place. I only know they exist from things Olivia said. And I've always been certain they were in the library. She must have mentioned something about them being in the library at one point. But now that you mention the library above the dining room...she never specified *which* library."

"Does anyone ever go up there?"

Mrs. W shook her head. "I do, only to dust. The books are antiques. Delicate. If you're going to work in there, please be gentle. There's nothing so old you can't handle it, but some of them are valuable. It's a wonderful little space, but not very practical. We tend to appreciate it from the dining room. Almost no one goes inside."

"May I have the key?"

"Certainly. Do you know how to get in?" A sly smile curled the sides of Mrs. W's mouth, and I shook my head.

"Here, I'll show you, let me dry my hands off."

I waited as she wiped her hands with a dish towel, neatly folding it and laying it beside the sink before disappearing into her office off the kitchen. She returned with a shiny brass skeleton key on a long, bottle-green ribbon.

I followed her down the hall, through the entry, and up the stairs to the second level. I'd only been up here once, the day we'd moved in. The second floor of Winters House held only two bedroom suites, the largest occupied by Aiden and the other, only slightly smaller, by Gage.

Just to the right of the top of the stairs, Mrs. W stopped. Reaching behind a small bronze statue of a dancer, she ran her fingertips down the wood paneling on the wall, feeling for something. Some change in texture, a bump, or a hole.

I couldn't tell, but I did see the flex of her arm as she pressed her thumb against something. A moment later, a small square sank into the wall and slid to the side, revealing a keyhole. I never would have seen it, the lines of the square disguised by the pattern of the paneling. She used the key to turn the lock and the door swung open, appearing as if from nowhere.

"The wood panels do a perfect job of hiding the door," I said, marveling at the way the designer had lined up the pattern with the shape of the narrow doorway.

"I know. I polish it carefully to keep dust from settling into the cracks. The elder Mr. Winters, the children's grandfather, was apparently full of secrets. He liked his fun."

Mrs. W hung the key around her neck and nodded her head to the open doorway. "As I said, be gentle with the books. You can open the door easily from the inside, but if you take a break, prop it open because it will lock behind you."

"Thank you," I said.

For a moment I wished I could say something about the argument I'd overheard, but I didn't know Mrs. W well enough. I did know she believed in keeping her personal life separate from her professional life. She wouldn't appreciate my butting in. She definitely wouldn't appreciate my telling the rest of the family what I'd overheard. And I wouldn't. Probably.

"Good luck," she said. Her feet echoed down the hall, then the staircase, as I slipped through the open door into the secret library.

The view of the Winters family dining room from the second level was imposing. From above, the space was somehow even more grand, the wide stone fireplace majestic, the long shining table with almost throne-like chairs at either end fit for royalty.

It was hard to believe I'd been eating breakfast and dinner there every day for more than two weeks. Oddly, it was somehow not hard at all to imagine Violet sharing that table with Aiden.

My baby sister had grown up in more ordinary circumstances than the Winters family, but she'd always had the seeds of a queen inside of her.

An empty place in my heart, a hole, jagged and unfinished, had filled at the knowledge that Vivi was safe and happy with Aiden Winters.

Obviously, I didn't think about what it really meant that she was *with* Aiden. In my mind, they sat side-by-side and held hands, because my little sister was never going to do more than that with any man, even after she was married.

If I admitted there might be more between them I'd go back to wanting to punch Aiden in his perfect nose, and Vivi would kill me.

Hand holding and other things aside, I knew Aiden Winters would do anything to keep her happy. That was more than enough for me. And this—this family, this house, these people—were everything she deserved. Weird then, that I had more right to them than she did.

I still hadn't absorbed the fact that I was related by blood to half of them. That Anna Winters, their beloved dead mother, had given birth to me first. That I was, in fact, the oldest in the family. Not a Winters. Not by blood. Anna had been a Marlow.

Not that I wanted to be a Winters. They may have been rich as sin, but I didn't do too badly myself, and their kind of money came with attention I didn't want. Scandal, and pain, and loss. I'd had enough of my own. I didn't want theirs, too.

Somehow, Aiden must have convinced the rest of them to let me search alone because the dining room remained empty, the silence interrupted only by Mrs. W clearing the breakfast dishes. I stood, leaning against the door, and studied the long wall of books. The narrow walkway. The waist-high railing of wood and dark iron.

I didn't know what I was looking for.

Patterns.

It's a side benefit of being a coder. My brain loves patterns.

If there was a secret compartment hidden here, there

would be a pattern to show me where it was. I let my eyes skim the shelves, unfocused, looking for the bigger picture.

Something in the color or the shapes.

Something in the way the books were spaced.

Nothing jumped out on my first pass. Or my second. I narrowed my gaze and looked for details, taking in each shelf one by one, studying them first horizontally, then vertically.

Still, nothing jumped out at me. I walked to the center of the library and leaned against the railing. It was hard to get the full scope this close. At least twelve feet of shelves extended on either side.

My peripheral vision blurred as I tried to process the entirety of the library at once. I let my eyes relax and began to scan again. Right to left. Top to bottom. Left to right. Floor to ceiling.

A few times, I thought I saw something, but when I checked it was only a book that hadn't been pushed all the way on the shelf or had been put back in the wrong place. Unlikely either were on purpose.

If the younger generation of Winters had no idea where to find the secret compartments, that meant no one would have touched them since Hugh and Olivia Winters had been killed nearly fifteen years before. And while this library was rarely used, it hadn't remained untouched since then.

At the least, Mrs. W came into clean. Anything that was slightly out of place was unlikely to be a clue. Methodically, I walked to the far end of the library, leaned into the corner created by the rail and the side wall, and began to scan the shelves again, just as I had the first two times.

Once with my eyes taking in every detail, and a second

time with my eyes unfocused, absorbing the whole rather than the parts.

That was when I saw it. From this angle, there was a pattern to the spines of the books. Not color. Not shape. But the print on the spines. While the bindings all matched—no hodgepodge of volumes here—some of the bindings had an embossed fleur-de-lis at the base. It was small and subtle. From my other positions on the narrow walkway the pattern hadn't jumped out at me, but from where I stood in the corner I could see they formed a line pointing to the bottom shelf, dead center.

Crouching down, I carefully removed the books from that section, stacking them neatly to the side, maintaining the order so I could replace them exactly how they'd been.

Right there, waiting for me on the back of the shelf, was a small black iron latch. I hooked the latch and pulled. The back panel of the shelf rose smoothly to reveal a hole in the wall.

My heart thudding with anticipation, I pulled out my phone and flicked on the light. I thought about calling the others. They'd want to be here to see what was inside. I told myself to get up or call out.

I did neither.

Breath short, heart racing, all I could do was stare. The last hidden compartment had contained secrets about me. Letters my biological father had written to Anna Marlow after she'd left him. After he'd gotten her pregnant with me.

I hadn't seen those letters yet. I hadn't asked. I knew if I did they would give them to me, but, while I hadn't decided how I felt about Anna Winters, I knew exactly how I felt about William Davis.

He'd been psychotic. Evil. He'd brought pain and death to this family, and I hated the thought that even a drop of his blood ran in my veins. Whatever he'd had to say to Anna, I wasn't ready to see it.

Just because the last secret compartment had answers to the mystery of my origins didn't mean this one would.

But it might.

Leaning in further, I shone the bright white light from my phone into the dark space.

It illuminated a rectangular wooden box covered with a thin film of dust. Scanning the light over all four corners of the compartment, I made sure the box was the only thing inside before I set down my phone and reached for my prize.

CHAPTER NINE

CHASE

The compartment, and the box itself, were bigger than I expected. I guess I'd imagined I'd find something small.

At about a foot square and a hand's width tall, the wooden box had weight to it. Enough weight that when I opened it I didn't expect to find letters.

More letters.

My heart sank. I didn't want to deal with letters. Letters were so personal. Trinkets I could handle. Everyone had trinkets. I thought of the top drawer of my dresser, now dumped into a box I'd unpack at some indeterminate point in the future.

Movie ticket stubs, a lanyard from a conference I'd enjoyed, a golf tee from the last disastrous time Violet and I had tried golfing together. No idea why, neither of us enjoyed the sport, but we'd laughed ourselves stupid in the process.

Trinkets I could handle. I didn't want letters.

I thought about calling out to the crew diligently searching the main library downstairs.

Something stopped me. The letters, still in their envelopes, were addressed to Anna at what I assumed was her childhood home in Alabama. They'd been stacked in the box in chronological order.

I opened the first and pulled out the folded sheet inside. Strongly slanted script, written in a heavy hand, addressed to Anna Marlow. I scanned to the bottom and saw they were signed by James Winters.

Double checking the postmark, I realized these were the letters he'd written when she'd dropped out of college. When she was pregnant with me. The first started simply.

Dear Anna,

Art history isn't the same without you. I think I'm going to fall asleep at least once a week for the rest of the semester. I don't know what happened with William, he won't talk about it, but he's been an ass, so I'm sure it was all his fault.

I hope you were telling the truth when you said this was only a short break. I miss you. If you don't want me to write, or don't want to write back...if it's too soon, I understand.

James

My hands shaking a little, I folded the letter, slid it back into the envelope and moved it to the bottom of the pile. I stared at the next letter before I pulled it from the envelope.

Anna,

Your aunt Janet sounds like my aunt Amelia. I'm glad you're enjoying the time with your family. I wish you'd tell me why you won't come back. I'm holding you to your promise to be here for the summer session. If not summer, definitely fall.

Everything seems slower without you. Dimmer. Not just art history.

William has been insisting that you two will get back together. Is it true? You don't have to tell me if it's too personal a question.

If you have time I want to hear more about life at home.

James

THE NEXT FEW LETTERS WERE SIMILAR, SHORT AND mostly filled with news about school, but here and there James revealed his growing feelings for Anna. I suspected those feelings had existed long before she left school.

I'd bet James Winters had been in love with Anna when she'd still been dating his best friend.

As I moved through the stack of letters they grew longer, more heartfelt, and finally filled with his devotion to her. Her return letters were not in the box, but somewhere along the line, she must have confessed what had happened. Why she'd really left school.

Based on a few comments from James, it seemed he'd visited her, and I wondered if he'd known the truth before he'd arrived in Alabama. Either way, her pregnancy with another man's child didn't dissuade him. In one of the last letters he said,

Dearest Anna,

You have to make the right choice for yourself. I can't make it for you and I won't pretend to try. But know that I love you. If you want to keep your child I'll raise him as my own. I know this is one of the hardest decisions you will ever make, and I want you to know that I'm yours, no matter what. I wish I could make this easier for you. I wish for a lot of things, but mostly I wish for your love and your good health. And above all else, I wish for you to return to me as soon as you can.

Yours Always,

James

I sat there and stared at the yellowed paper in my hand, at James Winters' strong slashes of ink, and wondered. What kind of man had he been? Would he really have taken me in and raised me as his son?

I couldn't picture that life.

I was estranged from my parents. Suzanne and Henry Westbrook had adopted me, raised me, and kicked me out when I no longer fit their plans. They'd been the source of so much pain and rejection.

But if I'd been raised here in this house the oldest child of Anna and James Winters, I wouldn't have my sister. I couldn't imagine a life without Vivi. I wouldn't want one. I'd adored Vivi the moment Henry and Suzanne had brought her home, with her gold and platinum curls and those odd lavender eyes.

She'd attached herself to me from the first day, her tiny baby fingers wrapping around my thumb and squeezing so hard I wasn't sure I could get her to let go.

Suzanne and Henry hadn't been the affectionate type. They'd been stern, with lofty expectations, and when we failed them—as we often did—they'd treated us to icy disdain until we could earn back their love.

Not Vivi. She was reserved with strangers, but since infancy, she'd given me her whole heart. I'd given her mine in return.

No, even if Anna and James would have been the perfect parents, I still wouldn't trade my little sister for them. Not for anything.

I couldn't quite decipher the feelings in my chest. Most of my life I'd hated Anna Winters. And I had to wonder—if James would have taken me, would have married her even pregnant with another man's child, then why hadn't he?

I put the letter away, sliding it to the bottom of the pile, and scanned the next few. There was no mention of the decision she had yet to make. Only news about school, James telling her how much he missed her, that he'd sent her a gift, or flowers. One letter alluded to a visit.

The last letter in the pile, however, was not addressed to Anna in James' slashing script. It was addressed to James, and the return address was Anna's.

My hands shook as I pulled it from the envelope, trembling so hard the letter fell through my fingers and almost fluttered through the rail to the dining room below.

My heart lurching, I snatched at it, catching the edge and pulling it back. I wasn't sure I wanted to read it. I had to read it. Knowing who my mother was, knowing the back-ground, was one thing.

Holding in my hands a letter she'd written? That was different. The paper rattled as I unfolded it and took in her looping messy scrawl. Not yet a doctor and already she had the requisite awful handwriting.

James,

I love you all the more for your understanding. For your acceptance. I'll never be able to tell you how much it means. Yet, it doesn't do a thing in helping me figure out what to do.

Why is that? Knowing that you love me anyway, that you'll take me with or without this child, should make everything easy. It only makes it harder.

I know that you mean it. I know that you love me, and you would love this child. But what kind of home can we give him now? We're so young. You have years left of school, as do I.

My entire life I've been working toward one goal. One dream. If I keep this child, I don't think it will ever come true. I can't envision a future that includes both the baby and medical school. What kind of life is that for him?

Either I resent him, or I abandon him to nurses and nannies. Assuming I could afford the childcare in the first place. I know you want to get married, and I want to marry you more than anything. But your parents will be furious. And if they cut us off, we won't be able to afford a child anyway.

I am selfish. I am a low, horrible, selfish person. Because I love this baby. I do. He moves inside me, and I feel his kicks, and I want to know him. I want to hold him in my arms, to kiss him, to teach him to walk, and ride a bike, to read him stories. And if I choose that future, I give up all of my dreams. I don't think I can do that.

I want children. I want to be a mother. But not right now. I have two paths in front of me, and I cannot follow them both. I know whatever I choose I will regret it for the rest of my life.

All my love,

Anna

THIS LETTER, I RETURNED TO ITS ENVELOPE AND SLID in my pocket.

This letter was mine.

I couldn't process her words and what they meant. Couldn't process the rush of compassion for her pain over the choice she'd had to make.

Or the resentment that she hadn't chosen me. That she'd chosen her career. That she'd chosen her dreams and forgone any hope of ever knowing mine.

There was no mention of William Davis in any of the letters, aside from James' brief comments that he hadn't taken their breakup well. I'd wondered if Anna and James had sent me away because they'd been worried about Davis.

That didn't quite make sense, knowing they'd remained friends with him until his obsession with Anna had gotten them killed. I set the stack of letters from James to Anna aside and felt along the bottom of the box. It was lined with black velvet, but there was something else there, a dark envelope that almost disappeared against the fabric. I hooked a fingernail under the edge and pulled.

I hadn't seen one of these in almost 20 years. An envelope of photographs, with the name of the drugstore where they'd been processed—long out of business—printed on the back. I shook the photographs into my hand and sucked in a breath of shock.

I blinked hard at the moisture prickling the back of my eyes. The face looking at me was so like my own, so like Vance and Annalise, and even Gage, who I'd heard resembled his father. A young Anna Marlow, lounging on the grass in a courtyard at what I guessed was Emory University, she was identical to pictures I'd seen of Annalise at the same age.

The resemblance shouldn't have been a surprise, considering it was the reason for William Davis' obsession with Lise, the reason he'd stalked her relentlessly until he'd died in his last attempt to claim her.

In the photograph, Anna was laughing, blue eyes bright, hair gleaming platinum in the sun. I slid that picture to the bottom of the pile and looked at the next. My heart clutched to see Anna, heavily pregnant in a hideous flowered smock of a dress, sitting on a porch swing beside a man who could only be James Winters.

There was an engagement ring on a chain around her neck. I could guess her fingers were too swollen from pregnancy to wear it yet.

He looked at her with such tenderness. In her eyes, I saw love, but also fear. Hesitation. Uncertainty.

Emotion swamped me, too much at once. Envy and pity and anger, and a deep, wrenching, horrible sense of loss for these people who should have been mine and were gone.

Her children, her real children, needed to see these pictures.

Methodically, I replaced the photographs, then the letters—except for the one in my pocket—back in the box and closed the lid. Pressing the heels of my palms to my eyes, I forced my roiling emotions under control.

The Winters family was so eager to reach out, to bring me into the fold, and I knew if they sensed the slightest bit of weakness on my part they would be all over it. Asking me to talk. Wanting me to tell them how I felt.

It was nice to know they cared, but these feelings were mine. Until I figured them out, I didn't even want to share them with Vivi. I didn't want to be fixed or reassured. I had to work through it myself. I closed the secret compartment and replaced the books.

In the main library, Vivi stood at the top of a ladder, Aiden at the base, arms crossed over his chest, glowering up at her. She was laughing, and I caught the tail end of what she'd been saying.

"...worried. You'll catch me,"

"Not if you land on my head," Aiden said sardonically. His eyes caught mine as I passed through the open door and immediately sharpened. "Chase, what do you have there?"

Taking a deep breath, I said, "I found one of the secret compartments. You're going to want to see this."

Silence fell over the room. Vivi started down the ladder so quickly Aiden reached out to steady her, and with a look of exasperation, closed his hands around her hips and lifted her off before she could slip.

Amelia was comfortably ensconced on the couch, a blanket over her lap despite the warmth of late summer. She reached out her hands and said, "Come on then, give it here!"

I didn't move. Belatedly, I noticed that not only was Gage here, so was Vance, his two and a half-year-old daughter sitting comfortably on his hip. I knew the secret compartment search was Amelia's pet project, but this box, these letters and pictures, belonged to Anna's children.

I crossed the room and held out the box to Gage. His dark blue eyes were wary as he took it from my hands. Without a word, Vance handed Rosie off to Sophie and turned his full attention to me.

"What did you find?" he asked evenly.

I started to speak, and the words caught in my throat in an embarrassing squawk. Clearing it, I tried again. "Letters. Letters from your father to your mother." Vance's eyes squinted at me and I corrected, "To Anna."

He wanted me to call her my mother, too. I couldn't. She wasn't my mother. For better or worse, Suzanne Westbrook was my mother. She had her faults. A lot of them. Starting with her belief that hugs made for unruly children and ending when she kicked me out for getting a tattoo and a motorcycle, despite the fact that I'd paid for them myself, had good grades, and mostly stayed out of trouble.

I wasn't a perfect child, so I was gone.

Even so, she was my mother.

She'd nursed me through the flu, given me a safe home and a full belly. Made sure I had a top-notch education. She'd given me Vivi, the most reliable source of love and affection in my life.

I knew from everything they'd said that Anna Winters had been a wonderful mother. But she wasn't *my* mother. She'd made her choice, and maybe after I read that letter to James a few thousand times, I would understand it better.

I knew what it was to have dreams. To want something so badly you'd do anything to have it.

I'd made my dreams come true, and I'd had a far easier path than Anna Marlow. I'd been on my own after my parents cut me off, but I'd had scholarships and a part-time job to smooth the way. I'd worked my ass off for years, but that wasn't the same as being an unwed mother who dreamed of medical school and a career as a doctor.

Making my dreams come true had required dedication. Hard work. Creativity. For Anna, it had required all of that and more. Sacrifice. Pain. She'd made choices no young woman should have to face. I could imagine what she'd been through, but I didn't really know.

I was well aware she could have chosen to end the pregnancy. It might've been difficult back then, but Anna had connections. I had no doubt if James had put a word in the right ear, Anna could have solved the problem easily enough without even leaving school.

She hadn't done that. She'd chosen to give me life. I appreciated it. Obviously. It still didn't make her my mom. Before Vance or Gage could say anything, I went on, "There are pictures. Of her when she was pregnant with me—" My voice caught a little, but I pushed through, "Of her with your father. You'll want to see them. If Lise is at her house—"

"I'll call her," Vance said, pulling his phone out of his pocket. With a look at Aiden, "We never gave Chase the other box."

"What other box?" Vivi asked, looking between Aiden, Gage, and Vance.

Sophie was so focused on Rosie, I knew that while she hadn't missed a word, she had no interest in jumping into the conversation. More worrisome, Aunt Amelia was uncharacteristically quiet, and she wouldn't meet my eyes.

Looking between Vivi and me, Aiden said gently, "The box of letters from William Davis to Anna. We found them when Davis broke into the house, opened the first compartment, and tried to steal them. We put them back in the box and set them aside. They should go to Chase."

Great. Letters from my sociopathic sperm donor to the mother who'd given me up. Just the kind of nighttime reading I was looking for. Forget a good techno-thriller. Let's read through years of obsession that resulted in four deaths.

Vivi knew what I was thinking because those lavender eyes went dark as they met mine. "Maybe they belong to you, but you don't have to read them. You don't. There's nothing you need to know about William Davis except that he's dead. He was crazy and he's dead. He has nothing to do with you."

She was right, and she was wrong.

I wouldn't exist without William Davis. And I wasn't one to hide from my problems. I could pretend he didn't exist, but that didn't erase the past. It didn't change the blood running in my veins. Maybe it was time I learned exactly how crazy he'd been.

I shrugged a shoulder, trying for nonchalance I knew I didn't pull off. Proving again that they were good people, everyone in the room let me get away with it.

"Vivi, it's okay. I'll take the letters. Doesn't mean I have to read them right away. It's not that big a deal. I didn't even know him."

Vivi wasn't buying it either, but she let it go.

Aiden gave Vivi's hand a squeeze and crossed the room. He knelt in the corner of the room, reaching deep into an empty shelf and removing a wooden box.

He handed it to me.

I eyed it the same way I might a grenade missing its pin. If I could have figured out a way to leave without touching that thing, that innocuous box that held my legacy of pain and evil, I would have.

Fuck my male pride, part of me wanted to take off running if it would let me avoid facing what was in that box.

The ravings of a madman, one who had been smart enough, clever enough, to hide his madness for a lifetime.

I couldn't bring myself to do it. When had I ever run from anything?

William Davis was dead. He couldn't hurt me now.

How wrong I was. I'd lived long enough to know the past can always reach out to cause pain.

The wooden box was cool in my hands. The moment I took its weight, I knew I couldn't stay in that room, in that house, a second longer.

Making some excuse, shutting out the sounds of my name called behind me, I took off, the tight band of panic around my chest only easing when I cleared the gates of Winters House and drove away.

CHAPTER TEN

CHASE

I didn't even think about where I was going. I didn't think about anything at all. The wooden box sat on the passenger seat of my car, a ticking bomb I wasn't ready to defuse.

I blanked my mind. I didn't want to think about the Winters family. I didn't want to think about Anna, or James, or William Davis. I had a violent and childlike urge for it all to just go away.

I wished I'd never found the file in my parents' basement. I wished I'd never moved to Atlanta, never forced my path to cross that of the Winters family.

Never discovered who my father was or learned that my mother was more than a name in a gossip column.

I was parallel parking on the street two blocks down from Annabelle's Café when I realized where I was. Who I'd come running to.

My subconscious was a lot sharper than the working part of my brain.

At the thought of seeing Annabelle, the knot in my gut

relaxed. She bristled with energy all the time, but it wasn't a nervous energy; it was active and productive. Underneath that buzz was a rock-solid sense of resolve. Of calm.

Annabelle knew enough of the background to make it easier than talking to a stranger, but she wasn't one of them. By her own admission, she was an outsider. I needed to talk to someone who didn't have an agenda, even if that agenda was my happiness.

I felt bad for running out on Vivi, but I knew in my gut that she would try to lead me around to accepting my place in the Winters family. A place I wasn't sure I wanted.

I didn't belong to them. I belonged to myself.

Picking up the box, I cradled it in my arms, awkwardly pulling my keys from my pocket and locking the car door.

The café was hopping. Midmorning on a beautiful Saturday and everyone was out shopping.

Even so, Annabelle glanced up from behind the counter, and the moment her eyes lit on my face she knew. I don't know how, but she knew something was wrong. With a word to the barista standing beside her, she stepped back, poked her head in the kitchen, and then she was coming around the counter, walking towards me.

"What happened?" she asked, concern clouding her warm brown eyes.

"I..."

I couldn't blurt it out in the middle of a crowded café.

Annabelle didn't wait. Closing her hand around my arm, she led me down the hall, past the restrooms, past her office, to a door with a deadbolt lock. Pulling a key from her pocket, she opened it and led me up a narrow set of stairs.

At the top, the door opened into a packed storage room. So packed, it took me a moment to realize that it wasn't a storage room, it was a living room. Or it had been.

Turning sideways to weave through the shelves and stacks of supplies, everything from paper cups to gigantic bags of sugar and flour, I followed Annabelle through another doorway into a makeshift studio apartment complete with galley kitchen, what looked like a tiny bathroom, and a futon neatly made with a quilt and pillow.

As if seeing it through my eyes, Annabelle's cheeks flushed. "It's not much. I, well, when I expanded—"

"Is this where you live?" I asked, trying to keep the judgment out of my voice. My freshman year dorm room had resembled a prison cell, and it had been more luxurious than this.

Annabelle's things were stacked in plastic storage containers, haphazardly piled in the corners. She barely had room to move around in here. Her cheeks flushed darker, and she gave a jerky shrug of one shoulder.

"I know, I know. It's ridiculous. But, see, I expanded into the storage room downstairs three years ago, and I had to borrow money to do it. I don't like that. It makes me nervous. So, instead of getting an apartment, like I probably should have, I turned my living room into the new storage room and I've been camping out here."

"For three years?" I asked, looking around the tiny, cramped space again.

She'd been living like this for three years? Carefully, not wanting to hurt her feelings, I said, "You look like you do a good business down there. Good enough that you could afford more than this."

"I do. I do a really good business. I didn't have any trouble borrowing the money I needed, honestly. But, like I said, I don't like that. It makes me nervous. I like to own what I have. And I had some financial setbacks a while ago, came close to losing the café and it's made me overly cautious.

"I want to buy a house. I know I won't be able to do it all with cash, but I was thinking if I could save up enough for a big down payment, I could keep my mortgage small. Then I'd have more money in the long run. I'm getting close."

"That makes sense," I admitted.

Most people weren't willing to sleep on a futon in a glorified storage room to save money for a down payment on a house, but I wasn't going to give her a hard time for being fiscally responsible. Even if she was taking it to an extreme.

It also answered my question of how much of a life she had outside of work. If this was where she went when she wasn't in the café, the answer was 'not much of one'. But I'd already suspected that.

"Sit," she commanded, gesturing to the futon across the room.

I did, balancing the wooden box on my knees. I still hadn't opened the thing. I still didn't want to.

Annabelle busied herself in the kitchen making a cup of coffee.

"I didn't mean to interrupt your work," I started to say, but she waved me off.

"I was due a break anyway," she said, "and Grover just came in off of his. He can handle my spot in the front for a while."

"So he showed up today?" Grover was the hipster, man-bunned barista who kept flaking on Annabelle. I'd been too distracted to spot him when I'd come in.

"He was even on time," she said with a little laugh. "I almost passed out from the shock"

I didn't say anything, only pressed my sweaty palms to the satiny surface of the wooden box and stared down at it.

"So, what's in the box?" Annabelle asked, coming to sit beside me and handing me a steaming cup of coffee.

"Have you heard about the search for the secret compartments in Winters House?"

"Amelia and Sophie's project? In the library?"

I nodded.

"I've heard enough. Why? Did you find that?" She started to reach for it, and I tightened my grip on the box.

When her hands dropped I reached in my back pocket and pulled out Anna's letter.

"No. This is the box they found after the break-in." I wasn't ready to say William Davis' name. "I got the bright idea to search the secret library above the dining room. I found a box of letters and pictures. Almost everything in there was from James to Anna—the letters, I mean—and there were some pictures of her—"

I cut off, suddenly realizing that I had no idea how much of the story Annabelle knew. Sure, she was tight with the Winters family, but inconvenient pregnancies and children given up for adoption weren't necessarily topics of conversation, even among friends.

For a moment I thought I should keep my mouth shut, and then I decided, *fuck that*. Annabelle was my friend, and this was my story, too. I had the right to talk to a friend if I wanted to. Feeling a shadow of my adolescent belligerence, I took a breath and started to explain.

"I don't know how much of this you know," I said. "But, apparently, Anna Winters and William Davis had a child when they were in college. She didn't tell him she was pregnant. She dropped out of college, went home to have the baby, and fell in love with James Winters through letters while she was gone. She gave the baby up for adoption, came back to school, married James, had a bunch of kids, and pretty much lived a fairytale until—"

I snapped my mouth shut. Annabelle had known Anna Winters. Had loved her. And while I might be resentful and angry, Annabelle still grieved.

"And you were that baby?" she guessed.

"You got there quickly," I said, feeling a little sick. Again, I wished all of this would go away. "Yeah. I'm the baby."

Annabelle didn't say anything. She reached out, prying one of my hands from my grip on the box and taking it in hers with a tight squeeze. All she said was, "Chase."

"How did you know?"

"You look too much like Vance for it to be a coincidence. I didn't know about Anna, though now that I'm thinking about it, it kind of makes sense. But I knew you had to be related to them somehow."

"Why didn't you ask?"

"Not my business," she said.

"How does it make sense? None of this makes sense to me."

I hated the part of me that wanted to understand Anna Winters. I hated the part of me that cared. I could still remember the rage I'd felt when I learned I was adopted, learned the people I thought were my parents had lied to me my entire life.

And then when I dug into the records and discovered that Anna Marlow had ditched me to become Anna Winters, I'd turned all that anger on her.

All that anger, that unhappiness, masked the part of me that was desperate for a piece of the woman who might have been my mother but had chosen not to be.

How to explain this to Chase?

To Chase, for whom every mention of Anna Winters was like picking at an open wound. His resentment and anger were so clear, and he had a right to them. I might have felt the same way. But the Anna in his mind wasn't the Anna I knew. The Anna I still missed.

"She died when I was nine," I said. "But I was there a lot. And she..."

I stopped, tipping my head back to stare at the ceiling as if the right words would appear somewhere among the exposed pipes and beams.

"She loved her kids so much. She worked a lot. She was a doctor and that doesn't generally lead to a light schedule. She wasn't just a doctor, she was a surgeon. On-call, long hours. And even as a little kid, I knew that as much as she loved her job, and she did love it, she felt guilty because it meant she was away from her children. Away from her family. I remember one night—"

My throat closed, and tears pooled in my eyes. She'd

been gone for so long, but Anna Winters had been a constant in my life, almost a second mother, and her loss at such a young age had hit me hard. She'd been vibrant, full of life, and then she was gone.

Chase's eyes went wide with alarm and he said, "Hey, hey, Annabelle, we don't have to talk about this. I didn't come here to make you sad."

"I want you to know, though. I don't think she ever forgot about you. She was late one night when I was there for a sleepover, and she missed putting Lise to bed. She never liked to miss putting her kids to bed. It was a thing with her. She would move heaven and earth to be home to tuck in her babies. And if she got called in to the hospital and couldn't do it... I was only a kid, but I could tell she hated it. She hated that part of her job. Maybe when she got into the hospital and scrubbed in for surgery she forgot about that and focused on how much she loved what she did.

"But in those moments when she was getting ready to leave the house, I could see it in her. As a kid, I didn't really get it. But Lise and I talked about it when we were older. It made Lise a little cautious about the idea of ambition. About wanting a career in the single-minded way her mother had because Lise remembered the price Anna paid for it. The guilt that ate at her. But now—"

I stopped as Chase shoved a letter into my hands. Anna's letter. Chase got up, setting the wooden box on the futon beside me and paced to the windows that looked down on Highland Avenue.

Slowly, not sure I was ready to see what was inside, I pulled the folded paper out of the envelope to see Anna's flowing, messy script. She'd been so young when she'd written this, young and facing a decision that had no right answer.

Hot tears streamed down my face at this glimpse inside the mind of a woman I'd loved, but only known as a child knows an adult, never as a grown woman.

In seeing this, seeing the decision that haunted her, so much made sense. Those nights I'd wake to find her sitting beside Lise's bed, stroking her daughter's hair off her face and watching her sleep with love and pain in her eyes.

Had she been looking at Lise and thinking of the child she'd given up? Doubting, and wishing she'd done it differently? Reading this letter, I knew her decision never sat easily, no matter how many years went by.

I refolded the letter and slid it back into its envelope, wiping away the tears on my cheeks with the back of my hands. My voice cracked when I spoke.

"She knew she'd regret it. She was right. She would have regretted it either way. It was different back then, you know. There weren't as many women pursuing a medical degree, for one. Med school would have been hard enough.

"I don't know that Annalise's grandparents would have disowned James. Honestly, it seems unlikely, but I never knew them. I always heard they were a lot more hard-line than Hugh and Olivia or James and Anna, so maybe her guess was right. And if James had been kicked out of the family business... He loved that company like Aiden and Gage do. It would have killed him. I'm not saying what she did was right—"

"Does it even matter anymore?" Chase shot out, with more than a trace of bitterness. "Was there really a right or wrong? She had me," he said, shrugging both shoulders and shoving his hands in his pockets. "She gave me life and then she gave me to a family she thought would take good care of me. Who *did* take good care of me. I'm not judging her."

"For someone who isn't judging, you seem pretty pissed off," I said neutrally. He had a right to be pissed. He had a right to feel however he wanted to feel. But Anna had done the best she could.

Chase let out a long breath and sank onto the futon beside me. "I am," he admitted. "And it's so fucking stupid, Annabelle. I don't have anything to be mad about. She made her choice, and in a lot of ways, it was a good one. She made sure I would have a good life and she wasn't sure she could give me that. Knowing what we know now about William Davis it's possible she kept me safe by giving me away. We'll never know what he would have done if she'd come home with me and married James. Obviously, he was unhinged..."

I hadn't even put that part of it together, and at the thought of William Davis—that stodgy, parental stand-in who'd hidden a monster beneath his bland façade—thinking about that man close to a defenseless infant who was in his way? I didn't want to consider what he might have done.

"Oh God, good point," I said. "Did those letters say anything about William?"

"No. Nothing. Not really. James mentioned in the beginning that William wasn't taking the breakup well. After that, nothing else. But Vance gave me this."

He looked at the wooden box beside him. Picking it up, he handed it to me. The wood was cool and silky beneath my fingertips, the box lighter than I expected.

"Is this what I think it is?" I asked.

"If you think it's the box William Davis broke into Winters House to get and left behind when he almost got caught, then yes."

"So, these are William's letters to Anna," I said, looking

at the box as if it were filled with roaches and poisonous spiders. I didn't have to read the letters to know their contents would be toxic.

"Exactly," Chase said grimly.

"Have you looked inside yet?"

"No. I couldn't. I came downstairs and I gave them the box with James' letters and the pictures of Anna. It was sad, but it was filled with so much love. Those pictures and letters were all about love. And then Vance gave me this—this box of poison—and I just—"

He let out another gust of air as if his ribs squeezed too tightly on his lungs. "I just left. I couldn't stay there and look at these. Their parents died because of him. And his blood is in my veins. He's a part of me. I wouldn't be alive if—"

"Stop," I shot out, grabbing his hand and shaking it hard, jerking him out of his thoughts. He looked up to meet my eyes. "Stop, Chase. Just because he was a part of the process that gave you life does not mean that he has anything to do with you. From everything I know, William Davis came from two perfectly normal, perfectly nice people. He has a brother and a sister around here somewhere and neither of them are crazy. Sometimes people go wrong. It doesn't mean it has anything to do with you."

"Annabelle, you know that's bullshit. Sometimes this stuff is genetic."

I squeezed his fingers tighter and shook his arm again. "And most of the time it's not. I'll agree, there must've been something wrong in William Davis' brain. You don't get that unhinged..."

I looked at the floor between my feet. It had been less than three months since William Davis had almost killed Annalise. The fear and pain—the shock—were still raw.

"I don't know how you get that deranged," I said. "The

way he went after Lise was fucked up. So, yeah, I'll agree there was something wrong with him, but we have no idea if it was genetic. And by now, don't you think you'd know? It's not like you're a little kid. If you were going to be a sociopath, I'm pretty sure we'd have seen the signs by now."

Chase appeared to think that over. I'd only known him for two weeks. Maybe he *was* a sociopath. I wasn't an expert on deranged minds, but I was sure most sociopaths knew how to hide their crazy. William Davis had been particularly good at it. But William Davis had always left me cold. The way he looked at me as if I were a bug, suitable only for being squashed beneath his shoe. Not good enough for the Winters children.

I'd always thought there was something off about him, but I'd assumed it was a normal reaction when someone doesn't like you. I didn't get anything like that from Chase.

I didn't entirely trust my judgment of him as a man. I wasn't good at picking boyfriends. In that context, I was a shit judge of character.

But in general? When it came to friendship? There, my track record was stellar.

Chase was my friend. He was a good guy. He didn't have crazy hiding inside him. I was sure of it.

I looked down at the box on the futon, still unopened. "Are you going to read them?" I asked.

"Do you think I should?"

I didn't have to consider. "No, I don't."

Chase, who'd opened his mouth to interrupt, shut it and stared at me for a second before he took a breath and said, "That's not what I thought you'd say. You strike me as the kind of woman who faces her problems head-on."

"I am," I agreed. "But this isn't your problem, Chase. William Davis was a lot of people's problem. He left a wake of destruction and death behind him. He was responsible for James and Anna's murders. He killed Olivia and Hugh himself. He terrorized Annalise, and she's lucky he didn't take her with him when he died. Leave him to the dead. He has nothing to do with you. You look like Anna. You remind me of her."

"I do? How? I know I look like her but—"

"No, not the way you look. I mean, yes, obviously the way you look. Your hair, your eyes, you and Vance and Annalise all look so much like her. But that's not what I mean. I mean the way you show up here with your laptop and work for hours without taking your eyes off the screen.

"I see her in your ambition. Your drive. Your focus. That's Anna. That part of you comes from her. Between the three of you, you're the only one who lived his ambitions from the start. The rest of them all got sidetracked by the past.

"They've made successes of themselves—well, Lise is working on it—but Vance and Gage disappeared. Vance into drinking, Gage into the Army. It took them years to find their way back to themselves. But you—you sound like you hit the ground running in high school and never looked back."

Chase's cheeks flushed a very appealing pink and he let out an embarrassed laugh. "I guess I did," he said. "I've never had a problem going after what I wanted."

There was a flash of intent in his eyes when he said he didn't have a problem going after what he wanted. I ignored it.

"There's nothing in you from him. You don't need to read those letters to prove that. And trust me, if what he wrote to Anna is anywhere close to as creepy as what he did to Lise, you don't want that in your head. You don't need it."

When I mentioned what William Davis had done to Lise, Chase squeezed his eyes shut.

"You were around when it started," he prompted.

"I was. And at first, we thought it was a game. We thought it was one of the boys in school who had a crush on Annalise Winters and was too shy to say anything. I'll never forget when we realized it was more than that. He left her a note. I don't know how to explain it. It wasn't so much what he said. I can't remember word for word, but it was basically that he loved her and someday they'd be together, but the tone of it was off. Creepy.

"We knew this was no teenager. We hadn't told anyone until then. It was a fun little secret. And then it was scary. It was a cat and mouse game to him, I think. It still seems like yesterday when she left. She was so in love with Riley and so heartbroken, knowing she was the reason he'd almost died."

"It wasn't her fault," Chase said. "She wasn't responsible for that."

"She wasn't," I agreed. "But she felt like she was. They were both dumbasses. If he'd told her he wasn't really a college student—"

I shook my head in disgust. "True love and the two of them fucked it up for over a decade. But Davis had her head screwed on backwards after so many years of messing with her.

"She wasn't thinking straight. I don't think she got it together until she came home. Until she had to deal with Riley again." I studied Chase's face, the set of his chin, and the roil of emotion in his blue eyes.

My voice gentle, I said, "I haven't known you that long. Only a few weeks. And maybe you're a really good liar. But I don't see that in you. I never thought Davis was her stalker, but he always creeped me out. The stiff, old guy who was always telling us what to do.

"He was a square peg in a round hole, you know? I always put it up to being ridiculously rich and out of touch with the rest of the world. Instead, it was that he was a sociopath."

Chase laughed, the pain wiped from his eyes by amusement and the line of tension in my shoulders relaxed. He looked down at the box again.

"I don't know what to do with this," he confessed. "I feel like I can't throw it away, but I don't want it. I don't want anything to do with him or his letters."

"Leave it here," I offered, without even thinking about it.

"What?"

"Leave it here," I said, knowing it was the right thing. "Stick it on one of the shelves in what used to be my living room. Hide it behind a bag of flour or sugar. It won't go anywhere. If you ever decide you want it back, I'll give it to you. It shouldn't be at Winters House, and you don't want it in your new place when you finally move in. Just leave it here. Leave the past in the past."

Chase stood picking up the box and looked down at me. "You're a good friend, Annabelle Woods."

I stood, smiling up at him. "I know." I took the box from his hands and carried it to the storage room, shoving it in a corner behind a giant bag of sugar. "Brownie to go?" I asked.

Chocolate couldn't fix everything, but it didn't hurt.

"Always," Chase said.

I felt his eyes on my ass as we went down the stairs and tried to ignore the little flutter in my belly I got when I knew he was looking at me, not as a friend looked at another friend, but as a man looks at a woman he wants.

I was doing so well on my dating ban. I was finally

getting my life back on track. I did not need to turn it upside down by falling into bed with my new friend.

I needed to keep doing what I was already doing.

Working my ass off and saving money.

Not dating.

Even if a part of me really wanted to. But only if it was with Chase.

CHAPTER TWELVE

CHASE

I pulled open the door to Annabelle's Café, my lips already curving into a smile, my heart beating faster at the thought of seeing Annabelle.

She'd become the high point of my day, the minutes and hours with her snatches of time, stolen and treasured.

Day by day, it was getting harder to wait. I was late tonight. It was almost eight, and I was hoping Annabelle would let me hang out while she closed, get some work done. Maybe help her out.

Hipster man-bun guy still hadn't agreed to move back to nights and she was still closing the café alone. I'd never tell her straight out that I happened to show up shortly before eight and stay until she was done because I didn't like her alone in the café at night.

She'd beat me over the head with one of her cast-iron skillets for that. Didn't make it any less true.

My gut twisted into a knot when I saw the café was mostly empty except for a man in a suit, briefcase in hand, talking to Annabelle at the counter.

I couldn't hear what they were saying, but I didn't like the body language. His or hers. He leaned forward, getting in Annabelle's space, his slicked-back blonde hair gleaming in the bright overhead lights, his smile smarmy.

Predatory.

Annabelle stood, shoulders stiff, arms crossed over her chest, teeth gritted, eyes narrowed in a glare. Something feral inside me clawed its way out of my chest and I had to consciously force it back.

I wanted to take the guy by the arm, rip him from the counter and shove him forcibly out of the door. Annabelle was beautiful. It wasn't her looks, it was everything about her. Her smile, her boundless energy.

It didn't surprise me to know she attracted male attention. Hell, she'd attracted mine the first time I laid eyes on her. But this guy didn't seem to get that she wasn't interested.

I hated the tightness in her jaw. The clench of her fists.

Her voice was low, but I caught a snatch of the conversation and it turned my gut to ice.

"You need to go. Now. I'm done talking to you."

Whoever this guy was, he wasn't a customer looking for a date. This was something else.

As I walked into view, Annabelle's warm brown eyes settled on my face and sheer relief washed over hers. She flashed the bright, brilliant smile that always dove straight to the center of my heart, bringing light everywhere she cast it.

"Hey," I said.

"Hey, Chase, I was wondering where you were." To my utter shock, Annabelle came around the counter and walked up to me, fitting herself to my side and sliding an arm around my waist, beaming up at me, affection and familiarity written all over her.

The guy at the counter took a step back, his dark eyes turning to stone. "Who the fuck are you?" he demanded.

Leaning into me, resting her cheek against my chest, Annabelle gave him a cool smile. "This is Chase."

She didn't offer his name, and I didn't ask for an introduction. As happy as I was to finally have Annabelle in my arms, her need for reassurance, for a barrier between her and this guy, was alarming.

She'd been so careful to keep a distance between us.

Whatever was going on with this guy, it was bad.

I wrapped my arm around Annabelle, holding her tight to my side, angling her slightly behind me as I studied the guy who'd been bothering her.

Dark suit, slicked-back blond hair, pink tie. Expensive briefcase, good shoes. He looked like all the other corporate drones at Winters, Inc. Not the right guy for Annabelle.

And yeah, I know, I was working at Winters, Inc., too.

But, number one, that was only temporary. I worked for myself. I didn't want a boss, even if that boss was family.

And number two, I didn't wear a suit. I wore whatever the hell I wanted.

So far, Gage and Aiden didn't seem to give a shit. They just wanted the work done. Neither of them would cut that kind of slack for a regular employee, but there were benefits to being family.

I couldn't resist dropping my cheek to the top of Annabelle's head, breathing in the vanilla scent of her shiny, cinnamon hair. She melted into me a little and I turned my head to press a kiss to her hair.

"Long day?" I murmured.

"Mmm," she answered, settling into me even more.

I closed my eyes for a heartbeat. If I could end every day like this, I'd be a happy man, even if it meant I'd soon be doing dishes or mopping the floor. Annabelle paid me in brownies and sandwiches. Considering that she was a fucking fantastic cook, it was an excellent trade-off.

"Annabelle," he barked, infuriated to have lost her attention. She went stiff in my arms, burrowing further into my side.

"Don't ever talk to her like that," I said in a low voice, conscious that there were still customers in the café. This asshole might not care about embarrassing Annabelle, but I did. "I think Annabelle wants you to leave."

I dropped my mouth to the side of her face and whispered, "You want him gone?" She nodded into my chest.

"She wants you out," I reiterated. "Go before I call the police. This is her place, and she has the right to refuse service."

The guy stared at us for another second before shaking his head in dismissal. "This isn't over, Belle."

Annabelle straightened a little and met his eyes. "It is over. I meant what I said. Don't come back."

"We'll see." At that parting shot, he stormed through the front door. The second it shut behind him, Annabelle tried to ease away from me. I tightened my arm.

In a low voice, I asked, "Who was that? Why was he bothering you?"

"It's no big deal." She tried to pull away again, and again I tightened my arm.

Under my breath, I said, "Hang on a sec. I want to talk to you, and I know you don't want your customers to hear."

Getting my point, Annabelle stayed where she was, but instead of soft and pliant, she was stiff, trying to put distance between us even if it was measured in millimeters.

I shouldn't have taken advantage, but I couldn't resist nuzzling my cheek against the top of her head one more time. She smelled so good. Warm sugar cookies with a hint of something beneath that was all Annabelle.

I wanted to strip off her clothes and see if she smelled that good everywhere. I wanted to make her come and see her smile at me, relaxed and replete. I wanted to stay like this, my arm wrapped around her long, lean frame, her body tucked into mine. Protected. Safe.

I planned to have all of those things eventually. But not yet. Annabelle wasn't ready. I would push on little things, like kissing her hair when I had her in my arms, but on the big stuff, we were on her timeline, not mine.

Annabelle wasn't a quick fuck. I wanted so much more than that from her. And more required trust. I could wait for trust.

I'd been on the sidelines for some of Violet and Aiden's courtship. I'd missed the beginning, fortunate for them because if I'd been around it never would have happened in the first place.

Aiden Winters was not who I had in mind for my Vivi. But, neither of them had trusted the other. Not really. Not where it counted. That lack of trust had almost torn them apart.

No one could tell me I didn't learn from my mistakes. I never saw a mistake as failure. I saw it as a lesson, and the best lessons were those someone else had to learn for me.

So, trust. I would be patient. Annabelle was worth waiting for. It still took everything I had not to turn her in my arms and put my mouth on hers. If I didn't suspect she'd drive her knee straight into my balls, I might have been tempted to try it.

My gut said it wasn't time. Not yet. I hadn't been waiting this long to fuck it up now.

"You're not going to tell me?" I murmured against her temple, my lips barely tasting her skin.

"Why? Are you going to go after him and beat him up?"

"Don't try to distract me. It's not a joke. Why was he bothering you?"

Annabelle sighed, the tension leaking from her shoulders. She melted into me again, shaking her head against my chest, brushing her temple against my lips. "Chase, I promise, I have it under control."

"Does that happen a lot?" I asked, knowing she wasn't going to explain. "Customers bugging you?"

"He wasn't a customer. And not really. Sometimes. Trust me, annoying customers hitting on you happens a lot less to baristas than it does to bartenders and cocktail waitresses. I know. I've done that, too. At least here I get to make brownies and I don't get my ass pinched. Most of the time."

Fighting down the growl that rose in my throat at the thought of some guy putting his hands on Annabelle's ass, I said tightly, "Anybody pinches your ass, you point me at him and I'll make sure he never touches anyone again without permission."

Annabelle shook against me and I realized she was silently giggling. "You don't need to beat up every guy who comes in and hits on me," she said, the laughter warbling in her words.

"I do if they're making you uncomfortable."

I said what I'd been holding back. If I wanted her to trust me, I had to be honest, even if she wasn't going to like it.

"I don't like you closing by yourself. I know this is your place, and I know you can handle it. But I don't like the way it looks to customers, you here on your own, and them knowing you're vulnerable. What if somebody hides in the bathroom when you lock up? Do you have an alarm system? I've never seen you set an alarm."

"I check the back and the bathrooms after I flip the sign," she protested, "and I do have an alarm. I usually set it from upstairs."

"Can you set it from down here? When you lock the door at eight?"

"I guess. There's a panel in my office in the back hall. I don't usually bother."

"You should bother. If you won't do it for yourself, will you do it as a favor to me?"

"Chase, this is the Highlands. There are bright street-lights right outside the front door and there's still street traffic at 8 o'clock, people going to restaurants and bars. It's not like I'm isolated."

"Not entirely. But you're alone, and your customers know that. You should fire what's-his-name if he's going to keep leaving you to close by yourself."

She planted a hand against my chest and pushed. I didn't loosen my arm and she said, "Don't tell me how to run my business."

I sighed and pressed my lips to the top of her head again. "I'm not. Do whatever you want with what's-his-name. I'm not trying to tell you how to run your café, I'm asking you to be more careful with yourself. There's a difference. I don't want anything to happen to you. And there are a lot of sketchy dudes out there who see a woman like you and—"

I cut myself off. Neither of us needed to put into words what that kind of guy might want from Annabelle. And why she might not be safe in her shop by herself at night.

"I want you to be more careful, that's all."

"I'll set the alarm," she agreed.

"Thank you," I said, pressing one last kiss to the warm skin at her temple before dropping my arm and stepping back.

There was a flush on her cheekbones and a glitter in her eyes when she stepped away. She couldn't quite meet my gaze. I hoped that meant she liked being in my arms as much as I'd liked having her there.

"Did you eat dinner?" she asked.

"Not really. I grabbed something from the vending machine by my desk. Lost track of time. You have anything left over?"

"You know I do. I always have leftovers for you. Go grab your spot and I'll bring you some dinner."

"Only if you let me help you close."

"I'm not going to turn down free labor," Annabelle said, with a saucy grin.

She pointed me in the direction of my favorite armchair, currently unoccupied. It was a little too close to a group around the couch who were deep into a board game, empty coffees and plates surrounding them.

It was probably rude to sit so close when there were plenty of other seats, but the armchair was my spot, and the café closed in ten minutes. They had to wrap up the board game anyway. If they wanted to keep Annabelle open past closing, they'd have to order a lot more than a few espresso drinks and some pastries.

Knowing Annabelle, she probably didn't plan to kick them out. This wasn't the first time I'd interrupted a game in progress. Annabelle had actually rearranged the chairs in that section slightly, pulling my favorite armchair a little away from the couch configuration. She'd moved it just far enough that the people who took over the couch and coffee table for board games rarely tried to pull it into their circle.

It was still close enough that I could glower at any lingering patrons as it neared eight o'clock. By the time I had my laptop out, Annabelle was sliding an Americano, decaf and black, fragrant and steaming, onto the table to my right. She'd serve a customer whatever they wanted at seven fifty-nine, but me, she gave decaf.

She said if I wanted to stay up all night working, I could make my own damn coffee. Annabelle's coffee was too good to argue, so I took what she gave me and drank it happily.

She was right, I didn't need to be staying up all night staring at my laptop screen. The days of marathon coding sessions were over. I wasn't twenty anymore.

Well, they were mostly over. It still happened now and then, but generally, I was an early to bed, early to rise kind of guy. In my twenties, I'd been fueled mostly on caffeine & junk food to counter my lack of sleep, but not long before I turned thirty, I'd noticed a spare tire creeping around my gut and found myself getting short of breath when I took the stairs.

I wasn't ready to lapse into mushy middle age at twenty-eight, so I'd ditched the junk food and took up running. Then free weights. A few years ago, I'd gotten into a high-intensity interval program that packed an hour of strength building into twenty sweat-soaked minutes.

I appreciated efficiency, even when it kicked my ass. Especially when it allowed me to indulge myself with Annabelle's decadent brownies.

I'd cut out most of my junk food habit, but chocolate wasn't junk. Chocolate was chocolate. A necessary food group. Plus antioxidants and all that. It's good for me.

Coffee in hand, I sipped and reviewed a section of code

I'd been working on earlier in the day. My project would move a lot faster if I had a team working with me, but I wasn't yet ready to share the app I was developing. I hadn't decided exactly what I was going to do with it.

I typed and tested and typed some more, quickly losing track of my surroundings. I didn't look up until Annabelle flopped onto the couch only a few feet away and propped her sneakered feet up on the coffee table, crossed at the ankle.

Startled, I looked up to see her lounging back, a wide, satisfied smile on her face and an ice cold bottle of beer in her hand. A plate with a thick sandwich and slice of cake sat on the corner of the coffee table closest to me.

CHAPTER THIRTEEN
ANNABELLE

C hase was lost in whatever he was doing on his laptop. Customers finished up their board games and brought their empties to the counter, slowly filtering out of the café on their way to whatever they'd planned for the rest of the evening. He noticed none of it, his eyes intent on the screen, fingers flying over the keyboard.

I liked to watch him like this, when he didn't know I was looking. When he couldn't read too much into it. I loved the focus in his eyes, the way he was so into his work. He'd tried once to explain his new project, but technology wasn't my thing unless it involved an espresso machine.

It was something about coordinating social media posts and viral reach. The café had a Facebook page and I liked to post pictures of my baked goods on Instagram, but that was the extent of my experience with social media. Viral reach sounded like something I didn't want to catch.

It didn't matter; the important thing was that he loved it.

It was clear that in the current upheaval of his life, work was his anchor. Work, and it seemed, the café.

He was here almost every day. It had gotten so that I checked the clock around seven thirty every night wondering when he'd show, feeling a little anxious if he hadn't turned up by eight.

I can't explain it. He wasn't my boyfriend. For so many reasons he wasn't going to be my boyfriend. But if I was being honest with myself, Chase was more than a friend. What I felt for him wasn't casual. That leap of my heart, that flutter in my belly when he pushed open the door... They were trouble.

I watched him raise his head and blink as if brushing away the cobwebs, finally realizing the café was empty and we were alone. He looked over at me and, of course, the first thing he said was, "You have beer?"

I tipped the bottle back and took a long sip before I answered. "Not for customers," I said. "I don't have a liquor license."

"I'm not a customer since I haven't paid you for anything."

"Good point," I conceded with a nod at the plate on the table. "Eat your dinner and I'll think about giving you a beer."

"I'm not going to turn down that deal."

I rested my head back on the couch and stared at the ceiling, smiling to myself. Chase picked up his plate and bit into the sandwich, his eyes lighting with pleasure. I pretended not to watch out of the corner of my eye.

I didn't want him to know how much satisfaction I got out of feeding him. I knew he had Abel at Winters House available at all hours to make him whatever he wanted. And still, Chase came here.

I'd made the double chocolate cake with mocha icing for him. Relaxed for the first time in hours, I let my eyes wander around the room. My feet ached and my shoulders burned from hauling trays and supplies, but I was happy all the way to my tired bones.

"What are you smiling about?" Chase asked through a mouthful of turkey, bacon, and avocado sandwich.

I lifted my head off the back of the couch and took another long sip of beer. "I love this place," I said simply. "I love every inch of it. And I don't care that it's a crazy amount of work. I don't care that I don't have a life. Because I made this and it's fucking awesome."

"It is," he agreed.

It was. I'd worked in the café in high-school and college. I'd taken a job there my senior year to pay for my prom dress and I'd fallen in love.

From the moment I tied on my apron, I'd known this was my place. The rich scent of coffee beans, the hiss of the espresso machine. The chatter of satisfied customers and sense of community.

I'd loved the place from the start, but I'd always known it could be something more. I had a vision in my junior year of college and was already imagining starting my own place after I graduated.

I'd paid close attention to all of the details involved in running the business. Ordering, planning, scheduling, budgeting. I made myself indispensable to the owner, and in return she gave me more and more responsibility, allowing me to learn everything I needed to know.

When she'd decided to sell halfway through my senior year all I'd been able to think was *finally*. Finally, it's going to happen.

That last semester of senior year had been crazed, first

putting together the business plan, trying to talk her into waiting while I worked with Aiden to get the money I needed, all while juggling exams and projects, making sure I did well enough to graduate.

All I remember from that period of my life is an overwhelming sense of relief when I had both my diploma in hand and my name on the front of the building.

Annabelle's Café.

The day my name was painted on the plate glass window, I'd started a long-term commitment that meant endless hours, financial risk, and sleepless nights. Sore feet and chapped hands. Early-morning alarms.

I loved it all. The exposed brick walls, the black iron of the tables and chairs. I'd loved painting the pipes overhead and choosing the faux antique tin ceiling panels.

Finding the overstuffed velvet couch I was sitting on. Hunting up Chase's favorite armchair in a consignment shop, purchased at a steal. Every piece of the café was a part of me, and I loved all of it.

Chase followed my eyes around the place as if seeing it for the first time. "Did you do the ceiling or was it here?" he asked, looking up at the vintage style tin squares painted in an antiqued, slightly metallic black. It was a subtle detail, but like most subtle details, it made the difference.

I grinned at my ceiling, then at Chase. He had a good eye. Most people wouldn't have noticed the ceiling like he had. "That was me," I said. "It wasn't very budget-friendly. Aiden and I had words about it. But even he gave in when I convinced him how good it would look. They look like tin—that's partly the paint—but they're made of an acoustic material that dampens the sound so it's not so echo-ey in here."

"How long did it take before you turned a profit?" he asked, looking concerned.

"Almost from the beginning," I said and couldn't help smiling to myself. "I was lucky. I'd worked here since I was seventeen, years before I bought the place. I knew most of the regulars and they knew me. I knew what sold and what didn't sell. I knew what people liked. And I knew what people wanted that the old owner wouldn't do."

"Like what?"

"Well, better coffee for one. She insisted that people didn't really know the difference and she went cheap. But people do know the difference, at least some of them, and I got a lot of appreciation when I kicked up the quality. The baked goods, too. She ordered out. I didn't have time to bake for her back then, and she was not good in the kitchen. Her sandwiches were okay, but she always used too much salt in her cookies and brownies."

"How do you use too much salt in brownies?" Chase asked, wrinkling his nose in disgust.

"I have no idea. But she did. She contracted out for the pastries and baked goods, but the margins were thin, and waste was a problem. She burned through money when she didn't have to. I do a lot better now that I keep the baking in-house."

"You do better because you bake like an angel," Chase said as he devoured the slice of chocolate cake with his eyes. It wouldn't last long once he finished with the sandwich.

I flushed at his compliment. "I've always like to bake. My mom and I used to do it together. Some of my best recipes are hers, or things we made up together. I love coming in in the early mornings when no one else is awake and making treats people will enjoy all day long."

Chase smiled at me, a gentle, sweet smile heavy with

affection and just enough heat to spark the tummy flutter that made me so nervous. I looked away.

He said, "You had good business from the first day, then."

"I did. Not like it is now, but enough to keep the lights on," I said distractedly.

Things with Chase were sliding off track.

We were friends. We had to stay friends. I already looked forward to seeing him too much. I knew what he wanted. I knew why he was here. And if I wasn't honest with him, we were both going to end up hurting ourselves. And each other.

I didn't want to do that. I loved his affection. I loved his attention. I loved talking to him. Being with him. I wasn't going to risk what we had over sex. I couldn't do it, and he needed to understand that.

I drained the rest of my beer and set it on the coffee table. The easiest way to do something hard is to get it over with. Like ripping off a band-aid. I braced myself for the pain and did what I had to do.

"I'm not going to go out with you," I said quietly. I rested my hands on my knees and stared at the open sign on the front door, turned inward to indicate the café was closed.

I waited for Chase to argue with me. To tell me I was wrong, that he'd talk me into it.

He didn't say anything, just watched me, carefully, confusion and a little irritation in those vibrant blue eyes.

Finally, he said, "Will you tell me why?"

I nodded once and tried to think. It was my fault I'd raised his expectations. I shouldn't have used him as a shield against Tommy, shouldn't have pretended he was my boyfriend and thrown myself into his arms.

Touching him had been a mistake. I didn't need to know

how good it would feel to lean into him, his strength and heat, the kiss he'd feathered across my temple. His touch left me giddy and lightheaded and it wasn't going to happen again.

I couldn't let it happen again or everything would go to hell and I'd lose him completely.

I chewed on my lower lip, my lip balm long since worn away, and thought about where to start. Finally, I said, "I'm only going to tell you because I don't want to lead you on. I don't want to be unfair to you."

"Why don't you let me worry about what's fair?"

"No. You need to understand. It's not you. I don't really go out with anyone. Especially not customers. Never customers."

"Annabelle, I'm not just a customer. For one thing, customers pay for their food."

I made myself laugh and flinched at the hollow, forced sound. Chase's brows drew together. He knew I was faking and he didn't like it either. I had to get this over with.

"Was he a customer?" Chase asked, interrupting my thoughts. "The guy who messed you up so badly you won't even let me take you out to dinner?"

"Yeah," I spit out. "He was a customer. And then he was my husband."

Chase jerked back as if he'd been punched. I figured he knew I'd been married. It's not like it's a secret.

His eyes hard in an expression that was both annoyed and territorial, he asked, "Was that him? Earlier?"

I hated that I had to say *yes*. Unable to force out the word, I nodded.

"How long were you married?" Chase asked, his voice carefully even.

He leaned forward as if he wanted to get up and sit next

to me or reach out and take my hand. I dug my fingers into the cushion of the sofa and hoped he'd stay where he was.

"Only two years. We dated for a year and a half before we got married. He used to come in for coffee every morning after the rush. He was charming and sweet. Thoughtful. He started bringing me things. Flowers. A book he thought I'd like.

"He talked me into a date, and then another. He completely swept me off my feet. Roses, limos, expensive restaurants. He was in marketing for a huge pharmaceutical company and he made a lot of money. I didn't like him because of that stuff. He was a really good guy. We fell head over heels in love. Whatever happened later when everything went to hell, I really believe that those first few years he was in as deep as I was."

"What happened?" Chase asked, his words clipped, their edges sharp.

"I don't know," I admitted. "I mean, I can tell you the events that occurred, but I still don't know why. We were together a year and a half before we got married and we never talked about things changing. After the wedding, he didn't seem to mind that I kept working so much. He said he understood that I was running my own business.

"Back then I was still trying to pay back Aiden and buy him out. Tommy was trying for a big promotion and he worked all the time, too. At first, our schedules matched. Then he got the promotion, and everything changed."

I stood up abruptly, needing a second. "Do you want a beer? I want another beer."

Chase nodded and I turned on my heel, escaping to the kitchen. In the two minutes it took me to grab two beers from the fridge and come back I tried to figure out how to tell the rest. I wanted to be honest with Chase, but I couldn't bear to give him the whole truth.

The cruel comments. The way Tommy would pick me apart, leaving me feeling like a failure. Like I was a bad wife and a bad person because I was selfish and self-centered and I didn't know how to give.

I couldn't bring myself to be that vulnerable, to open up the worst moments of my life for comment and judgment. I still didn't understand how my sweet, charming, loving husband had turned sour and distant and cruel.

I sat back on the couch and opened the beers, handing one to Chase. I wasn't sure IPAs went with double chocolate mocha cake, but the flavor combination didn't seem to bother him.

I was going to stick with the facts. He only needed to know the facts. He didn't need a big sob story about heartbreak and tears.

CHAPTER FOURTEEN

ANNABELLE

"So, the good times didn't last?" he asked, prompting me.

I took a slug of beer before I answered. "No, they didn't last. He asked me to marry him, and I said yes. We were in love. I wanted to be together. I was so sure everything would work out. We didn't do a big thing, went to Vegas for the weekend and I came back with the ring on my finger. So stupid."

I couldn't help the bitter laugh. "I knew by the way everyone reacted... I wish we'd planned a real wedding because it would have given me time to think. Time for my friends and my parents to talk some sense into me. Time for them to tell me what they saw that I didn't. Maybe that's why he came up with the idea of Vegas. Maybe he already knew they didn't like him. I don't know. I never asked."

"What happened? How long after the wedding did things change?"

"Not long. Maybe six months. Tommy got his promotion and he cut back on work. He was keeping normal hours, but the café was still open until eight. He started asking why I wasn't home to cook his dinner. Why did I have to work so late? Why did I have to get up so early?

"He wanted me to hire help, but it wasn't in the budget if I was going to pay Aiden back and buy him out. Then he wanted me to contract out the baked goods, but there was no way I was doing that. Selling my own product made a big difference in my bottom line, and I love the baking.

"He already knew all of that. We used to have long conversations about the café and what it meant to me. He never said he wanted me to work less. He never told me he wanted me to change."

I scraped my thumbnail against the label of the beer, peeling up a thin foil strip, watching it curl and fall to my lap. I hated thinking about my failed marriage to Tommy.

Hated remembering the helpless sense of failure, of losing something and not knowing how to save it without giving up everything I loved about myself in the process. I forced myself to finish.

"Then, he wanted to invest in the café. He said if he gave me more money it would be easier to hire a manager. I could oversee things from home instead of being here all the time."

"You'd hate that," Chase cut in. "This is your place."

"I thought he understood," I said, still staring down at my bottle of beer. "I didn't want to let him buy in. At that point, I'd finally paid Aiden back and bought him out. The café was all mine. I was proud of myself for accomplishing so much only a few years out of college, but Tommy didn't get it.

"He was furious I wouldn't let him buy in. Things were still okay at that point, but I had this feeling in my heart, in my gut, that if I let him own a piece of the café, he'd use it as leverage. He was looking for a way to get what he wanted, which was me at home taking care of him."

"He sounds like an asshole," Chase growled, glaring at the piece of cake sitting in front of him.

"But that's the thing, Chase. He wasn't. Well, later he was. But he didn't start that way. He didn't start out as an asshole. Things didn't really get bad until I decided to expand and I went to Aiden for a second loan. Since I'd already paid off the first and bought out his investment, he didn't even make me write a second business plan."

I laughed at the memory of Aiden agreeing so easily when I'd expected him to put me through the ringer.

"It must not have been a very big loan," Chase commented.

"It wasn't," I agreed. "The space we're sitting in now used to be part of the storage area, and the apartment upstairs was a real apartment. I lived there before I married Tommy, and no one was using it. I didn't want to rent it out. I own the building, and I could have, but I didn't like the idea of a stranger living over my café.

"I borrowed the money from Aiden, turned this section into more seating and moved the storage upstairs. Tommy said it was a slap in the face that I took Aiden's money and not his. He didn't understand that I didn't want to mix our marriage with my business, especially when he was so resentful of the café in the first place."

"He was jealous," Chase said. "He wanted you to take all the passion and creativity and drive that you pour into your café and spend it on him instead. He wanted a claim on what was important to you."

Chase had hit it exactly. "How'd you guess?"

"I know the type," he said. "I bet he was mad about the money, but more so that it came from Aiden. To a guy like that, taking money from Aiden Winters instead of him would have been like cutting his dick off."

I burst into laughter. My shoulders shook so hard, I leaned forward, almost spilling my beer in my lap before I slid it on the table and smacked a hand over my mouth, trying to hold in my giggles.

When I could finally speak I said, "That's exactly how he acted. Like I tried to impugn his manhood by taking money from Aiden. It just made sense. Aiden had been a partner in the business, he knew everything he needed to know, and he was more than happy to lend me the money. I knew he'd give me a decent interest rate and he'd treat me fairly. He knew I'd pay it back quickly, which I did. But Tommy acted like I'd betrayed him on the deepest level. I didn't get it."

"You wouldn't," Chase said.

"What does that mean?" I asked, annoyed. "What do you mean 'I wouldn't get it'?"

"I mean, you wouldn't get a guy like that. He's inherently selfish. He wants what he wants, and he's mad at you for not toeing the line. He thinks because he put a ring on your finger you're supposed to rearrange your entire life to suit him.

"Of course, you wouldn't get that. You're *not* inherently selfish. You're focused on your goals, but that doesn't make you selfish. Did you expect him to stop working long hours for that promotion just because you wanted him around?"

"No, never," I said. "He put so much of himself into his job. That promotion meant everything to him."

Chase lifted his beer in my direction, tilting the neck toward me in salute. "See? That's why you don't get it. Because your instinct is to support someone you love, to try to make that person happy. His instinct is to figure out how to make it easier for you to make *him* happy. Not the same thing."

I'd never thought of it like that. Honestly, I'd resigned myself to the idea that I was selfish. That I wasn't a good wife. Maybe Chase had a point.

"I didn't see it at the time, but taking the money from Aiden was the beginning of the end. Tommy got distant. Busy. He did that passive-aggressive thing where he would ignore me to get a response and then when I didn't give him one, because I didn't know he was playing a game, he would get even more distant and then he'd explode in a rage when I didn't understand that I was supposed to come to him apologizing for... I don't even know. He started taking little digs at me—"

I snapped my mouth shut. I wasn't going to get into that stuff. If I started to recount the things he'd said, I wasn't going to be able to hold it together. The only reason I was telling Chase this was so he could understand why we needed distance between us.

I knew him well enough to know that if I fell apart in front of him, he would not be okay with distance.

I needed to hold it together and I needed to finish the story.

I needed him to understand why I kept saying no.

Why I was going to keep saying no.

"He told me he was going after another promotion at work, and I believed him. The expansion here was under-way, and I was distracted. I guess I was naïve. I figured we were going through a rough patch and we'd get through it. Relationships take work. Even good ones. Nothing is perfect all the time.

"I thought maybe he needed time to realize that my borrowing the money from Aiden wasn't a big deal. To figure out how we could match our schedules in a way that worked for both of us. I thought once the renovation was done and he got the next promotion we could get into a new groove and things would be better."

I took another long sip of my beer and pulled my knees into my chest, bracing my heels on the edge of the sofa.

"I was selfish, too. I had so much going on here, and it was easier to focus on business. Tommy was ignoring me because he wanted me to pay attention, and I let him because I was frustrated, and I didn't understand why he was so angry with me. He was my husband. I shouldn't have let him ignore me. I shouldn't have been distracted."

"Let me guess," Chase asked, his voice cold and cynical. "You caught him cheating."

My eyes slid closed and I winced. "Nope. I did catch him out to dinner with another woman, but he told me she was a rep for a hospital he was working with and it was a business dinner. He had business dinners like that all the time, and I believed him. Until his date's best friend called me a few weeks later and told me to go to a certain hotel downtown, to a specific room, and knock on the door.

"She said her friend was there with my husband and if I didn't believe her I should go check it out for myself. I did. Tommy answered the door with a towel around his waist and a naked woman in the bed. I went straight home, packed my things, and moved into what was left of the apartment upstairs. And I called Aiden to get the number of his divorce lawyer."

"I hope you took him to the cleaners."

"Not exactly. Stephanie Marks, the lawyer who handled Aiden's divorce, and then mine, is really good. Amazing. She's a pit bull underneath the polish and designer suits.

But she's expensive. I dipped into my savings. Deep. I knew he'd come after the café."

"And he did?" Chase asked, not sounding surprised.

"He tried. He tried to take everything. Stephanie kept him from touching anything that had been mine when we got married. Fortunately, I'd been pouring almost all the profits back into the café. I pay myself a small salary, but I wasn't saving for a house yet.

"Tommy had a nice place and we'd been living there, so it made more sense to reinvest my profits. Stephanie kept him from getting the business, but he dragged it out as long as he could, hoping to drain my reserves until I couldn't afford to fight anymore. By the time it was all over, my savings account was pretty much empty. I had a nice shiny divorce decree, the café, and not much else."

"You didn't go for alimony," Chase said, as if he didn't need me to answer.

"No, I didn't. I didn't want anything of his. I only wanted him to go away. And I couldn't afford it. Going after alimony would have meant more billable hours and I could barely pay Stephanie's fee as it was."

"How long ago was your divorce?" Chase asked.

"Three years. It's hard to believe it's been that long. When I left him, I moved upstairs and I focused on work, saving money to build back my emergency fund, and later to buy a house. After the divorce, I didn't want to date again. It seems simpler not to. I can't go through that again."

"Why is he bothering you now? What was that about tonight?"

"If I tell you, you have to swear you won't say anything," I said.

I didn't need Chase running home to Winters House

and spreading stories about Tommy and me. Tommy was my mistake, not theirs.

"I don't know if I can do that when I don't know what you're going to say."

That was one of the things I loved about Chase. He was honest with me, even when I didn't want to hear it.

"Then I'm not telling you," I said quietly. "I'm not trying to be a pain, but Jacob is getting married in a week and I don't want this bothering him."

"He wants an invite to the wedding," Chase guessed.

I should have known he'd figure that out if I mentioned Jacob. The long day was muddling my brain.

"Yep. I just have to ignore him until the weekend, and he'll forget about me again."

"Until he wants something else," Chase said, through gritted teeth.

"Pretty much."

"That's bullshit."

"That's Tommy. He thinks I owe him because I ruined his life. You know, because I was such a horrible wife."

I hated the bitterness in my voice. I wanted to be done with it. Done with Tommy. But he refused to let me go.

Chase sat back and picked up the slice of cake. I would have thought he was completely relaxed, but the muscle on the side of his jaw ticked as he carefully, precisely, pressed the side of the fork into the cake and cut off a bite. He chewed and swallowed in silence before he spoke again.

"What's your plan then?" he asked, his voice neutral. "You're going to stay single for the rest of your life? Be married to the café? Are you going to take a bag of coffee beans to bed at night? Grow old and gray by yourself?"

I pressed my forehead to my knees and didn't answer.

I didn't have an answer.

Did I want to grow old alone? No, of course not. Who does?

But if the alternative is what happened with Tommy? Yeah, alone sounded pretty good.

Chase wasn't going to let it go.

"You can't let one guy ruin your life, Annabelle. If you don't want to date me—okay, I don't get that because I think we'd be great together. The more time I spend with you, the more time I want to spend with you—but if you don't want to date me, fine, I'll figure out a way to live with that. But you can't let this guy steal the rest of your life from you. You deserve better than that."

"I'm not letting him steal the rest of my life," I protested, suddenly angry. "I'm not giving him anything else of mine. Not him and not any other man. I'm keeping what I worked for. I'm keeping what's mine. I'm living my life the way I want to, and no one's going to take that from me."

"And it doesn't get lonely?"

I mumbled into my knees, not wanting to look at him.

"What was that?" he pressed.

I said grudgingly, "Loneliness isn't the worst thing in the world."

"No, it's not," he agreed, "but it's not that great, either."

"Look, I do like you, Chase. I like hanging out with you. I like having you around. But I feel like you're biding your time until I agree to go out with you, and I don't want to play you like that. Because it's not going to happen. It's not. And if you're looking for someone—"

My voice cracked and I swallowed hard. "If you're looking for someone, a relationship, you're wasting your time with me."

"What if I say I'm okay with being friends?"

He wasn't okay with it. I already knew he wasn't. "Not if

you're saying we're friends but you're really waiting for me to change my mind."

"What if I promise not to push?"

I started to argue back, and he interrupted.

"You can't control my feelings, Annabelle. You can't tell me not to be attracted to you. You can't tell me not to like you, not to enjoy your company. You can't tell me I shouldn't want to see you at the end of the day.

"You can ask me not to push. You can tell me, honestly, that you don't want to go out with me, and I can agree to accept that. But you can't control my feelings. And I *can* control my actions."

He was making sense. But he was also talking his way around my objections. "As long as we understand each other," I said, thinking we didn't understand each other at all.

"Fine," Chase agreed. "So you should go to Jacob and Abigail's wedding with me."

My mouth dropped open, but before I could launch into an argument he cut me off again, raising his hand, palm out.

Did he give me the hand?

I was gritting my teeth when he said, "As friends. Just as friends. I'll keep my hands to myself, and I won't expect a kiss at the end of the night. I promise. I just want someone to hang out with. Half of Atlanta is going to be there and almost everyone I know is in the wedding party. Unless you already have a date."

"I wasn't planning to bring a date," I said, shaking my head slowly, knowing his plan was full of holes and a terrible idea.

"It'll be fun," he cajoled. "I'm a good dancer. I bailed out of dance class early on, but I can still manage some moves. I won't drink too much and embarrass you, and if you want to drink too much, I promise I won't take advantage. Scout's honor."

"Were you a Scout?" I asked, with one eyebrow raised.

"I got kicked out. But I still have my honor."

I stared at him for a very long time, the gears in my brain turning sluggishly, the voice in the back of my head telling me to *say yes, say yes* and every ounce of caution, every scarred piece of my heart, cringing in fear.

Finally, I opened my mouth to speak and heard myself say, "Okay. Just as friends."

"Just as friends," he agreed, but I already knew he was lying through his teeth.

CHAPTER FIFTEEN

CHASE

I had a date with Annabelle. Finally.

Except it wasn't really a date. Did that count as progress?

I'd take what I could get. Obviously.

I'd never put this kind of time into wooing a woman. I hadn't needed to.

In high school, I was the dangerous rebel type. Not really, not on the inside, but on the outside the girls ate that shit up.

I never had a girlfriend. None of the girls in my private school were willing to risk their parents' wrath if they brought me home. Since I wasn't angling to sit at the table for Sunday dinner that worked out fine for me.

In college, and after, all my energy went into my projects. There were women here and there, but no one serious.

I'd never met a woman who made my soul go still, just so I could soak in everything she was. I'd never met a woman I simply wanted to be near.

To hear her voice.

To see her smile.

Annabelle drew me in. Her honesty. Her boundless energy. She had a light inside her, and I only wanted to bask in her warmth.

Okay, no. I didn't only want to be near her.

I wanted her naked.

Wanted her in bed, wanted my hands, my mouth, all over her until all that limitless energy was focused on me and me alone.

Did that make me a selfish bastard like her ex? No. No, I refused to think that might be true. I wanted Annabelle for herself. I wanted Annabelle to have her dreams, wanted to help her make them come true.

I didn't want to take from her any more than she would take from me. I wasn't her ex, but I was starting to wonder how long it would take her to see that.

I cranked up the speed on the treadmill in the workout room at Winters House, going fast enough that I couldn't think about much more than the burn in my legs and a desperate need for oxygen—one of the side benefits I'd discovered in exercise.

I started to stay in shape because I liked my brownies, but exercise was one of the few things that quieted my racing mind. Sex worked, too, but that wasn't always an option. With Annabelle firmly warding me off, exercise was it.

I ran until my legs felt like jelly and I was soaked with sweat. The house was quiet as I wobbled my way upstairs. Violet was in Athens for a long day of classes. Aiden and Gage were already at the office. Sophie and Amelia had left early for an appointment on the other side of town.

In the stillness of the mostly empty house, the murmur

of voices from the kitchen hit my ear like a shout. I caught the sound just before I pushed open the door and froze, my fingertips pressing against the wood.

Abel and Mrs. W.

I let out an inaudible sigh and dropped my hand to my side. I could go back down the stairs, traverse the hall of the lower level and come up the secret staircase into the library, but by the time I did that, Abel and Mrs. W might be done talking.

I didn't want to eavesdrop, but I'd wait a minute, maybe two, before I gave up and tried a different way.

I couldn't hear exactly what they were saying, only snatches of words and the tone of their voices.

Abel's was drawn tight, frustrated. Almost angry. He spat out, "Helen, tell me what to do. Tell me what you need, and I'll give it to you."

They could have been my words, my thoughts for Annabelle, and the love in them made my chest ache.

Mrs. W replied, her voice low and indecipherable through the heavy wooden door. I couldn't make out what she said, but her anguish came through loud and clear.

The kitchen went silent, and I stood there wondering if they'd left or if they were doing something other than talking. Breath held, I waited, and jerked back, startled, as heavy footsteps stomped past the door and down the hall.

Abel, clearly not happy with the result of their conversation.

I knew how he felt.

Slowly, I pushed open the door to the kitchen to find Mrs. W leaning over the sink, brushing beneath her eyes with her index fingers, drawing in a little hitching breath.

She was crying. The indomitable Mrs. W was crying.

I needed Sophie. Or Violet. Both of them were close to Mrs. W. They'd know exactly what to say.

I had no fucking clue. I barely knew her, but I knew enough to understand that she'd hate for me to see her in a moment of weakness. I turned my back on her and opened the refrigerator, giving her another moment to compose herself.

From the corner of my eye, I watched her banish her emotions, a mask of cool, professional competence descending over her face.

"I didn't see you there, Chase. Can I get you something for breakfast? Abel—" Her voice cracked, and she broke off, sucking in a breath of alarm at the way her pain had spilled over, washing away her facade of control.

Letting the door swing shut, I turned to face her. "Sorry, I didn't mean to eavesdrop. I didn't really hear anything, but I know you and Abel were having an argument."

"Well, I apologize. We should keep our personal business—"

"Don't apologize," I said. "There's nothing to apologize for."

"It's not appropriate to discuss personal matters in the house. Now, can I get you anything?"

"I'm good. I'm going to make a protein shake."

I hesitated, knowing I was about to be incredibly rude. But I had to know.

"Look, this is not my business, and if you want to tell me to go to hell, feel free. But I need to know. Why won't you marry him?"

"You're right," Mrs. W said stiffly, "it isn't any of your business."

I shifted uncomfortably. "It's just that I know how he

feels. Annabelle—" I stared at my feet. I didn't need to say more than that. Mrs. W had known Annabelle since she was a little girl

Letting out a long breath, Mrs. W's shoulders slumped forward the tiniest bit. She shook her head at the floor before she gave another sigh and said, "Would you like a cup of coffee?"

"I'd love one, thanks." I settled back to lean against the counter and waited, watching as she pulled mugs from the cabinet and doctored my coffee exactly the way I liked it.

Mrs. W knew all about the denizens of Winters House, even the temporary ones like myself. I kept my mouth shut and gave her time to pull her thoughts together.

Handing me the heavy stoneware mug, she said almost conversationally, "You know, I came to Winters House when I was only twenty. I was engaged. He was in the Army. He wasn't career. He wanted to go to college and we didn't have the money. It seemed like the best plan. He'd serve his country, go to school, and when he got out we'd be married. I only planned to be here a few years."

"What happened?" I asked, knowing that whatever it was, it had been life-changing. Catastrophic. All these years later, and Helen Williamson still had not recovered.

She drew in a deep, slow breath to steady herself. "He died when I was twenty-two. We'd been married for only a few weeks. I wanted to be a June bride, so we went ahead with the wedding, even though he wasn't out yet. He was in a jeep accident on base. An everyday errand. He wasn't in combat. He wasn't doing anything dangerous. The tire blew on a soft shoulder and flipped his jeep into a ditch. It never should have happened.

"I came to this house a young woman with a ring on my

finger, expecting to stay only until I became a bride. Instead, I never left."

Mrs. W paused, staring down into her coffee mug. After a short breath, she put it on the counter and busied herself arranging squares of shortbread on a small, round plate.

Her fingers lingered over the cookies, giving the coarse grains of sugar on top a caress. Shortbread was a Winters family tradition, but I'd learned from Violet, who'd learned from Sophie, that Abel didn't make the treat for the family.

He made the shortbread for Mrs. W because it was her favorite.

Neither of them were openly demonstrative people, but these cookies were his love letter to her, an everyday way to show her she was in his thoughts. In his heart.

Her dark eyes stared at them with remorse before she pushed the plate toward me. Remorse for their fight? Or remorse because she wouldn't marry him?

If Mrs. W's story was any example, I was in big trouble. Thirty years later, and she was still afraid to risk her heart. Annabelle's scars were only a few years old. What chance did I have?

"Is it the memories?" I asked. "Is it that you can't love someone else the way you loved him?"

Mrs. W let out a sad laugh. "No. I loved Peter. I loved him with everything I had. We would have had a good life together, but he's been gone a long time, and I'm not that girl anymore."

"Then what's holding you back?"

Mrs. W picked up a piece of shortbread and held it to her lips, inhaling the buttery, sweet scent. She bit into one corner thoughtfully.

"I'm afraid of change. When I say it like that I sound like such a coward. I buried my grief for Peter in this family. All the love I had for him, I gave to these children. To their parents. I don't regret a moment of it.

"My grief might have drowned me, but Jacob had just been born and Olivia had her hands full. She needed me. They all needed me. I found a family when I'd lost the one I wanted. The Winters were a blessing."

"They see you the same way," I said crunching into my own piece of shortbread. "That doesn't mean they don't want you to have a life."

"I know that," she said shortly, glaring down into her coffee. "I'm old and set in my ways. All I've done is here. This is all I know how to be. I don't know how to be a wife. What if I can't put him first? What if I'm too old to change and I ruin it? Abel is—" She cut off, her eyes going soft and a blush rising to her cheeks.

"Abel is in love with you," I said quietly, knowing I spoke the truth. I'd heard it in his voice. His love and his anguish that he might not win the woman he needed more than life.

"He says he is, but he's lived so much more than I have. He's traveled all over the world. What if he gets bored with me? What if it doesn't work and he leaves and the household is disrupted—"

Gently, I said, "You're making excuses."

"I know," Mrs. W snapped at me, her dark eyes skewering me for my impertinence. "I know they're excuses and that doesn't make it any easier to put them aside."

She wasn't wrong about that. Still... "And you're not old. Stop saying that. You're what? Late forties? That's nothing."

"I'm fifty-five," she corrected primly, reminding me of Vivi when she was annoyed. No one did icy disdain quite like my baby sister, but Mrs. W could give her a run for her money.

"Fifty-five is still young. Age is another excuse."

"I don't feel fifty-five," she confessed. "I feel ancient."

"And how does Abel make you feel?" I pressed.

That blush hit her cheeks once more, accompanied by a tiny, secret smile. "Like I'm twenty again. Like I'm a young, foolish girl with a crush."

"I know the feeling," I said, thinking of the way my heart jumped in my chest when I saw Annabelle.

Straightening, she busied herself clearing the counter. "I shouldn't be talking about this with you."

"It's okay, I'm not part of the family."

Her hands fell still and she dropped the tin of short-bread to the counter with a clatter. "Is that what you think? That you aren't part of this family? Is that why you keep running off to Annabelle's?"

I examined the toes of my running shoes, unable to meet her eyes. A lump in my throat kept me silent, and I shrugged one shoulder like a guilty child.

"Chase," she said in a soft voice, "You may have been lost for all these years, but you belong here."

"I'm not a Winters."

"No, but you're Anna's. And she missed you every day. She did what she thought was right, but that didn't mean she didn't wonder what might have been. And she'd be over-joyed to know you're here. That you're with your family. Finally. Don't ever say you don't belong here."

I said the only thing I could. "Yes, ma'am."

"That's better."

I was done talking about my complicated connection to the Winters family. I wanted to talk about Annabelle.

"Annabelle's afraid of change, too. Her husband hurt her so badly she thinks she's better off alone. I don't know how to change her mind."

"How do you know you should?" Mrs. W asked, a shrewd look in her eye. "What do you want from her?"

"I don't want anything *from* her, I want *her*," I said simply. "I want to be with her. Want to be a part of her life. She keeps pulling me closer, then warning me off. She says we can be friends, but no more."

Raising an eyebrow Mrs. W said tartly, "Have you considered the possibility that she doesn't like you?"

"I did," I said with a laugh before popping the rest of the shortbread in my mouth and chewing. "But I know she likes me. She feeds me dinner all the time, and she won't let me pay. She lets me help her clean up when she closes. A few nights ago, her ex was bothering her and she pretended I was her boyfriend. She let me give her a hug. Would she do all of that if she didn't like me?"

Mrs. W took a sip of coffee, staring at the ceiling, lost in thought. Setting the mug on the counter with a decisive click she said, "No, she wouldn't."

"She said it's not me, that she doesn't want to go out with anyone. Is it like that with you and Abel? Or is it him? If someone else asked you out, would you feel differently?"

"No. No, absolutely not." Her response was so immediate, so visceral, I knew she was telling the truth.

"And if you could marry anyone would it be him?"

She stared blindly out the kitchen window and nodded slowly. "We've been dancing around this for over a year."

"Anyone who can tell Aiden Winters what to do and make him listen can face a challenge head-on," I said quietly. "Good things don't always come when we're ready for them."

I put my coffee mug in the sink and turned to go. Her voice stopped me.

"Her husband was not a nice man," Mrs. W said with

such heat I was sure she was calling him much worse in her head.

"They used to come over for dinner all the time. At first, I thought I was reading him wrong. They were so in love and he treated her like fine china. But later, he was awful. I always thought it was that promotion he got after they were married. Suddenly, he wanted a wife like the other executives. Someone who would stay home and take care of him. Someone who would follow his lead and set aside her own dreams."

"Asshole," I murmured under my breath.

A thin smile stretched across Mrs. W's face.

"Yes. He was. He started tearing her down all the time. Nothing was good enough. *She* wasn't good enough. She started to fade away. The boys wanted to do something, try to catch him cheating, anything to get him away from her. But Annabelle took her vows seriously and they were afraid if they interfered she'd cut them out of her life."

"Was it bad the whole time?" I asked.

"Mostly the last year. I was so relieved when she found him in that hotel room and filed for divorce, I cried."

As if what I'd said earlier had just filtered through, her gaze sharpened, and she said, "What was he doing in the café? Is he bothering her?"

I shifted uncomfortably. Mrs. W loved Annabelle, but still... "I told her I wouldn't tell anyone."

"She wants to handle him herself." I nodded.

"That girl," Mrs. W muttered, shaking her head at the counter as she wiped it clean.

"He's not going to bother her," I promised.

"Don't give up on her," Mrs. W said fiercely. "He did a number on her, twisted her head all around, but if you care for her, don't give up. Annabelle is worth waiting for."

"I know she is."

Mrs. W nodded, dismissing me. Before I left, I said, "Don't give up on yourself. The best things in life are always scary. Doesn't mean they're not worth the risk."

Mrs. W said nothing, only frowned down at the counter, scrubbing at an invisible spot and avoiding my eyes.

I headed down the hall for a shower. It was out of the way, but maybe I'd stop in at Annabelle's place for breakfast. I needed to see her face, needed a shot of her smile, before I started my day.

Mrs. W didn't need to tell me not to give up. I wasn't planning on it. Annabelle needed me, even if she wasn't ready to admit it.

CHAPTER SIXTEEN
CHASE

"How are you still a good dancer, when you got kicked out of dance class after only a year?" Vivi asked as I whirled her in a circle.

Giving her the smug, superior smile that is the province of older brothers, I said, "I'm just that good."

She giggled, her eyes scanning the ballroom and landing on Aiden, currently dancing with Annabelle. Annabelle was smiling up at him. Her expression sent a stab of jealousy through my heart.

Stupid, I know.

Aiden was crazy in love with Vivi, and Annabelle wasn't interested in him. Didn't matter. I was still jealous. Wanting and not having Annabelle was making me a little crazy. I could admit it, if only to myself.

Violet glanced up at my face, back to Aiden and Annabelle, and her smile became a frown.

"You've set yourself up for a challenge, Chase," she said quietly enough not to be overheard by the other dancers.

"I already know that."

"You sure you don't want to move on? I like Annabelle. It's not that, but—"

"What? What do you know?" I demanded.

Vivi shook her head. "I don't really know anything. Aiden said that her ex really messed with her head. Said he was a royal asshole and the only reason they didn't beat the shit out of him was because they were worried it would hurt her case in the divorce. He was already going after everything she had."

"I know all that," I said. "But that's all I know. I can't figure out how to prove to her that I won't hurt her the way he did."

"You can't," she said simply. "The only thing you can do is be who you are. Keep being her friend. Keep being there for her. She likes you. Sometimes I catch her looking at you, and it's not the way you look at a friend."

"That's my plan, it's just taking a lot longer than I thought it would," I said, disgruntled.

Vivi laughed at me, her eyes flashing with affection and amusement. "You know, it wouldn't hurt for you to wait to get something you want for once. When was the last time you had to work for a woman?"

"That's not the point," I protested, annoyed.

Vivi raised an eyebrow and said nothing. I scowled down at her, but she was immune. That was the problem with little sisters. They always knew where to poke at you to get a reaction.

The music ended, and I led her back to Aiden, growling under my breath, "Just in time. I'm ready to get rid of you."

She laughed again. The sound of it brightened Aiden's dark eyes and sent a smile curling across his face as he reached for her hand and pulled her from my side.

Before she left me, she reached over, poked me in the chest and whispered, "You'll never be rid of me."

I squeezed her hand and gave her a gentle shove toward Aiden, ignoring the little pang in my heart as I did. Any day now, he was going to slide a ring on her finger. It was only a matter of time at this point.

I had no doubt it would happen eventually. And then my little sister would be someone's wife. She'd always be my baby sister. But she'd also be his. It wouldn't be the two of us against the world anymore. She had Aiden.

I wanted her to have Aiden. I did. And I would be proud as hell to give her away at her wedding. That didn't mean a small part of me didn't envy her. And it didn't mean that a tiny part of me didn't hate him a little for taking her away.

I looked down at Annabelle, wrapping my arm loosely around her shoulders, and mused that if only emotions were logical my life would make so much more sense.

"They look so good together," she said, watching Aiden lead Vivi to the bar for another glass of champagne.

"I guess," I said grudgingly. She was right, Aiden's height and dark hair and Vivi's gleaming blonde and odd periwinkle eyes. His air of command and hers of icy composure. They might have been made for each other.

On the other side of the ballroom, the newlyweds caught my eye and I nodded my head in their direction.

"You could say the same of those two."

Jacob stood with his arm around Abigail, the smile on his face so wide I thought his cheeks must hurt, and the pride in his eyes as he looked at his new wife unmistakable.

Abigail glowed with happiness. I didn't know Jacob that well. I spent a lot more time with Aiden and Gage, and I'd been hanging out here and there with Vance. I knew

Charlie from the work she was doing on my house and I'd hit it off with her husband Lucas and Lise's husband Riley.

But Jacob was something of a workaholic—a family trait —and he and Abigail lived in the building he owned in Midtown, called Winters House like their family home.

We'd seen each other at family dinners and I talked to Abigail here and there, but I wouldn't say we were friends. Still, I'd been around them enough to see how deeply Jacob loved his new wife and how devoted she was in return.

Unlike the rest of the family weddings, which had been fairly modest, Jacob and Abigail seemed to want half the state to witness their wedded bliss.

The wedding and the reception were at Château du Jardin, a vineyard and resort in the countryside about an hour outside of Atlanta.

I don't know how good the wine was—I hadn't tried it yet—but the grounds and resort were over the top in the best way.

Luxurious didn't even begin to describe the accommodations. Jacob and Abigail had been planning the wedding forever, I'd heard, and it was huge. At least five hundred people, maybe more.

They'd been married in the atrium at sunset, the pink and gold rays streaming through the glass roof, the light gilding Abigail as she strode down the aisle on Aiden's arm. Her parents were both gone and she didn't have any family to speak of, but Vivi confided that Aiden had been deeply touched when Abigail had asked him to do the honor of giving her away to Jacob.

The ceremony had been just long enough to give it a sense of circumstance, but not so long we were shifting in our seats, wondering when it would be over.

For a bride, Abigail had been calm and collected the

few times I'd seen her during the day. Jacob, on the other hand, had been a bundle of nerves.

He'd reserved every room in the resort for family, and we'd all arrived before lunch to take advantage of the pool and other amenities. Abigail, always the perfect hostess, had drifted from one group of guests to another, welcoming us all with warm affection and a serene smile.

Jacob, under the auspices of avoiding his bride until the wedding, had paced their suite, rearranging the roses he'd ordered for Abigail and nursing the same warm beer for hours.

I'd stopped in the room for only a minute, not wanting to intrude, and had a beer with Aiden while we watched Jacob pace.

"Relax, man," Vance said, biting into a chip and shaking his head at his cousin. "It's not like she isn't going to show."

"I know that," Jacob had snapped, irritably.

"Then what? You're not having cold feet. Are you?"

We all understood Vance's disbelieving tone. Jacob and Abigail had been engaged for over a year and the few times I'd seen them, they looked madly in love.

"Don't be an idiot," Jacob snarled. "I just want it over with. I want her to be my wife now. I don't know what we were thinking with this circus. I don't want to wait until sunset."

"You were thinking," Aiden said reasonably, "that you want to share the most important day of your life with your friends and family. You were thinking that your bride wants a sunset wedding, and you want to give it to her. You were thinking that you want the entire city to see how much you love her when you make her your wife."

"Not the entire city," Jacob grumbled.

"Most of it," Vance laughed under his breath.

"Well, I was an idiot. We should have eloped. Then we'd be done with this and she'd be mine."

"She's already yours," Aiden said in that same reasonable tone that I could see was driving Jacob nuts.

Siblings. When you didn't love them more than life, you planned inventive ways to murder them.

"Why don't we go down to the gym and you can run off your mood," Vance suggested. "If you look at Abigail with that face when she comes down the aisle, she's liable to turn and run."

"You're funny," Jacob had said with a glare, but he'd let his cousin drag him to the fitness center and push him on a treadmill.

Aiden and I had wandered off, he to find my sister and me to hunt down Annabelle. I found her leaving her room wearing a swim cover-up. After a quick stop by my room so I could change into my suit, we'd killed a few hours at the pool.

Annabelle in a bathing suit. She wore a modest one piece, but my brain and body didn't care. She was still mostly naked.

I lay on my stomach and watched her talk to Charlie, ignoring the murmur of their voices in favor of daydreams of tugging one strap, then the other, off her shoulders, of pulling that conservative suit down her body until every inch of her was bare.

That was how the day went. Always by her side, always surrounded by other people.

She'd sat beside me at dinner after the ceremony and had been monopolized the entire time by an old friend who'd been seated on her right. I had only one dance with her before Aiden claimed her, and it looked like Evers Sinclair was on his way to do the same.

I gritted my teeth. I was trying to prove to her that I was a good bet. Throwing a jealous temper tantrum would not help my case. Evers had left his date across the room with his brother, Axel, and Axel's wife.

Coming to a stop in front of us, Evers gave me a chin lift and said to Annabelle, "Are you going to dance with me or what?"

"In a minute, I'd love to. Just let me finish my champagne."

"Let Chase hold it for you," Evers complained.

"So impatient. Chill out," Annabelle said, then, tilting her head to the side and gesturing subtly to the couple in the corner, "What's going on with Cooper? Who is he with, and why do they keep arguing?"

Evers glanced at his older brother, currently in the corner, hands on his hips, glowering down at his petite date, who scowled back up at him.

"I didn't know Cooper was seeing someone," I said.

I knew all of the Sinclairs well enough, except for Axel, who lived in Las Vegas. Lucas and Riley worked for Sinclair Security, and I hung out with all of them here and there.

The Sinclair brothers had spent most of the summer doggedly trying to discover what had happened to their father, carefully and systematically untangling the threads of the mess Maxwell Sinclair had created and then left in their laps.

Evers had dropped out of sight for a while, working an angle on the case, according to Lucas. He hadn't made much progress in the investigation, but he'd reappeared with a woman at his side. I'd never seen her before, and no one else seemed to know her, but her last name was Winters and she and Evers did not look like they'd just met.

Knox, the middle brother, had left Atlanta for over a

month and returned with company. Based on the way he held his date in his arms as they danced in a dark corner, I thought that while he might not have been happy about what he'd discovered while he was gone, he'd agree the trip had been worth it.

But Cooper... Cooper had been holding down the fort in Atlanta, chasing leads from the main office while his younger brothers had been out in the field.

He'd said something the last time I saw him about being ready to make his move, and I'd assumed he was talking about his father's case, but watching him, the tension in his shoulders and the angry glare in his dark eyes, I wondered if he hadn't meant the woman in front of him.

"That's not his date," Evers said, shaking his head and rolling his eyes to the ceiling. "That's our office manager, Alice."

"You sure she's not his date?" Annabelle asked as we all watched Cooper close his fingers around Alice's upper arm and haul her from the ballroom, teeth gritted. She let him pull her away, stomping along beside him, her jaw clenched as tight as his, rage spitting from her eyes.

Evers shook his head again, this time in clear amusement.

"Maybe that means he's going to figure his shit out sooner rather than later."

Annabelle hummed in the back of her throat, and I wondered why it seemed like everybody was getting the girl except for me.

As if he read my thoughts and found them amusing, Evers plucked the champagne glass from Annabelle's hand, lifted it to her lips, said, "Drink up," and tilted it into her mouth.

She sputtered a little as she swallowed, but laughed.

Evers shoved the glass into my hand and pulled Annabelle to the dance floor where he swung her around in a fast-paced combination of a swing dance and a foxtrot.

I wasn't quite sure what he was doing, but he and Annabelle were having fun.

I was getting tired of watching her dance with other men. I wanted her to dance with me. I wanted her in a dark corner, or up in my room.

I just wanted her, and the waiting was starting to wear thin.

Annabelle was laughing when she came back. "Having fun?" I asked, my irritation fading at the happiness in her eyes.

When was the last time Annabelle had a night off? I'd bet it had been years. I wasn't going to ruin it for her by being a jealous grouch.

My mood lifted when she pulled away from Evers to take her place by my side, sliding an arm around my waist, leaning into my chest, her shining cinnamon hair spilling over the sleeve of my suit.

I looked down to see another glass of champagne in her hand.

"How much of that have you had?" I asked.

"I don't know," she said, looking at the full glass and blinking as if it had appeared in her hand out of nowhere. "A few? I haven't been keeping count."

"Maybe you should take it easy."

I knew she didn't drink much. A beer after work sometimes, but that was it. Champagne could hit hard, especially if you weren't used to drinking, and I didn't think she wanted to deal with the hangover in the morning.

Sound rumbled in the back of her throat. "Hey, not

telling you what to do," I reassured. "If you're hungover, I'll bring you the aspirin."

She relaxed into me again and took a sip. It felt good, standing there with her, smelling her warm sugar cookie scent, feeling the way her body fit to mine. I hadn't even kissed her yet and it felt like she belonged exactly where she was.

By my side. In my arms.

My mind drifting, I watched the couples across the room. Evers had reclaimed his date and she leaned into him, looking up into his face, her eyes bright with emotion. Not lust, not the flash of an affair. Something deeper. Something that took time to grow.

"Why don't I believe those two met while he was looking into his father?"

"Because they didn't," she said simply. "They've been seeing each other, kind of, for a while."

"I never heard him mention a girlfriend."

Annabelle shrugged, a little smile playing across her lips.

"How did you know?" I demanded, not liking that smile over another man's secret, even if he was an old friend and the secret was his love for another woman. Fuck, but I was turning into a jealous bastard.

Annabelle shrugged one shoulder. "Evers comes by for coffee a couple times a week. Usually when we're not that busy. I don't have time to hang out like I used to, but we always get a few minutes to catch up."

I knew it wasn't reasonable. I wasn't a jealous guy. I'd never been jealous before. I'd never had a woman I cared about enough to bother. I'd always figured, hey, if she wanted someone else, she was welcome to go.

But with Annabelle...

Maybe it was all the waiting. Being close, but not close enough. Wanting to touch her and holding myself back.

When I thought of Annabelle and Evers having coffee together, sharing confidences, my stomach turned sour and I heard myself say, "Are you sure he's coming by for coffee?"

CHAPTER SEVENTEEN

CHASE

Annabelle burst out laughing and flung her hand toward Evers and Summer, champagne sloshing over the rim of her glass.

"Are you kidding me? Forgetting the fact that I've known Evers since I was a little kid, and he is so not my type, Evers is very, very taken."

My brain accepted Annabelle's logic. She didn't seem to have romantic feelings for any of the guys she'd grown up with and I trusted her. I could take her at her word. A part of me still hated that I couldn't stake my claim and make sure every single person here knew that she was mine.

She *wasn't* mine.

Not yet.

She sipped her champagne, still comfortably tucked into my side, her slight weight warm against me.

Across the room, Mrs. W danced with Abel. She looked like a queen, her mahogany hair on top of her head in a complex arrangement of braids, her dark gray dress severe, yet majestic.

Abel had packed his broad shoulders and bulky frame into a charcoal suit. They shouldn't have looked right together. Mrs. W was elegant from her head to her toes and Abel looked like exactly what he was: a former Navy man, burly and grizzled and gruff.

But he held Mrs. W as if she were the finest china. The flush in her cheeks gave away how much she liked it.

Leaning down and whispering to Annabelle, I said, "Abel asked Mrs. W to marry him and she said no. More than once."

Annabelle's eyes went wide. "I heard there was something going on, but I didn't realize it was serious. Why won't she say yes?"

"I asked her the other day," I admitted, wanting to hear what Annabelle would say. Wondering if she would see herself in Mrs. W.

"You asked her? Like, came out and asked her?"

"Well, I kind of walked in on Mrs. W after they were fighting. I think she wanted me to pretend everything was fine, but I couldn't do it. So I asked."

"What did she say?"

"That she was scared."

I stared down into Annabelle's beautiful brown eyes and saw the wariness creeping in.

"She was married a long time ago, when she first came to Winters House."

"What happened?" Annabelle breathed.

"He died," I said gently, "and she's gotten used to being on her own. To being alone. She loves him, but she's scared."

Annabelle said nothing, leaning into me, staring up into my eyes, emotions clashing in the depths of her own.

Fear, wariness, and the faintest hint of hope. I pinned every one of my dreams on that flicker of hope.

Annabelle cleared her throat and looked away, her gaze landing across the room on the dancing couple, the curl of Abel's thick arm around Mrs. W's slender waist. Her tentatively happy smile.

They looked like any other dancing couple, but everyone who knew them recognized what it meant for Mrs. W to dance with Abel here, in front of family. In front of the world. It was subtle and personal, but it was a statement all the same.

Annabelle sipped the last of her champagne, and I plucked the empty glass from her hand. "Hungry?" I asked, looping my arm through hers and leading her around the dance floor to the hall outside the ballroom. The catering staff had set up another bar, along with tables loaded with food ranging from savory appetizers to every dessert I could imagine. And, of course, the wedding cake.

The official cutting of the cake had come and gone an hour before, Jacob smiling down at Abigail, love beaming from his eyes as he gently and carefully fed her a bite. No smashing the frosting into this bride's face.

When he was done, he'd cradled her face in his hands, kissing each cheek before pressing his lips to hers.

I'm a guy. I have a limit on mushiness, and even I got a little tear in my eye at that. Jacob's tenderness, his open affection, was almost exclusively reserved for his bride. He was ruthless in the board room, yet treated her as if she were the most precious thing on earth.

They'd been too distracted by each other to take more than the ceremonial taste of their cake. I wasn't going to make the same mistake.

Originally taller than the bride, the cake had been tiers upon tiers of creamy fondant, covered in flowers of platinum and the palest pink, on vines of barely-there green.

Elegant and elaborate, each flower had been carved by hand and painted with delicate precision, resulting in a three-dimensional watercolor of a garden, reminding me of a Monet come to life.

Even better, the buttercream frosting hid layers of moist lemon-basil cake separated by strawberry jam.

When I first heard the cake was lemon-basil, I'll be honest, I thought it sounded revolting. It was supposed to be a cake, not a stir fry.

Annabelle had rhapsodized over the cake long enough that I had a feeling I was off base, but really. Lemon-basil?

If the way it smelled counted for anything, it was going to be delicious. The serious dent the guests had put in the rows of dessert plates on the table told me lemon-basil with strawberry jam was a hit.

Annabelle picked up one of the small plates with a narrow slice of cake, pinched off a bite and popped it in her mouth. She tasted, rolling her eyes to the ceiling before she closed them, humming a little in the back of her throat.

"Are you eating that cake or communing with it?" I asked, snagging a slice of my own before I tugged her down the hall and around the corner into an alcove. Annabelle barely noticed, so intent on the cake.

Finally, she swallowed and said, "I wanted to get all the flavors."

"I thought it was lemon-basil. With strawberry." I looked at the slice of cake on my plate, wondering what secrets it hid.

"It is, but there's more. Something else. Maybe thyme?" She broke off another tiny piece and set it on her tongue, closing her eyes again as she absorbed the nuances of the cake.

Doing that cute humming thing again, she swallowed

and murmured to herself, "Not thyme. Maybe lavender. Just the smallest bit."

"Can't you ask Abigail?" I interrupted.

"I will, but I want to figure it out for myself."

She took a third bite, bigger this time, and closed her eyes again, breathing in slowly through her nose to let the scent and taste wash over her senses. I did the same, wondering if I could pick up the nuances that seemed so apparent to Annabelle.

I tasted sweet, then vanilla, reminding me of Annabelle, the green of the basil and the tart of the lemon. But lavender... I wasn't getting that. Clearly, I was not cut out to be a pastry chef.

I'd finished my entire slice by the time Annabelle was on her fifth bite, this time carefully savoring the frosting and murmuring to herself, "No basil? Not with..."

I swiped a finger full of frosting from the side of her slice and held it up to her lips. She closed her mouth around my finger so easily I knew she hadn't thought about what she was doing. Her eyes shot up and locked on mine, her tongue swiping across my fingertip.

I waited for her to back away, to pull her mouth from my finger. She didn't.

She sucked harder. My cock went rock hard. I lay my palm along her cheek, feeling the muscles flex in her jaw as she took one last lick of frosting from my finger.

She swallowed. I turned her face to mine and drew my finger from her mouth.

I brushed my lips against hers, giving her all the time, all the space in the world to back away.

I wanted this. I needed it. I lay awake every night dreaming of this. I had so many fantasies of Annabelle, and every one started with a kiss.

She froze for a second, for a heartbeat, her lips parted slightly. Every muscle in my body was drawn tight, my hand still cupping her cheek. I tugged her forward the tiniest bit, sliding my other arm around her back, urging her closer.

She let me pull her body to mine, let me tilt her face to the side and part her lips with my own, inviting me in. I took her mouth, tasting sugar and vanilla. Lemon and basil. Strawberry.

And Annabelle. Underneath it all, the sweet, perfect flavor of Annabelle.

Backing up until I hit the wall of the alcove, I pulled her into the shadows, fitting her between my legs, plastering her to my body, surrounding her until she was finally, finally mine.

She made a sound of want, her breasts pressed to my chest, nipples sharp points through her dress. I could have stayed there all night, and all the next day.

I might have if a tipsy wedding guest hadn't stumbled down the hall, taking a wrong turn into the alcove and elbowing Annabelle in the back.

She jumped like a scalded cat, only my tight hold keeping her from losing her balance and tumbling to the floor. The guest murmured, "Oops!," and laughed raucously as she tottered in the other direction.

Annabelle leaned back, trying to put space between us, and I reluctantly, regretfully, let her go. She took a step away, wobbling on her heels. I reached out to close my fingers over her elbow, steadying her without making her feel trapped.

Our kiss felt like a victory, but I knew better than to press my advantage. The last thing I wanted was to send her running scared. Eyes wide and a little confused, she lifted her hand to her mouth and touched her lower lip with her index finger

"I–"

"Can we do that again?" I asked softly.

Annabelle started to shake her head abruptly. She stopped and touched her finger to her lower lip again, swollen and red from our kiss.

"I don't know."

"Do you want to?" I asked carefully, knowing that if she said *no* I was going to find the biggest bottle of whiskey I could and drink every drop. Nothing else could drive this need from my body.

If Annabelle didn't want me after that kiss, she never would.

"I do," she admitted, her eyes dropping to study her toes, brightly polished in her spike heel sandals. Under her breath, so quietly I almost couldn't catch the words, she said, "I do want to, so much."

"Will you?"

Desperately wanting to reach out and take her hand, to pull her back into my arms where she belonged, I held back, knowing if I did I risked scaring her away.

She looked up at me, eyes swimming with tears. Remorse stabbed my heart. I wanted her. I wanted this. More than sex, than attraction, in the past few weeks she'd become one of the best friends I've ever had.

I knew her past, knew she had hurdles to overcome if she ever chose to be with me. Knew that breaking down her barriers might hurt along the way. But knowing that and seeing the cost, seeing those tears, seeing the war between fear and desire and something more than affection in her eyes left me desperately uncertain.

I wanted her to say yes. To admit that she cared for me,

that she wanted me, that we should ditch the reception and go straight upstairs to strip each other's clothes off and have each other until we passed out from sheer exhaustion.

I didn't want her to cry.

I didn't want this to hurt.

"Annabelle," I breathed, lifting a hand to wipe away the single tear that spilled over her lashes. "Don't. Don't cry. Forget it happened. We'll go back to the way it was and forget this happened. I swear—"

Her tears welled deeper, spilling over her cheeks faster than I could wipe them away. Her eyes locked on mine, searching for something.

If I'd known what it was I would have given it to her.

I would have given her anything.

Her tongue peeked out from between her lips and she surged forward, knocking my hands aside, grabbing my shoulders and dragging my mouth down to hers.

Relief was a blade slicing through me, slicing through my restraint.

My arms were too tight. My mouth too hungry.

Annabelle didn't seem to care.

She molded her body to mine, her lips, her tongue, kissing, nibbling, tasting, biting. Absorbing me, taking everything I had to give and returning it in even measure.

I kissed her until I was lightheaded and halfway to pulling down the zipper of her dress, peeling away the silk to finally see the woman beneath.

Reason filtered down the hall in the form of somewhat drunken laughter, reminding me that we were anything but alone.

I pulled back just enough and whispered, "Let's go upstairs."

Annabelle said simply, "Yes."

That was all I needed to hear. Sending Jacob and Abigail a silent thank you for insisting that their closest friends and family use the rooms they'd reserved in their names, I held Annabelle's hand tightly in mine and pulled her, a little impatiently, down the hall to the back staircase.

No way was I taking her to the elevator bank, beyond the main bar. I wasn't running the risk of her changing her mind, and I knew she wouldn't want everyone to see her with kiss-swollen lips and tear-reddened eyes.

Neither of us wanted to make explanations. We just wanted each other.

Fortunately, my room was on the second floor, a mere two flights up from the ballroom. The metal fire door clanked shut behind us, and Annabelle slid off her sandals, looping the straps over her fingers, laughing as she ran up the stairs with me close behind.

Annabelle crying was a stab to the heart, but Annabelle laughing...

Annabelle laughing was the most beautiful sound I'd ever heard. Especially since she was laughing on the way to bed with me.

We chased each other down the hall like children, tumbling through the door of my room only to skid to a stop at the sight of the bed. Annabelle flashed a look at me, part desire and part nerves.

It almost killed me to say it, but I had to, the memory of those tears too fresh to forget.

"We don't have to," I started.

Annabelle gave a hard shake of her head, sending her gleaming cinnamon hair flying.

"I want to. I want to, Chase. I want you. I'm tired of thinking and being afraid. I just want you."

I was already reaching for her, ignoring the twinge in my chest that she'd said *I want you*. Not something else.

What had I expected? For her to profess her undying love to me? We'd only just kissed.

Deep inside, where I shoved emotions too messy to think about, I needed so much more than simple *want* from Annabelle.

I needed everything.

Reminding myself that this, right here, was more progress than I'd made in weeks, I pulled her into my arms and kissed her again, shoving all my unruly feelings and wayward thoughts deep down where they couldn't get in my way.

This was not the time to doubt. This was the time to revel in finally having Annabelle exactly where I wanted her.

In my arms and under my mouth. Under my hands.

I didn't reach for the zipper on her dress until she tugged at my tie, pulling roughly at the silk, tearing it free and pitching it to the floor so she could go to work on my buttons, yanking until she parted the fabric and shoved the shirt off my shoulders.

I undid the cufflinks, hearing them drop to the floor, not caring where they rolled, helping her drag the shirt down my arms.

Careful not to snag her hair, I eased the narrow zipper down the inseam of her dress, the dark silk parting to reveal creamy, smooth skin beneath.

She dropped her arms and the fabric fell away.

A t the sight of her, my mouth went dry, and my hands, fumbling with my buckle, went still. Her tall, lean frame was wrapped like a gift in black lace, so sheer it was almost nonexistent.

Her breasts, pert and little more than a handful, were pressed together by a bustier that perfectly matched the thong beneath. Her eyes glittered with heat.

I was reaching for her before I thought to do it, my fingers itching to touch all that skin.

I wanted Annabelle all the time.

At the end of a sixteen-hour day, sweaty and exhausted, in a coffee-stained T-shirt and torn jeans.

I'd want her wearing a trash bag.

But this, this confection of black lace with those spike heels and all that shiny cinnamon hair falling around her shoulders... This was beyond my wildest imagination.

She didn't notice me staring at her. Reaching out, she traced a fingertip over the tattoo on the right side of my chest, a design based on a circuit board, narrow lines and small circles in a branching grid-like pattern that wouldn't mean much to most people but meant everything to me.

Her touch was light, barely there. Lips parted and breath shallow, she traced her fingers along the pattern, dropping them to run along my ribs, then down, down, to skate across my hipbone.

Suddenly impatient, I picked her up and turned, laying her across the bed, leaving her there for a second while I shoved at my suit pants and kicked off my shoes.

Then I was on her, pulling her into my arms, my mouth on hers.

Saying I loved the black lace was a massive understatement, but I wanted it gone. I didn't want anything between us. I just wanted Annabelle. All of her, naked and open to my eyes and my body.

I fumbled with the hooks on the back of the bustier, pulling it free and baring those perfect breasts to my eyes. Cupping one in my hand, I closed my mouth over her nipple, pulling hard, teasing her with my lips and tongue, sucking and licking and tasting, drinking in the sounds of her moans.

Her hand closed over my cock, and I lost my breath.

I'd spent a lot of time fantasizing about what Annabelle might do if she ever got her hands on my cock, and none of it came close to the sheer pleasure of her fingers wrapped around me.

My mouth fell open against her breast as I pressed my face to her skin, shuddering a little at the effort of holding back. Reaching down, I pulled her hand away with a twinge of regret.

"Too good. I've been dreaming about you for too long. It's going to end before it starts if you keep doing that."

Annabelle answered by sliding her legs apart and urging me on top of her.

Too fast.

Too fast, but the head of my cock slid against her, slick and hot even though I hadn't even touched her yet. My body disconnected from my brain, I pressed forward, her tight, wet heat closing around my cock before I realized what I was doing and jerked back.

Condom.

Condom, you asshole.

Annabelle wasn't thinking straight. Annabelle had had at least five glasses of champagne, and I'd bet everything I had that she hadn't had sex in three years. Her brain was muddled with champagne and lust.

I wasn't much better, but I should've remembered the condom.

"Don't move. Don't fucking move."

I hadn't planned for this. Not exactly. But I'd hoped. Hoped enough to pack a box of condoms. I ripped at the cellophane outer layer, wondering why they made these things so fucking hard to open.

Frustrated and tantalized by the view of Annabelle reclined on the bed, legs still spread, propped up on her elbows, those sweet breasts on full view, hard nipples shiny from my mouth and pointing at the ceiling, her brown eyes heavy-lidded with desire, her mouth swollen from my kisses.

I jammed my thumb through the plastic and tore the cardboard box in half, snatching out a condom and opening it, suiting up in record time.

She welcomed me, wrapping her legs around my hips and her arms around my neck as if she'd been waiting for me for a lifetime. I pressed my forehead to hers, drowning in her eyes, as I pushed inside, dizzy from the sheer, blissful pleasure of her tight heat closing around me.

It almost killed me, but I went slow. So slow. She was tight. Almost too tight, and the last thing I wanted was to cause her any pain.

When I was seated to the hilt, I pressed my mouth to hers, kissing her in little bites. Her lips, her cheeks, her chin, her eyelashes still salty from tears.

She rocked up into me, grinding her clit into the base of my cock, and we both shuddered. I wanted to go slow, draw it out, make it last, but Annabelle moaned beneath me and my restraint snapped.

Cupping a hand over the curve of her ass, I pulled back and drove inside. Her fingers dug into my shoulders, hanging on, her open mouth hot against my neck, her moan filling my ears as I fucked her hard, mindless, thinking only of her sounds of pleasure, chasing them, building her up until she screamed out my name.

I fucked her through the orgasm, barely letting her catch her breath before I pulled out and slid down her body, pressing her legs wide with my shoulders, my mouth closing over her pussy, licking and tasting, sucking her clit hard. Her fingers sank into my hair, pulling, the pain its own kind of bliss.

I didn't care that my cock throbbed against the comforter, so ready to come. Once I got inside her again I wouldn't last long. But I needed to hear her, to feel her come for me one more time.

Something in the back of my head whispered that this might be my only chance.

When it was over, she'd regret it, and that would be it.

When it was over and the champagne and desire had faded, I might never get to touch her again.

I would take what I wanted now.

I drove two fingers inside her, sucking her clit and fucking her with my hand until she broke apart, pulling my hair and clamping her thighs around my head until I was deaf, blind and all I knew was her taste and the sweet, musky scent of her pussy.

Tremors wracked her body, fading bit by bit until her legs fell limp and wide, her fingers losing their grip on my hair.

Opening my eyes, I looked up to see her lazy grin, her lips parting to say, "Please. Come back. Please."

She didn't have to ask again. My grateful cock slid inside her heat. At the touch of her mouth on mine, her tongue flicking out to taste herself on my lips, I spilled inside her with a groan, half ecstasy, and half regret that it hadn't lasted a lifetime.

I had just enough energy to get up and take care of the condom before collapsing back into the bed and dragging the comforter over us. Annabelle rolled into me, nuzzling her face into the hollow of my neck with a satisfied sigh.

Her leg draped over mine, arm thrown across my chest, she drifted from a doze into sleep. I held her, hoping this wouldn't be the end. Sleep pulled me under before I was ready, the champagne and long-awaited orgasm overcoming my desire to stay awake.

Sometime in the night, I opened my eyes to see the other side of the bed empty. I was reaching out to touch the still warm sheets when the door of the bathroom clicked open and a light flicked off. Annabelle's long hair draped over her shoulders, hiding her breasts from view as she came back to bed, sliding beneath the sheets and into my arms as if she'd never left.

This time I went slowly, tasting every inch of her until

she was sobbing beneath me with pleasure instead of tears, and I came inside her as hard as the first time, my need no less desperate despite having her only hours before.

I held her against me and hoped with everything I had that she'd still be here when I woke up.

CHAPTER NINETEEN
ANNABELLE

I noticed the headache first. You'd think I would have noticed the six feet of man in bed with me, but I hadn't had that much champagne in years.

Almost as long since I'd woken up with a man in my bed.

It took me a minute to get my bearings.

Throbbing head, check.

Scratchy eyes, check.

Dry mouth, check.

Tender between my legs? Oh, yeah. That.

Rolling to my side I looked at Chase, relaxed and defenseless in sleep. I resisted the urge to trace the line of his cheekbone with my fingertip.

He was like me. He never slept in. I already knew I wouldn't be able to fall back asleep, but I didn't have to wake him up.

I waited for the rush of regret.

Waited to start second-guessing myself, to wonder what the hell I'd been thinking.

It never happened.

I watched Chase sleep, his blonde lashes fanned against his golden cheeks, his face relaxed as it never was when he was awake.

So much focus, no matter what he was doing. He had the gift of giving 100% of his attention, all the time. Defenseless in sleep, he reminded me of a boy, all his responsibilities, his ambitions, his goals set aside for the moment.

I hadn't been sure. Sure that I wanted him, yes. I'd known that since the first time I laid eyes on him. How could any woman not want Chase Westbrook? Then later, more than attraction, I'd wanted *him*.

I'd been blessed in my life. Like everyone, I've had some rough spots, but I've always had the best of friends since before I was old enough to appreciate what that meant.

And still, in such a short time, Chase had become necessary. The friend I wanted most, all the time.

Now I had to admit to myself that he'd always been so much more than a friend. That I'd always wanted this, always wanted what we'd done the night before.

What I hoped we'd keep doing.

And if it went wrong?

The thought tore at my heart, tore at the scars I'd built up since my divorce.

Chase was worth the risk.

He was worth everything.

And if it went wrong, I'd survive. I'd find a way.

I thought of Mrs. W and Abel. I knew how she felt, being hurt and finding safety, then being terrified to let that go. Terrified to try again and risk the pain.

Chase was a gift.

He'd offered himself to me, and if I turned my back, I deserved to be alone.

He was beautiful. His heart. His patience. His body. Oh, his body. It was everything I'd imagined and more. The lines of the circuit board tattoo spread across his chest. I traced my finger above them, almost, but not quite touching him, and found a tiny, delicate violet hidden between the circuits. How could I not adore a guy who got a tattoo for his beloved baby sister?

His shoulders were broad, muscles more defined than a keyboard jockey should have. I wanted to let him sleep in, but I couldn't imagine he'd mind if I woke him early by...

Out of the corner of my eye I caught sight of the clock and barely managed to stop my shriek of alarm. Nine twenty-seven.

Nine twenty-seven.

The wedding breakfast started at ten AM. It would be, as you'd expect from Jacob and Abigail, decadent and formal.

I was un-showered, had sex hair, and a wrinkled dress I'd left on the floor.

It would take at least ten minutes to get down to the formal dining room and find our seats. Which left me barely twenty to get back to my room, get dressed, and be there on time.

The last thing I wanted was to stumble in late. They'd know why I'd slept in. They weren't stupid. But the night before was ours. I wanted it to stay that way, just for a little while.

I thought about waking Chase, but I knew men well enough to know that he would not appreciate how much time I'd need to get ready.

He'd roll out of bed, stand under the shower for five minutes, throw on his suit and be done.

As much as I'd love to do other things in bed with him, I had no time.

Less than no time.

Sliding out of bed, I snatched my underwear and dress off the floor, ducking into the bathroom. I didn't bother with the bustier, rolling it tightly in my hand. I could shove it in Chase's suitcase for now.

The last thing I wanted was to be caught walking down the hall with my underwear in my hands.

Not happening.

I yanked up the zipper, finger combed my sex hair until it looked more tousled than recently bedded, and opened the door to the bathroom.

Chase lay on his side, propped up on an elbow, his eyes wide and lit from within until they narrowed on my dress and flashed to the sandals on my feet.

As if a switch had been flipped, the light went out.

My stomach sank.

Something was wrong. "I—"

"Sneaking out?" Chase's voice was cold. Accusing.

"No, I—"

"I wondered if that's how this would go," he said looking away as if the sight of me hurt his eyes. "I should have known."

"Chase, the breakfast. I have to get dressed. I...I wasn't—"

His piercing blue eyes had gone flat, like stone. The sick feeling in my gut spread.

I thought... I thought this was...

Maybe I'd been wrong.

Maybe we were just friends and he wanted to get laid and all that flirting had been for fun.

I hadn't thought Chase was like Evers, one of those guys who flirted as easily as he breathed, but what the hell did I know about reading men?

I had a failed marriage behind me that said I did not understand the opposite sex.

Maybe I'd been so busy building walls against Chase, I hadn't realized I didn't need to bother.

In the end, he'd only wanted sex.

My tongue tangled, tripping over itself as I tried to figure out what to say. Another look at the clock on the bedside table told me I'd better think of something fast, or I'd be rolling into breakfast in last night's dress with my hair sticking out in all directions.

I didn't get the chance.

Chase sat up, the sheet pooling around his waist. He flicked his hair out of his eyes and speared me with a look so irritated, so dismissive, I felt no bigger than an ant.

"Don't worry about it," he said, with a shrug of one shoulder. "You might as well go. We're done. I get it."

"I—"

I went still, trying to understand what he wanted me to say.

We're done?

Done like this was a one-night stand? Or *done* like, like over? Like he had what he wanted and he didn't want anymore?

I'd been here before. In high school, and once in college. The sweet cute guy who laid in with the flirting and the invitations to dinner, calling and giving me flowers right up until I put out. Then nothing.

I knew my part in the script.

I hadn't thought I'd have to play it with Chase.

Just to make sure that I wasn't jumping to conclusions I said, "You want me to go. Because we're done."

"You're on your way," he said obliquely. "Don't let me stop you."

I should have expected it.

I didn't, and every word was a punch to the gut.

Dropping my head so he couldn't see my eyes, I nodded. I grabbed my tiny evening purse from the chair where I'd dropped it and made a beeline for the door, my cheeks burning, my eyes already starting to well with tears.

I heard my name as the door swung shut behind me, but I didn't turn around. I'd had a few too many glasses of champagne the night before, and I must have misunderstood.

At least I'd gotten a few orgasms out of it. I'd ended my dry spell in a spectacular fashion. And it was good to know that was all Chase wanted before I got in any deeper, right?

My room was at the other end of the hall and up a floor from Chase's. I trudged through the door, heartsick and numb.

Looking at the time on the clock, I let out a breath. I'd have to hurry if I wanted to make breakfast.

Not hurry, I'd have to move at light speed to get ready in time. I knew that. I knew the seconds were ticking away, and yet, when I stood under the hot spray of the shower, I didn't move.

I didn't wash my hair or shave my legs or scrub body wash over my skin.

I stood in the steamy heat and let the water wash away my tears, feeling sick at heart.

Sick and tired and so, so foolish.

CHAPTER TWENTY
CHASE

I knocked on Annabelle's door before breakfast, but there was no answer. I couldn't imagine she'd had time to get back to her room, get ready for the formal break-fast, and beat me downstairs, but if she was still in there she wasn't answering.

I thought I heard water running, but it was hard to tell.

I was unsettled. Off-kilter.

The look on her face when she'd walked out... Had I got it wrong?

I'd opened my eyes and she'd been gone, just as I'd expected. Then she was there, dressed, her hair everywhere and a tense, guilty expression on her face.

She'd been sneaking out.

There was no way to mistake that.

She'd gotten out of bed without waking me up, and was standing by the door fully dressed, looking guilty that I'd opened my eyes and caught her.

What was I supposed to do? Beg her to stay?

I was good enough for one night after a little too much champagne, but not good enough to wake up with.

Fine. She could stay locked up in her tower, alone for the rest of her life if that was what she wanted. I'd been begging for scraps of her attention long enough.

I told myself all that as I showered and got dressed, but it didn't sit right.

If Annabelle was going to have a one-night stand, why wait three years? If she wanted sex, she didn't need me for that.

None of the pieces went together the way I wanted them to. I tried to shrug it off. I'd see her at breakfast. We could figure it out then. Or after, on the ride home. I wasn't sure if an hour alone in a car with Annabelle was a gift or a curse.

It might be the most awkward hour of my life, but maybe not. Maybe we just needed to talk.

I told myself I was being a hopeful idiot.

I was so distracted, I didn't notice her empty chair until I sat down. I didn't know most of the other people at our table, so I focused on my coffee and watched the happy couple celebrate their morning after breakfast.

Jacob looked smug, his silver eyes warm rather than their usual ice, and Abigail wore a satisfied smile. Not quite as smug as her husband, but close. Her wedding may have been over, but she still looked like the happiest bride I'd ever seen.

Aiden stood up at one point, clicking a fork against his mimosa, the bright, crisp sound far too happy for my dark mood.

I didn't hear a word of his short speech and only barely registered Abigail sniffling and standing up to give him a tight hug, Jacob leaning over and slapping him on the back.

I did notice Annalise shoot me a glare as she stood and left the dining room, her heels clicking against the hardwood in angry taps. Riley met my eyes from across the room and slowly shook his head, his mouth grim. He glanced at the seat beside me, then back at me and shook his head again.

What the fuck?

I didn't have to wonder long.

A few minutes later Lise was back, sliding into Annabelle's chair and giving me a scowl. It was bizarre to see that angry look aimed at me from eyes so like my own.

"Just so you know, you're giving us a ride home."

"Us who?" I asked, not following.

"Us as in Riley and me. I just gave Riley's keys to Annabelle."

"Why the fuck would you give Riley's keys to Annabelle? Annabelle is riding with me."

"Yeah? Then where is she?"

"We overslept. I thought she was getting dressed," I said, hearing the words come out of my mouth and realizing I was an idiot.

First, I'd confirmed I'd spent the night with Annabelle, which she might not have wanted me to share with Lise. And second, it was obvious Annabelle wasn't running late.

She was running away.

"She's not getting dressed. She left," Lise confirmed.

"She's supposed to ride with me," I said, still an idiot.

Why was she running away? She was the one who snuck out. There were other tables if she didn't want to sit with me.

She didn't have to make a dramatic exit in a borrowed

car. I could take a hint.

"She doesn't want to drive home with you," Lise said. "I'm pretty sure she never wants to see you again. Whatever the hell you did, I hope you're ready to apologize."

"I didn't do a fucking thing," I growled back, shrugging a shoulder at Lise's annoyed grunt over my language.

"You must have done something. It's not like her to bail. It's not like her to cry, either."

I started to shove back my chair, ready to go after her and figure this out. Lise's hand closed over my wrist, stopping me.

"Don't bother. I watched her drive away myself."

"Why did you give her your keys?" I demanded.

Why was Annabelle crying? She'd walked out on me. I was the injured party here.

"Because she's my friend," Lise said slowly, as if I were a child. "I wasn't here for that whole thing with Tommy. We've been friends since we were kids and I let her go through that alone. Whatever's going on with you two, I don't care that you're my brother, I'm not letting you stomp all over her. If she needs my car keys—or Riley's—she can have them. She can have anything she wants. You'd better figure out a way to fix this."

She didn't give me a chance to respond, pushing her chair back and returning to her seat across the room with Riley.

Great. Now Violet, Aiden, Charlie and Lucas, even Vance and Maggie—everyone in the family had noticed that I was sitting at breakfast alone, my date nowhere to be seen.

Wonderful. I had no idea how this had turned around to be my fault.

I'd have to get through the rest of this breakfast, get back to Atlanta, and then I could figure out what the hell had happened.

We left Chateau du Jardin not long after the breakfast ended. Jacob and Abigail were staying another night, then leaving for a two-week honeymoon in Europe. The rest of us had to pack up and depart paradise to go back and face real life.

I wasn't looking forward to it. Annalise and Riley met me in the parking lot, bags in hand. Riley took the front passenger seat and Lise climbed into the back. She pulled out her phone and started texting, conspicuously ignoring me.

Fine.

We'd been driving for twenty minutes when Riley cleared his throat, gave me a sympathetic look and said, "So, what did you do?"

"None of your fucking business."

Lise already wanted to string me up by my balls. I wasn't having this conversation in front of her. She might have been my half-sister, but she'd made it very clear who had her loyalty, and it was not me.

"Come on, man. You must have done something. Annabelle is a fucking champion at gritting her teeth and doing what she has to do, even when it's killing her. The whole time she was getting divorced from that asshole, she never missed a day at the café. I never walked in when she didn't have a smile on her face. Even when I knew she felt like hell. So for her to bail on the breakfast? Come on, what the fuck did you do?"

Annabelle had quite the army of protectors, didn't she? Every one of my half-brothers and cousins had looked out for her for years. Now Riley? No wonder she only needed me for sex.

Dodging his question, I said, "How do you know her so well? You only got back together with Lise a little while ago."

"Jealous," Riley murmured under his breath.

"Fuck you," I muttered back.

Riley and I were friends, closer than I was to any of my new relatives, and normally we poked at each other for fun, but I was not in the mood.

"It's not me you want to fuck," he said in a low tone that wasn't quite low enough, based on the punch Lise threw into his shoulder from the back seat. "Sorry, babe."

"Asshole," she said affectionately.

Finally answering my question, Riley said, "I know Annabelle from when she was in college with Lise, and because most of Sinclair Security goes to her for coffee. On the rare occasions we have office meetings, we always get Annabelle to cater."

"Kind of out of your way," I muttered. Sinclair Security was in Buckhead. Not exactly around the corner.

Riley shrugged a shoulder. "That's what interns are for. Anyway, how I know Annabelle isn't the point. The point is she took our car and drove home and she'd been crying. We all know she spent the night with you, so I want to know. What the fuck did you do?"

"I didn't do anything," I burst out. "I woke up, caught her sneaking out on me, and that was it. I don't know why *she's* mad at *me*."

"What do you mean you caught her sneaking out on you?" Lise asked, putting down her phone and leaning forward.

"It's none of your business, but if you have to know—"

"I do," she interrupted, and I took my eyes off the road to glare at her in the rearview mirror.

"I mean exactly what I said. I woke up and she wasn't in bed and then she came out of the bathroom with all of her stuff heading for the door, dressed and ready to go."

"What did you say?" Lise pressed.

I focused on the road ahead and tried to think.

What had I said?

I'd been pissed off. I couldn't remember my exact words. I just remembered looking up and seeing her, the guilty expression on her face. She looked ready to flee and it felt like a slap. I opened my mouth and...

Shit.

What had I said?

Truthfully, and regretfully, I admitted, "I don't remember, exactly. I was pissed off. I think I said something about this being done. And if she wanted to go she should go."

"Are you sure she wanted to go?" Riley asked.

I didn't answer.

I had been.

I'd been completely sure she'd been on her way out.

Could I have been wrong? Could I have misread everything and then kicked her out of my room?

That would make me a Grade-A asshole, wouldn't it?

Staring at the road, and trying to think, all I could say was, "Shit."

From the backseat Lise chuckled, and I fought the urge to throw something at her.

It turns out little sisters are little sisters, whether you'd known them a lifetime or a few weeks.

Sometimes annoyingly right, and sometimes just annoying.

CHAPTER TWENTY-ONE
CHASE

Annabelle wasn't taking my calls.

I'd been trying for three days and every time the phone either rang through to voicemail or sent me there immediately.

So not only wasn't she answering, she was actively declining my calls.

I'd fucked up. There was no other way to look at it.

If I'd been right and all she'd wanted was a one-night stand, she would have expected to go back to being friends. Instead, she was shutting me out.

Because I'd hurt her.

Because I'd seen what I'd expected to see instead of what was really there.

I'd been so sure she was going to walk out on me, so sure that night had been my only chance with her, that I'd shoved her right out the door.

Now I was on the other side, and she wouldn't let me back in.

Fucking idiot.

I hadn't worked up the nerve to confront her in the café. For one thing, according to Lise, the last time I'd seen her I'd made her cry. The café was her place of business. It was her livelihood. Her customers kept the lights on and she lived there.

I wanted to see her.

I really wanted to see her.

But I couldn't bring myself to upset her while she was working. I thought about showing up right at 8 o'clock when she was closing, but something held me back.

Maybe I was afraid she'd lock the door in my face. Hell, she probably would.

I texted to ask her to talk, said I thought I owed her an apology. I was sure she saw the messages, but she never answered.

I planned to give her a few more days, and then I was going for the full court press. I'd messed things up, but if that was true, then I could fix this.

I *would* fix this.

I wasn't giving up on Annabelle, and I was not going to walk away.

My family thought the situation was fucking hysterical.

Nosy bastards.

They took to poking fun at me whenever they could, asking if I needed coffee and did I want them to pick me up something from Annabelle's. They weren't creative, but they didn't have to be.

It still stung.

Vivi was the only one on my side, though she'd made it clear she was only on my side out of a lifetime of loyalty. Not because she thought I was right.

All she'd said was, "What were you thinking? It took a

lot for her to let you in and then you threw her out the door? You're a moron. Do you want me to talk to her?"

That was my Vivi. Telling me how it was, and then offering to do whatever she could to make it better. She was a good sister, the best, but she couldn't fix this.

I was sitting at breakfast, ignoring both Aunt Amelia's taunts about getting a mocha and Vivi's sympathetic glances, when Lise's phone rang.

I was usually out the door and on the way to the office by then, but I'd been putting in late nights working on my new project. Anything to keep my mind off Annabelle.

I'd overslept.

Or not slept enough.

However you wanted to look at it, I was sleep deprived and running late. Mechanically shoveling scrambled eggs into my mouth between sips of coffee, I listened with half an ear as Lise said, "Hey."

Her voice was hesitant. Cautious, but friendly. The odd combination caught my attention and drew it further when she shot me a quick, wary glance, then deliberately looked away.

"What's going on? It sounds like a madhouse." She listened for a few minutes, then shoved the chair back from the table and stood up, not looking at any of us. "I'll be right there. Fifteen minutes, no more. Promise. Just hang on."

Going with my gut, I got up and followed her, grabbing her arm and turning her around before she reached the front door. "What's going on? What's wrong?"

Lise looked over my shoulder to the door, then at the ceiling, then my hand on her arm. I dropped it but asked again, "What's going on?"

"That was Annabelle. Grover and Penny ran off together. No notice, just didn't show up. Now she's alone over there in the middle of a rush and she has no staff. I worked cafés off and on for the last ten years. I know my way around a portafilter, and she asked if I could pitch in."

"I'm coming," I said.

Lise shook her head and stepped back. "Chase, I know you mean well, but she doesn't need—"

"She needs all hands on deck. I won't get in her face. I won't push. But I know my way around the kitchen. I can wash dishes. I can man the cash register. I can clear tables. She has at least three people on during the day, and you know it. Even with two of you, she's going to be slammed. I'm coming. I can help."

Lise sighed, shaking her head. "Okay, fine. We don't have time to fight about this and you're right."

Annabelle was not happy to see me walk in behind Lise. Her eyes went flat and blank, and she looked away, hiding her face from me.

My stomach turned over in a sour twist. My chest ached.

I'd done that to her. It didn't matter that I hadn't meant to.

I'd been so ready for her to hurt me that I'd hurt her first.

Fucking hell.

The first time she'd peeked her way through her shields and I'd fucked it up. Now she'd built them back up so tall I'd never get through again.

Let it go I told myself.

This wasn't about me.

This was about Annabelle and her fuckwad baristas who'd run off and left her alone during the morning rush.

I was here to help, not get in her face.

Lise went straight back behind the counter, grabbed an

apron, and hit the espresso machine, falling into the rhythm of taking orders and making drinks as if she'd never left the job.

I stopped in front of Annabelle and said, "Register or dishes?"

She stared at me, blankly.

I tried again, saying gently, "Do you want me to work the register or do dishes?"

She blinked and swallowed hard, her voice cracking as she said, "Dishes. Grab one of the bins, bus the tables, and then do the dishes stacked up in the kitchen. Please."

I could handle that. The next few hours passed in a blur of sounds and smells.

The clink of the tableware, the unending murmur of voices, the hiss and puff of the espresso machine, the clang of Lise smacking the portafilter to loosen the ground espresso.

The *ching* of the register and the click of tip money filling the jar on the counter, all drowned out here and there by the rush and churn of water in the kitchen as I busted my ass to keep up with the demand for clean dishes.

I washed and restocked and cleared and washed again. It was the first day of a sidewalk arts festival in the Highlands and the café was twice as crowded as usual. It was one of the worst possible times for her idiot baristas to run off.

Things didn't slow down until mid-afternoon when Annabelle came in the kitchen and started putting plates together.

She didn't talk to me. She barely acknowledged me.

But when she was done, she slapped a plate holding a turkey sandwich, apple slices, and a salted caramel brownie on top of the dishwasher before she walked away.

She wouldn't speak to me, but she was still feeding me. That had to mean something, didn't it?

I wasn't optimistic enough to think that washing a few dishes in her time of need was going to fix things, but I was in for the long haul.

I was refilling the bakery case when I realized that Lise had gone home.

Why would she have left me alone with Annabelle? She'd made it clear whose side she was on in this mess.

When Annabelle had a break at the counter I asked, "Where did Lise go?"

"She had a date with Riley for dinner."

"Dinner?" I asked stupidly. What time was it?

Annabelle answered my unasked question. "It's almost six. You don't have to stay. I can handle the rest myself."

"I'll stay," I said.

"Chase, you don't—"

"I'll stay," I said again. "I'm not going to bother you. I'm not going to get in your way. But I'm going to stay and help, okay?"

Annabelle swallowed hard and nodded, but she didn't meet my eyes.

Shit. I didn't know how to fix this. Everything I said was the wrong thing. I wanted to tell her I was sorry. That I hadn't meant it. That I'd been an idiot.

She didn't need to hear that now, while she still had customers. While she still had two more hours before close and then all the work of shutting the place down.

What was she going to do the next day? And the day after that? It would take time to find new staff.

I'd worry about that later. For now, I had tables to bus and dishes to wash.

Eight o'clock came before I knew it. I was used to the

café at this time of night, the ebb and flow of customers as people stopped shopping in favor of dinner or home.

The festival had the café packed right up until Annabelle ushered the last customer through the door. She flipped the lock, turned the sign, and sank onto the stool behind her in exhaustion.

I could imagine how she felt. I'd been on my feet all day, too, but I'd been in the back, doing my own thing. She'd been up front, charming customers, making everyone feel at home as she fed them and caffeinated them with a smile.

"Go up to bed," I said. "You look exhausted. I can close up."

"*I* look exhausted? How much sleep did you get last night?"

I was trying not to think about that. I leaned against the counter. "Enough. I've been working late on the project, but I got enough sleep. If this place is so crazy, when are you going to find the time to interview for new staff?"

Annabelle squeezed her eyes shut and shook her head. "Honestly? I haven't even thought about it. I have no idea."

"Fuck Grover and Penny," I said, startling a laugh from Annabelle. The sound was tired and faded, but it was a laugh.

"I'll come in tomorrow," I said.

Aiden, Gage, and my department would have to deal without me. We were almost ahead of schedule. A few days away wouldn't put us too far behind.

Even if it did, I didn't care. Annabelle needed me more than they did.

"Chase, you can't—"

"I can," I said. "Tomorrow you can run me through the register, and I can help with that, too. I know I can't pick up the espresso machine that fast, but I've handled a cash register before."

Annabelle sagged even further and looked at the floor. My gut burned seeing her so tired. So defeated. The burn was worse for knowing I'd played a part in that.

The customers were gone, and we were alone. I couldn't leave it like this anymore.

"Annabelle, I'm sorry. I fucked up. I know I fucked up. I thought—"

"Chase, it's okay. It's okay. You don't have to explain. I get it."

"I don't think you do. I wanted you to stay and I thought you were leaving and I didn't think. I just... I was an asshole."

"Yeah, you kind of were."

A laugh shook her chest, but the sound was so far from her usual bright, rich laughter that it hurt to hear.

Annabelle shouldn't laugh like that, gray and dark and empty.

She sounded beat up. Alone.

I hated myself for it.

"You can go," she said, unintentionally echoing my words from the day after the wedding. "I can handle the rest by myself. You already did the dishes. I just have to wipe everything down and—"

"And sweep the floors and wipe down the tables and wash the floors and put the games away... I know all the stuff you have to do, Annabelle. Let me help."

Too tired to argue, she shrugged a shoulder and started to wipe down the tables in the front of the café. I decided to give her some space and try again when we were done.

We'd closed the place down together so many times, we worked in synchronicity without speaking a word. Her sweeping, me mopping, putting everything to rights for the next morning.

When we were finally done, Annabelle walked me down the hall to the back door, stopping at the base of the stairs to her tiny studio.

Looking up at me, finally meeting my eyes, she said, "You really don't have to come back tomorrow. I appreciate it but—"

"I'm coming back tomorrow, Annabelle. At least until you get some permanent help."

"But your job—"

"They can do without me. I make my own schedule, anyway."

Quietly, so quietly I almost didn't hear her, she said, "I don't think I can do that. Have you here all day again. I just... I need a little space before we can go back to how things were."

"I don't want to go back to how things were, Annabelle."

"We have to. We have to go back or we can't go anywhere."

"Why? I messed up. I know I did, and I'm sorry. I got angry and I lashed out and—"

"I know," Annabelle said. "I know. And I can't do that again. I don't want that. That's the way it was before with Tommy. Everything would be fine and then he'd get upset about something I didn't even know I did and he'd lose it. He'd say things—"

Her voice choked off and she blinked hard. I sensed it was an act of courage when she raised her chin and met my eyes again.

"I can't live like that, Chase. Always wondering what I'm going to do wrong next. Always tiptoeing around hoping I don't set you off. It's too much. It's too hard. Everything that happened with us made me think of everything I want to leave behind me."

"Everything?" I heard myself ask, reeling from being compared to her asshole of an ex-husband.

I hadn't thought about what happened from her perspective. Hadn't realized what that must have felt like. She'd told me about her marriage, told me what he was like, but still, I hadn't seen it.

I have a temper, it's true. But the way I'd lashed out at Annabelle, jumped to conclusions and hurt her feelings—that almost never happened. I was a grown man and I was usually adult enough to keep my temper in check.

One slip, one time, and it was the very worst time to let go of the reins.

Again, I said "Everything? Did everything remind you of him?"

Reaching up, I cupped her chin in one hand and turned her face to mine, pain slicing through my heart at the sight of her wet eyelashes, dark and spiky against her pale cheeks.

She didn't step back.

Didn't pull away.

When I lowered my face and pressed my mouth to hers, she opened for me, kissing me back as if we'd never been apart. As if I'd never driven her off and lost her just when I thought I'd found her.

She pulled away before I was ready, pressing her palm to my chest, moving me back until feet separated us.

"I can't, Chase. I can't do this again. I'm sorry. I wanted to, and I'm sorry. I need you to go."

Annabelle pushed gently, backing me closer to the door. I wasn't going to make it harder for her.

She was a woman alone in an empty building with a man who she wanted gone.

If she wanted me gone, I'd go. That didn't mean I wouldn't be back.

I turned for the door saying only, "I'll see you tomorrow, Annabelle," before I walked out into the street, hearing the door close and lock behind me.

With a laugh, I realized my ride had abandoned me hours before, and I didn't have a way to get home.

Pulling my phone from my back pocket I opened a rideshare app and resigned myself to a wait.

In more ways than one.

CHAPTER TWENTY-TWO

CHASE

Annabelle let me in the door five minutes before open the next morning, but she did it with a scowl for me and a glare for Lise. Lise shrugged and went to put on an apron, mumbling under her breath, "You need the help."

Annabelle didn't acknowledge the truth.

She didn't want me there, but she was too smart to kick me out.

Quietly, keeping distance between us, she showed me how the register worked, and the day went more smoothly with both Lise and Annabelle working the espresso machine, making drinks, and serving food.

The dishes piled up, but we worked out a rhythm. When the line slowed down, Lise or Annabelle would take the register and I'd go to the back to catch up on the dishes. When people piled in the door, all three of us worked the front.

To be honest, I'm not exactly sure how Annabelle did this all day, every day. She never stopped moving. I like exercise. Love to work out, love to push my body until my muscles are shaking and I drip with sweat.

I did not love being on my feet for sixteen hours straight, carrying trays of dishes and food, smiling at customers when what I really wanted was for all of them to get the hell out so that Annabelle could sit down and put her feet up.

She needed more staff. She needed help.

A few days later, the arts festival ended, and the flow of customers died down to its usual busy-but-not-frenetic. She picked up one new barista, a college student with a year of experience who'd been working for a big chain coffeehouse and wanted something a little more funky. A little more personal.

The girl had purple dreadlocks and a ring in her nose, but she was fast, smart, and she took Annabelle's directions with a smile. She also showed up on time, which put her miles above Grover and Penny.

I, on the other hand, wasn't making much progress. Annabelle had been very careful not to let me close enough to kiss her again. And while she hadn't kicked me out, she rarely let down her guard.

She looked at me with wary, cautious eyes.

I hated it. I missed what we'd had. The comfort of her company.

I couldn't even think about the one night I'd had her in my bed.

That way lay madness.

Remembering her soft skin, her long, lean body wrapped around mine, her silky cinnamon hair like fire against the white sheets—remembering what I'd lost would make me crazy.

It was bad enough that she'd stopped smiling. Stopped laughing. Part of it was exhaustion, but the rest was me.

It seemed a high price to pay for one mistake. One moment of temper and she refused to give me another chance.

I was almost starting to resent her for it.

I might have if it hadn't been for Aiden.

I was in the library with Vivi, having a glass of wine before dinner, when Aiden strolled in, his dark eyes lighting up at the sight of my sister.

He poured himself a whiskey from the new crystal decanter and matching glasses on the tray at the bar.

Whiskey wasn't usually my drink, but if it had been I would have wanted that decanter and those glasses. Heavy, with a diamond-like shine, they fit perfectly in Aiden's big hand.

Vivi had destroyed the first set in a rare fit of temper. The Westbrook siblings didn't fly off the handle on a regular basis, but when we did...

At least Vivi had only damaged property.

Decanters and glasses were replaceable. Hearts were not.

I remembered the mess Aiden had been when she'd left him, hollow-eyed and miserable. But that was different. Aiden had been the one who fucked up.

Vivi had lost her temper, true. In the process, she'd destroyed a set of barware worth more than my first car, but her display of temper had been righteous. She'd been the injured party.

Every time I thought about hurting Annabelle, my gut twisted. My outburst had been anything but righteous. I'd been a coward, trying to protect myself at her expense.

I knew that, but how long was she going to hold it

against me?

That little seed of resentment settled its roots deeper into my heart.

I looked at the glass of wine I'd set on the coffee table, then to the whiskey in Aiden's hand.

I didn't want the wine. I didn't really want whiskey either.

The last time I'd indulged in whiskey had been after a fight with Vivi, and I could still remember the hangover. I already knew that whatever Aiden had in that decanter, it was light years better than the crap I'd been drinking in my condo.

He sat on the couch, too close to Vivi in my opinion, and sipped, his eyes moving between us.

"You two look serious," he said, sliding his arm around my baby sister and pulling her to his side.

She cuddled in, resting her hand on his thigh. I looked over their shoulders, out the window. I was happy Vivi was happy, but I still didn't like the PDA.

Vivi said, "We're talking about Annabelle."

Aiden's gaze sharpened on me and he said in a dangerously neutral voice, "What about Annabelle?"

"She won't give Chase a second chance," Vivi said, a little disgruntled.

"I wasn't aware she'd given him a first chance," Aiden said, that sharp gaze ready to slice me to pieces. I kept my mouth shut.

"You know she did," Vivi said, squeezing his leg. "At the wedding. Remember? And then she didn't show for the breakfast because—" She waved her hand in my direction.

"Because I was an asshole," I admitted. "I misread the situation and I said stuff I shouldn't have. I apologized," I said when Aiden leaned forward.

"What kind of stuff did you say?" he asked, his tone devoid of emotion.

Not a good sign. I wondered if my future brother-in-law and sort of cousin was about to beat the hell out of me.

"This isn't any of your business—"

"Tell me anyway," he ordered.

Bossy son of a bitch.

Anyone else and I would have told him to butt the fuck out. But Aiden was an honorary older brother to Annabelle. They'd been friends most of their lives, and he'd been there for her through her divorce.

If he understood how I felt, what my intentions were, he might help me. God knows I needed the help.

"Look, I woke up and she was leaving, okay? Or I thought she was leaving. I thought she was sneaking out. I thought she regretted it and was ditching me and I was pissed. And now she knows that I know I misunderstood, and I apologized."

"The last thing Annabelle needs is another guy yelling at her every time he doesn't get his way," Aiden said, his voice even and his brown eyes filmed with ice.

"But Chase isn't like that," Vivi burst out.

Aiden raised an eyebrow at her and she said, "He isn't. I can't remember the last time he lost his temper. He has a temper—" Vivi looked at me in apology. "You do. You know you do."

Meeting Aiden's eyes, she went on, "But ever since he was a teenager he's been so good about controlling it. Even when the whole thing went down with the company, I'm the one who went a little crazy—"

"I'm aware of that," Aiden said, dryly.

He would be, considering they'd met because she'd infiltrated Winters, Inc. to try to find a way to bring Aiden down and get the company back. She'd failed in that goal, but she'd fallen in love in the process, so her scheme had been worth it in the end.

Aiden looked at me, considering. "Interesting," he said. "You didn't lose your temper when you thought I stole your company, even when you realized I couldn't give it back. Even when you found out I was dating your sister. You weren't happy, and you yelled a few times, but that was it. Why did you lose it over Annabelle?"

I rubbed my palms on my thighs, suddenly feeling like a teenager being grilled by his date's father.

Anything other than honesty would be a mistake and I knew it. I wanted to tell Aiden that how I felt about Annabelle was none of his goddamn business.

"I'm in love with her. I haven't even told her that. Mostly because she wouldn't believe me. But I'm in love with her. I woke up hoping things between us had changed and I thought I caught her sneaking out. I overreacted. I know it. I told her that—not the love part but the overreacting part—and I apologized. I'm there every day, helping her in the café—"

"Yes, I know, considering your department has ground to a halt since you've been gone."

"I don't give a damn," I said. "You muddled along just fine before you found me, you can wait until Annabelle doesn't need me anymore. I don't give a shit about the algorithm or fixing the tech. I give a shit about Annabelle.

"She's working herself to the bone because those two flakes bailed on her. The new girl is okay, but Annabelle is still short-staffed. I'll come back to Winters, Inc. when she's settled. If you don't like it, fire me. I couldn't possibly care less."

Aiden said nothing, just leaned back into the couch and

studied me thoughtfully. Finally, he said, "The dickweed she married had a temper. A bad one. And when he decided their marriage wasn't shaping up the way he thought it would, he took it out on her. All the time."

I leaned forward, sick at what he'd said. "Did he—?"

Aiden shook his head. "He never laid a hand on her. Nothing physical, just words."

"Words can hurt worse than a fist," Vivi said quietly.

She knew. We'd both been on the receiving end of our parents' brand of discipline. Mostly telling us what disappointments we were. They'd never physically hurt us, but they were experts at slicing us to pieces with a vicious turn of phrase.

I thought of Annabelle, her bright smile and rich laugh, being berated and demeaned by that slick, overdressed desk jockey.

I was going to give the Sinclairs a call. Get his home address. Just in case.

"You really love her?" Aiden asked.

"I really do," I said. I meant every word to the depths of my soul. No hesitation.

It had happened so quietly.

Not the flash of attraction; I'd felt that the first time I laid eyes on Annabelle, the first time I saw her smile, saw her long legs eat up the floor in the café, the tight curve of her ass and the sway of her narrow hips.

Attraction was easy. Everything about her did it for me. But attraction, lust—that wasn't love.

Love was the sandwiches she made.

Letting me stay and work after she closed. Love was making sure I filled my stomach when I was too distracted to eat.

Love was helping her sweep and mop so she could go to bed a little earlier.

Love was the little things. Love was being there. I'd fallen in love with her day by day until I couldn't imagine not being with her.

Until the idea of the day passing without seeing Annabelle felt like misery.

"And what about the café?" Aiden asked.

"What about it?"

"You know she's a workaholic. She loves that place, and even if she finally gets some decent help, she's never going to turn it over to a manager."

"If she did, she'd lose half of her customers."

I thought about Annabelle's bright smile behind the counter, the way she remembered her regulars' orders and saved them treats she knew they'd like.

"Annabelle is that café," I said. "She'd do a decent business if she turned it over to a manager. But not like she does now. She's made it more than a coffee house. It's a home away from home for a lot of people. No one can do that but her. Nobody loves it like she does."

"What about when you guys have kids?" Aiden pressed. "If you love her, eventually…"

I swallowed hard. I hadn't thought about kids. I'd thought about Annabelle. I'd thought about Annabelle and my new house. Every time I walked through the place, every time Charlie gave me a tour of the progress, I imagined Annabelle living there with me.

If I couldn't win her back, living in that house would be hell without her. I'd even upgraded the kitchen with her in mind.

But kids?

I wanted kids. In a vague, someday-down-the-road kind

of way. Kids with Annabelle? Little boys or girls with that bright smile and her boundless energy?

Yeah. Yeah, I wanted that. The house had room. Just because I wasn't planning a nursery right this second didn't mean I'd forgotten about the future.

"What about when we have kids?" I asked. "What does the café have to do with kids?"

"Well, won't you want her to stay at home?"

Vivi punched his ribs and he flinched.

"Sexist much?" she asked. "Are you expecting me to quit my job when we have kids? Because I'm not busting my ass in grad school just so I can dust my framed diploma."

Aiden gave her an affectionate smile and kissed her temple. In a low, intimate voice no older brother should have to overhear, he said, "No, sweetheart, I don't. I expect that when we get to that point, you and I will figure it out together. Like we're going to do everything. We're a team."

"Damn straight," she said, smiling up at him, love beaming from her eyes.

I rolled my own and said under my breath, "Really? Do I have to watch this?"

"You still didn't answer my question," Aiden said, breaking Violet's gaze and pinning me with a hard look.

"I haven't answered because I don't know," I said, "but we'll figure it out. My work is flexible. I hate the corporate gig. You know that. The only reason I'm still at Winters, Inc. is because my tech isn't finished. Once you've got it rolling, I'm out."

"Yeah, I figured that part out already," Aiden said, his lips quirking in a half smile. "I don't suppose you're going to let us take a look at what you're working on now, are you?"

I raised an eyebrow. Not much got past Aiden Winters.

"I haven't decided yet," I said honestly. "But that's not

the point. The point is, I'm flexible. I work for myself. And yeah, I like the whole startup thing. I like the long hours. The adrenaline and the risk.

"But I also have plenty put aside, more than enough for a secure future for a family. And if we decide to have kids we can do it when I'm not in the middle of a project. I'll stay home with them. Besides, my house is five blocks from the café. Annabelle has that studio upstairs we could use as a playroom if we need to have the kids there but not under-foot in the café. We have options. We can figure it out."

"What if she gets pregnant and you're in the middle of starting a new company?" Aiden asked.

"Then I'll ditch the company," I said. "Seriously? You're asking me if I'd ignore my own kid over a tech startup?"

"I want to know how much thought you've put into this," Aiden said. "I want to know how serious you are."

"Pretty fucking serious," I said. "But don't you think you're jumping the gun? At the moment she's barely talking to me. Kids are not on the table when I can't get her to look me in the eye."

Sophie ducked her head around the door of the library, her cheeks flushed pink, tendrils of blonde hair curling around her face. She wore Abel's kitchen apron, the strings wrapped twice around her waist.

"Dinner's ready. It's been an age since I was in the kitchen, so I can't make any promises."

We all stood as Sophie disappeared to pass the message of dinner on to Gage and anyone else hanging around looking for a meal.

"Why is Sophie cooking?" I asked.

"Mrs. W and Abel are taking a few days off," Aiden said.

"Wait, what?" Vivi asked. "When did this happen? They were here at breakfast."

Vivi had been on campus all day, and as she did on most school days, had left before the rest of us were up and about.

"It happened today."

Aiden didn't offer any more information. His abrupt answer was not enough for Vivi.

She grabbed his arm to stop his departure from the room and demanded, "Well? They left together? Where did they go? When are they coming back?"

Aiden turned to face her, sliding his long fingers into the thick fall of hair down her back. He combed them through in a sweet, soothing gesture that I would have appreciated if not for the heat in his eyes when he looked at my little sister.

Quietly, but firmly, he said, "None of your business. They want privacy, and privacy they'll get. They'll be home soon enough and then you can see what you can pry out of Mrs. W yourself."

She scowled at him. Aiden loved Vivi to pieces, but he was loyal as hell, and if he'd promised Mrs. W and Abel he'd keep their secret, he would, even from Vivi.

If he wouldn't tell Vivi, the rest of us didn't stand a chance of prying a single clue out of him. We'd have to be content with the mystery until Mrs. W and Abel returned to solve it for us.

CHAPTER TWENTY-THREE

CHASE

I showed up the next day at five minutes before opening to find Annabelle waiting in the doorway, arms crossed over her chest, jaw set and eyes hard.

I looked past her to see the new barista, purple dreadlocks practically glowing in the bright lights. Someone else was beside her. A guy, a little older than purple dreadlocks, with a ring in his eyebrow and a colorful tattoo sleeve. He was setting up the espresso machine with what looked like competence.

"Another new one?" I asked, shoving my hands in my pockets.

"He left a place across town. He lives by Little Five Points and he was tired of the drive."

"So you're saying you don't need me." I shoved my hands in my pockets, hiding the pinch in my heart.

"I really do appreciate all of your help, Chase. It means a lot."

"But go away now?" I asked, with a raised eyebrow.

If she thought I was going to disappear and forget about

her, she was out of her mind.

"I think we need some time."

"Who's helping you close?" I asked.

"I don't need help to close, Chase."

"Yes, you do," I said. Leaning in, I pressed a quick kiss to the curve of her cheek and murmured, "See you later, Annabelle."

I turned and strolled down the block, leaving my car parked where it was. I was meeting Charlie at the house a little later, but she'd be there now. If Annabelle didn't need my help in the café, I'd check in with Charlie, help out a bit over there, and then head into work.

Might as well. Every hour I spent there was an hour closer to leaving Winters, Inc. More and more my head was in the new app and not on what remained of CB4 Analytics in Winters, Inc.

It had been good working with Aiden and Gage. Without that, I don't know how long I would have held back on getting to know the family better.

I didn't need the job at Winters, Inc. to be a part of the family, and I was getting impatient to shed the corporate straitjacket and go back out on my own where I belonged.

I could feel Annabelle watching me as I walked away. I was glad she had help, but she could use one more barista. I wasn't going to point that out. Not yet.

Charlie met me in the front yard, a wide smile on her face, her ocean-blue eyes sparkling.

"Almost there," she called out. "Kitchen's done! You have got to see this. You were right about the appliances, it's freaking gorgeous."

A thrill ran through my heart. I'd owned my own home before, but always condos. I'd never had my own land, even if it was the size of a postage stamp.

And the house... I stood in the front yard, hands on my hips, and looked at the house.

A hodgepodge of architectural styles that shouldn't have worked yet did, the house had the peaked gables of a Victorian combined with the beams and shingles of a rustic cottage. The windows, oversized and trimmed in black, poured light into the interior.

It was everything I never knew I wanted in a home and it was mine. Maybe mine and Annabelle's if I could convince her to take a chance on me. From the outside, it looked ready for me to move in.

Charlie grabbed my arm and tugged me to the front porch and the open door. The buzz of a saw poured through. The entry was covered in paint-splattered drop cloths.

Charlie was right. We were close.

I followed her in, through the front rooms, down the hall to the great room that made up the back half of the first floor. The kitchen filled one side, facing an open family room with a stone fireplace. Exposed beams ran the length of the room, tying the spaces together.

In the back, a wall of windows looked out to the small square of green grass between the house and the detached garage with studio above.

I'd put my office out there, saving the bedrooms in the house for me and Annabelle, guests, and someday kids. Weird how the thought of kids seemed so right. As right as the thought of sharing the house with Annabelle.

I refused to consider the possibility that I wouldn't win her over. I could be patient. I *would* be patient. Whatever she needed, I'd do it.

I left Charlie with a check for the final phase of the work, and her promise that I could move in within a week. I thought about Vivi. When we'd moved into Winters House all those weeks ago, she'd planned to move back out when the house was done. To keep living with me instead of Aiden.

He'd hate that, but he wouldn't stop her. Aiden knew how to be patient, too.

Vivi could live with me as long as she liked. My sister would always have a place with me. Always. We'd both been turned out by our own family, kicked to the curb when we'd displeased them one time too many.

We stuck together, and I would always look out for her just like she would always look out for me. I still wasn't going to let her move into this house. She belonged in Winters House with Aiden.

I knew it, he knew it, and she knew it. I didn't think she'd argue too much.

When I finally talked to her about it, she'd grinned at me with pink cheeks and agreed she didn't want to move again. Aiden was relieved, and everyone was happy, except for me.

I devoted myself fully to my pursuit of Annabelle. It was Vivi who gave me the idea.

When I'd cornered her in the kitchen of my new place and confronted her about staying with Aiden, she'd agreed, then countered by demanding to know my plan to win Annabelle.

"Plan?" I'd asked. "I don't have a plan, exactly. I was just going to keep showing up. Keep helping her close the café. Just be there, like I was before, until I wear her down and she decides to forgive me."

Vivi rolled her eyes at me as only a little sister can. "That's it? Just show up?"

"Hey, showing up is half the battle."

"No, I don't think that's it. It's *knowing is half the battle*. Didn't we watch cartoons together for most of a decade?"

"Whatever," I said, not interested in a critique of my courting methods from my sister.

"Not whatever," she said, clearly disgusted with me. "You need to do more than show up. She cares about you. She wants to trust you."

"So? Tell me what to do then, oh wise one. I don't think I could pull off your corporate espionage approach. I'm not getting a job in her café. First of all, because she already knows what I look like, and second of all, because that was pretty much the dumbest plan ever. You're lucky you didn't get arrested."

"Worked, didn't it?"

"Um, not exactly. Or did you forget the part where we didn't get the company back and you got fired?"

Vivi shrugged a shoulder and grinned up at me. "Whatever," she said, mimicking me. "Do you remember when we were kids and you used to torture me by leaving gross surprises in secret places? Like dead bugs under my pillow or a frog in my ballet shoes?"

I busted out laughing. I'd mostly forgotten that.

Vivi had hated gross stuff and her squeals of indignation when she found my presents had been well worth any punishment I earned.

"You want me to leave her dead bugs?" I asked.

"No, you idiot. Not dead bugs. Same concept, but maybe try flowers and chocolate instead of insects and amphibians."

Vivi could be a pain in my ass, but she was a smart one.

So began my campaign to win Annabelle.

I left her flowers at the back door where her employees

would find them on their way in and deliver them to her first thing.

I showed up at seven every night, worked on my laptop until she closed, and helped her clean the place up, over her objections.

I didn't push for more.

I didn't ask her out.

At first, I didn't even try to kiss her.

I did leave her gifts in places I knew only she would look.

In a pile of papers on her desk.

By the stairs up to her studio.

Tucked into the pocket of the apron she always wore.

Little things. Nothing extravagant, but gifts that showed her I'd been listening. That I knew her.

The flowers were red tulips, her favorite because the color and shape reminded her of the teacups her mom had when she was a little girl.

Earrings in citrine and amethyst, her two favorite semi-precious stones.

Chocolate truffles from the ridiculously expensive confectioner's shop in Buckhead she loved. She'd confessed weeks ago that they were a favorite indulgence, but she could never justify buying them, considering the expense for tiny bits of chocolate when she was a baker and spent her days to her ears in chocolate.

An audiobook she said she wanted to listen to, so she could pop on her headphones when she closed.

In choosing every gift I realized how well I'd come to know Annabelle. And how much I understood her.

The night I left her the earrings, but before she'd found them, I stopped before she ushered me out the door and turned, pulling her into my arms.

I held her loosely, giving her plenty of time to push me away. She stood still, staring up at me, eyes wide and dazed like a deer caught in headlights.

"I'm going to kiss you now," I said.

Her eyes dropped to my lips, pupils dilating. My cock hardened instantly, pressing uncomfortably against the thick fabric of my jeans. Fuck, a look from her and I was ready. I was turned inside out, so desperate for her I could barely stand it, and yet willing to wait as long as it took.

Her lips parted, the tip of her tongue tracing the edge of her teeth, and I lowered my head, waiting, hoping she wouldn't push me away.

She didn't. I took her mouth with mine, my tongue stroking hers. Claiming. Savoring. Just when she'd melted into me, boneless and pliant, I broke the kiss and stepped back, gritting my teeth at the effort of letting her go.

She blinked up at me, warm brown eyes wide and confused. She parted her lips to speak and I pressed my index finger against them, silencing her.

"Good night, Annabelle. I'll see you tomorrow. Sleep tight."

I dropped a kiss on the curve of her cheek and walked away, fighting the urge to go back, to pick her up and brace her against the wall, to strip off her clothes and fill her with me.

To give us both what we wanted.

I knew she wanted me. Annabelle wouldn't have kissed me like that if she didn't. She knew all she had to do was ask me to leave and I'd go.

I wouldn't use lust to cloud her mind. I wanted her to choose me. To trust me. And I wanted her to do it with her whole heart, not because she was dizzy with lust and need.

I had time. And I was going to use it well.

Every night it went like that.

Just like I had before, I showed up in the evening before closing. I brought my laptop and Annabelle made me coffee and a sandwich, always topped off with something chocolate she knew I'd love.

I never had to ask, and she delivered the food without comment. Slowly, carefully, I was easing us back into the friendship we had before.

Day by day. Step-by-step.

When she flipped the sign to CLOSED, I'd shut my laptop and bring my plate and cup back to the kitchen, starting on the dishes while she wiped down the tables.

Every night, at the end, I kissed her before I left.

Every night she came into my arms without hesitation.

Our kisses were getting longer. Hotter. A few times I'd slid my hand beneath her T-shirt, flicked open the clasp of her bra and filled my hands with her breasts, strumming my thumbs over her nipples and drinking in every whimper and moan.

One night, almost two weeks into my campaign, Annabelle surprised me by dropping onto the couch when we were done closing up instead of walking me to the door.

She had two open beers in her hand and held one out to me. I took it and sat beside her, sipping cautiously, waiting. So far, I'd been the one leading the way, coaxing her along, careful not to scare her off.

She sipped her beer, her eyes touching mine and flitting away. I missed her easy comfort with me. I understood her hesitance, but I didn't like it.

Trying to relax her, I asked, "Are you going to hire someone else to help you close?"

"Eventually," she said. "I want to get used to these two.

Why? You getting tired of helping me out?" It was the closest she'd come to teasing me in weeks.

"Nope," I said. "Anyway, I need the free meal. Mrs. W and Abel aren't back yet, and Sophie got tired of cooking for us. Vivi refused, I'm terrible in the kitchen, and I don't think Aiden and Gage can toast bread. Riley can cook, but he said flat out that he works all day and he's not filling in for Abel. Lise tried once and they begged her not to go near the stove again. They've all been living on pizza and take out. I'm the only one who's eating well."

"You should have told me, I'll send you home with sandwiches."

"No way in hell. You work hard enough. Those clowns can get their own dinner."

"No sympathy," she said, shaking her head.

"None at all," I agreed. "They can survive a few weeks without their personal chef. It's not going to kill them."

"So, you still don't know where Mrs. W and Abel went?"

"Nope. The only one who knows is Aiden, and maybe Gage. Neither of them are talking. Aiden keeps saying we can ask Mrs. W when they get back."

"I think it's sweet," she said with a little smile, and took another sip of her beer.

I made a sound of agreement and took a sip of my own. Aiden had mentioned they were due back any day now. I could wait to satisfy my curiosity.

"How is your project going?" Annabelle asked.

My heart lurched in my chest. It was an innocuous question. Not really that personal, but Annabelle had mostly been avoiding me for the last few weeks. When she talked to me, she was distant.

This—giving me a beer, asking me about my project—this was change.

Change was good.

"It's getting there," I said. "Aiden asked about it."

She laughed. "Yeah? What did you say?"

"That I wasn't going to tell him anything until I decided what I wanted to do with it."

"Bet he liked that," Annabelle smirked.

"He's not that mad at me considering I talked Vivi out of moving in with me and into staying with Aiden."

"Really? So your house is ready?"

"In a few days, yeah," I said. "Do you want to see it?"

Her eyes skittered away again. Damn. Pushed a little too far.

"Maybe," she said slowly. "Maybe, someday soon."

Not a rejection, but not an enthusiastic acceptance either. Well, I'd take what I could get.

Annabelle set her empty beer on the coffee table and shifted forward to stand. I reached out and snagged her hand in mine, tugging her toward me as I set my empty beer beside hers. She lost her balance, wobbling on the side of her foot. I turned her as she fell—right into my lap.

Exactly where I wanted her.

"Just give me a minute," I whispered against the shell of her ear. "Just give me a minute and then I'll go."

Annabelle turned her face to mine and kissed me. She tugged at my lower lip, sucking, opening my mouth to hers, her long limbs tangling with mine as she settled her slight weight against me.

The couch was long and deep. I lay back, pulling her on top of me until she straddled my hips, her mouth hungry on mine, her tongue darting into taste and stroke.

My hands closed over her ass, grinding her down into the erection pressed against the zipper of my jeans, the pain of it barely dulling my arousal.

Her kiss was fierce. Needy.

I gave her all she wanted and more, kissing her back with everything I had, not hiding my desperation. My sheer want of her. Her hair fell around us in a shining cinnamon curtain, stroking my skin with its cool length.

I slid a hand up the back of her loose T-shirt, pulling it from her sweat-damp skin, and flicked open her bra, tugging so the cups fell away from her breasts. Rolling her to the side, I shoved up the T-shirt and bra, hooking my hands under her armpits to pull her up my body as I slid down until my mouth was even with her breast.

Small and firm and just the right size, I closed my mouth around her, pulling hard on her flesh until she moaned, arching up into me.

My hand tight on the curve of her hip, I rocked her against me, sucking hard, moving from one breast to the other, forgetting that we were on a couch in her café, forgetting the tall plate glass windows in the front and that the lights were on back here.

Forgetting that we had to stop.

CHAPTER TWENTY-FOUR
CHASE

I don't know how far it would have gone if her phone hadn't rung. At the sound of it, she went rock solid.

Not pushing me away.

Not moving at all.

I panted against her skin, trying to catch my breath, trying to screw my head back on straight. I'd been about to strip her jeans off in the middle of the café. Never mind that we were alone, with the lights on and the front window twenty feet away, we weren't alone enough.

The phone stopped ringing, going to voicemail. A few seconds later, it started up again. Annabelle's face flushed bright red, and she gave up on trying to refasten her bra. She leaned over and snagged the phone off the coffee table. Without looking at the screen she swiped to answer.

I could hear him even from the other side of the couch, hear the slur in his voice as he said her name. The flush of passion drained from Annabelle's face, leaving her bone white.

Without asking, without thinking, I leaned forward and pulled the phone from her hand.

I already knew who it was, but when his slurred, angry voice hit my ear, rage fell over me in a red curtain. I sat completely still, my grip tightening on the phone, listening to Annabelle's ex-husband berate her.

"You fucking bitch. What the fuck? You told Winters I was trying to get an invite to the wedding? Fucking idiot. You were always a fucking idiot. You don't get anything about business. Now you pissed them off, and I lost an account over it. Goddamn fucking whore. You always ruined everything. I fucking got rid of you and you're still fucking ruining everything."

I stopped listening. Through my haze of fury, I looked over to see Annabelle, pale and shaking, watching me, her eyes wide. I realized she knew exactly how angry I was.

She wasn't afraid of Tommy and his drunken rant.

She was afraid of me.

Slowly and clearly, I said into the phone, "This isn't Annabelle, this is Chase. Don't ever fucking call her again. Don't call her and don't come near her. If I find out you have, you will regret it. Do you understand?"

"You can't tell me what to do, you fucking—"

"Just tell me you understand," I said, my voice even. Only a drunken idiot could miss my furious composure, but Tommy *was* a drunken idiot, and he missed it completely.

I ended the call without another word, navigated to his entry in her contact list, and blocked the number. Taking a long, deep breath through my nose, I let it out before I spoke quietly. Gently.

"I blocked his number. If he calls the café, I want you to hang up, okay?"

Annabelle nodded, some of the tension easing out of her tight muscles.

"If he comes by, lock yourself in your office and call the police."

"I can't call the police. The café, my customers—"

"Annabelle, this guy is not stable. So far all he's done is yell at you, right? He hasn't laid a hand on you? He hasn't hit you or hurt you physically?"

Annabelle shook her head, teeth biting into her lower lip until it turned white.

"You're sure?" I asked again. I didn't think she was lying to me, but I didn't want to be wrong about this. I had to know.

She shook her head again.

"Okay. But he doesn't get to talk to you like this. Ever. If you don't want to call the police, call me, or call one of the Sinclairs. If they can't come themselves, they'll send one of the guys."

"I can't—"

"You can. You absolutely can. Any one of those guys would move heaven and earth to help you, Annabelle. They don't talk about you behind your back, but I know from things they've said that they would have loved to go after Tommy when you were married.

"They'd jump at the chance to escort him from the café or help you with a restraining order. Promise me if he shows up here and I'm not around you'll call them if you won't call the police."

Another nod, but her teeth eased off her lip and her shoulders relaxed.

"I'm going to stay here tonight," I said, and at the flare of her eyes, I went on, "On the couch. I'll stay on the couch. I don't want you here alone."

"You don't have to sleep down here," Annabelle said, but the uncertainty in her voice, the wariness in her eyes, told me that I absolutely did have to sleep down here.

I slid across the couch until I was beside her and pulled her into my arms, resting my cheek against the top of her head and letting the familiar sugar cookie scent of her drive away most of my anger.

"I do, Annabelle. I want to spend the night with you, you have no idea how much. But not like this. Not when you're scared and off-balance. Go up to bed, and I'll be down here. You'll sleep better if you know you're not alone."

"Okay," she whispered. Leaning in, she brushed a kiss across my lips and it took everything I had not to pull her into my lap and pick up where we'd left off before the asshole had called.

"Thank you. You're a good man, Chase Westbrook. You're a really good man, and I'm sorry I'm such a mess."

My muscles tense with the effort of holding back, of giving her space and security when I wanted to wrap my arms around her and claim her as my own, I pressed my lips to the tip of her nose and said, "You're not a mess. You're human. Set the alarm and go up to bed, okay? I'll be down here all night."

She did as I said, taking the two empty beer bottles with her. They clanked as she tossed them in the recycling bin. The alarm beeped, set for the night, and she jogged up the stairs, her feet hitting the steps in rhythmic thuds.

The creak of the floor joists when she reached her futon assured me that she was going to bed. She needed her sleep. I knew she'd be downstairs at four to start her baking, and I'd have no problem sleeping through it. Maybe she'd send me on my way with a cookie.

I texted Vivi to tell her I wouldn't be home, knowing

she'd read all sorts of things into my message that weren't true. Yet.

Then I kicked off my shoes and stretched out on the couch, lulling myself to sleep with fantasies of all the ways I was going to beat the hell out of Tommy Mosler.

TOMMY MOSLER LIVED IN A TWO-STORY, TRADITIONAL colonial on the outskirts of Buckhead. Annabelle had said he'd married the woman he'd cheated with, but there was no sign of her car in the garage when I slipped in behind his sedan.

Like most people with their heads that far up their own asses, Tommy Mosler had no situational awareness. He had no clue I was behind him until I hooked my arm around his neck and dragged him off his feet, cutting off his oxygen and scaring the shit out of him.

He struggled for a minute. I let him, enjoying his fear. His panic. He deserved a lot more than that for everything he'd put Annabelle through.

When I got bored, I hissed in his ear, "Calm the fuck down. I just want to talk."

A lie, but he didn't need to know that yet.

He went still, his heart thudding in his chest, pulse beating frantically against my skin.

My voice so low it was almost silent, I said, "I'm here to deliver a message. Stay away from Annabelle. Don't talk to her. Don't come to see her. Don't fucking think about her. You are a memory to her. Get it?"

No response.

"Nod if you get it," I growled.

A quick jerk of his head. Thinking to take me by

surprise, he twisted his shoulders, trying to yank his way free.

Tommy Mosler hadn't grown up as the odd man out, hadn't grown up being picked on and beat up by the bigger kids. Tommy Mosler never had to learn to fight.

And Tommy Mosler was way outclassed with me.

I threw a punch into the side of his head, not hard enough to cause permanent damage, but hard enough to hurt like a son of a bitch. Normally, I didn't enjoy fighting.

I'd done it when I was younger to save my own ass, but I'd never gone looking for a fight. This was different. All I had to do was think about Annabelle, pale and shaking, her teeth cutting into her lower lip, still so afraid of this man, still so damaged by him that she couldn't even call the police to protect herself.

Not my Annabelle of the bright smile and boundless energy. My Annabelle was loyal and loving and sweet. This asshole didn't get another second of her life. If she couldn't deal with him, I would.

Dazed from the punch to his head, Tommy's knees turned to water and he folded, letting me take his weight. He was tall but skinny, and he didn't weigh much.

I held him easily and said in that same low, menacing voice, "You going to leave her alone?"

He nodded frantically.

I thought for a second. Nope, Tommy was a weasel, and weasels lied. A simple warning wasn't going to be enough. I'd thought this through. He might end up suspecting I'd assaulted him in his garage, but he wouldn't have proof.

The security camera only caught the front of the house. I'd scoped that out earlier in the day. I'd shoved a balaclava and a pair of gloves in my pocket before I left the house and slipped them on as I'd snuck in behind Tommy's car.

Not only couldn't he see my face, I wouldn't shed any hairs inside his garage. The only thing I'd touched was Tommy, and by the time I was done with him, no one would be able to pull a scrap of evidence off his skin.

Done with this, I tossed him away for me, hooking my foot around his ankle. He lost his balance and pitched forward, hitting the floor of the garage face first.

I was on him before he could get his bearings, swinging my fists into every part of him I could reach. I'd learned in the schoolyard exactly where to throw a punch to cause pain but no damage.

I wasn't going to kill him. Wasn't going to break his nose or his cheekbone or bruise his kidneys. But a dick-weasel like this didn't need to be permanently damaged.

He only needed to feel pain and fear more of it.

That I could do.

I hit him until blood streamed from his nose and several cuts on his face, until he curled on his side in a ball and wept, bubbles of bloody snot running down his cheek.

He begged, "Please, please. I won't bother her. I swear. I'll never see her again. Please, stop."

Satisfied, I stood and walked to the back of the garage where Tommy conveniently had a shop sink. As I washed the blood from my gloved hands I said, "You'll be fine. But remember this. Remember every second. Because if you come anywhere near her, I will find you again. And this? This will be a fond memory compared to what I'll do to you. Got it?"

"Got it. I've got it, I swear," Tommy blubbered.

I checked my shirt and jeans, but the fabric was dark enough to hide any stray drops of blood, Tommy had been thoughtful enough to keep most of those on his own clothes.

I let myself out the side door to the yard, flipping the lock on the handle to secure it behind me.

When I was standing on the lawn, still hidden by the shadows of the house, I pulled the balaclava off my head and shoved it in my back pocket along with the gloves. A moment later I was cutting across his backyard and through an empty lot to the side street where I'd left my car.

A minute after that I was gone, leaving Tommy Mosler with fuel for his nightmares and a clear understanding that he would never, ever, bother Annabelle again.

CHAPTER TWENTY-FIVE
ANNABELLE

I stared down at my phone, debating. It was eight-fifteen, and no Chase.

It wasn't like he worked for me. He didn't have any obligation to be here.

Really, it was a miracle he kept showing up. Any other man would have lost interest in me by now. Not Chase.

Sometimes my head was a brick wall, but even I was finally getting it. Chase was different. I could trust him. He was loyal. Dependable.

He was good. Everything about him was good.

Okay, he lost his temper one time. One time. Seeing him handle Tommy on the phone, watching him shut down his anger and get a handle on his emotions, I knew I'd been wrong.

Everybody had their bad moments. I'd just caught Chase in one of his.

Making a decision, I swiped open my phone and hit his name on the call list before I could think better of it. I almost thought it was going to voicemail when he picked up, a little out of breath.

"Hey, Annabelle, what's up?"

"Uh, nothing, really. I wanted to, um, check in. I—"

Could I possibly be any more lame? I didn't think so.

Why couldn't I just ask if he was coming by? Say I missed him, that the end of the day didn't feel right without him here.

I didn't need him to help, I just wanted to have him around. I'd baked brownies for him. Dark chocolate with a raspberry glaze.

All of those thoughts swirled in my head and jammed before they reached my mouth.

Chase's breath huffed through the phone. "Oh, shit. I didn't realize it was so late. Look, I can't come by tonight—"

"It's okay. It's okay. You don't have to come by. I can close the place on my own, you know."

He laughed, and the slam of a car door sounded through the phone.

"Yeah, I know, but I like helping. I've got something on tonight, but I was going to call you. Listen, I have some crazy news."

I sank into the armchair Chase always favored and propped my feet up on the coffee table, my day brightening at the sound of his voice. I'd rather have him here, but if I couldn't have that, talking to him was a close second.

"Crazy news? Crazy good news or crazy bad news?"

"Crazy good news," Chase said and I could practically see the smile on his face, the spark in those vibrant blue eyes. "Get this, Mrs. W and Abel are back."

"Where were they?" My mind spun through all the possibilities. A Safari. Scuba diving. Camping... No, not camping. Maybe Abel, but not Mrs. W.

Chase interrupted my meandering thoughts.

"They went to Disney and got married," he said, his voice filled with glee.

"No! Seriously?"

"Seriously. They're both tan and I've never seen either of them look so happy. I thought Abel's face would crack if he smiled this much, and Mrs. W has a rock on her hand."

"Like an Abigail-sized rock?" I asked. The ring Jacob had given Abigail was borderline obscene. She had the elegance to carry it off, but still, it was huge.

"Okay, not Abigail big, but big. The thing sparkles. She can't stop looking at it. We're all taking the day off tomorrow to help him move his things into her cottage, so they can have more privacy."

My heart swelled, and tears pricked the corners of my eyes. We'd all been wondering if anything would come of their flirtation. Wondering and hoping.

"That's so sweet," I said.

Chase went on, "We're having a party for them. Abigail has it set up, catered so Abel and Mrs. W don't have to do anything, but just family." He paused, and when he spoke again his words were uncertain. Hesitant. "Is there any way you think you could get the night off? Not tomorrow but the next night. Could you bribe one of the new hires to close for you?"

He asked as if he knew I'd say no. And if it were anyone else other than Chase, I might have.

The café came first. Not just because I loved it. It came first because it was my livelihood, and after my divorce, I'd come too close to losing it. Losing everything.

But this was Chase. This was Chase asking me to go with him to a family dinner, to celebrate the marriage of two people I'd known and loved for years. I didn't have to think for long.

"I'll work it out. Do you want to pick me up? Or should I meet you there?"

Relief heavy in his voice, Chase said, "I'll pick you up."

"I'll make it work," I said again. And I would. If I had to close the café early, I'd do it.

If I'd learned anything in the last few weeks, it's that the café couldn't be my whole life. I didn't want to be alone.

I didn't want to hide behind my walls with nothing but this place for company. And I'd learned that maybe, possibly, definitely, there was something—or someone—I loved more than my café.

It turned out I didn't have to close the café early. Bruce and Marie, my new hires, were more than happy to take the overtime I offered. I agreed to let them leave a little early off the dayshift, and they promised to be back by six to take over and close.

I was a little nervous at the idea of giving them a key when I hadn't known them that long, but at the end of the day, the café was just a place. It was insured.

The wedding dinner was about people. People I loved, and I wanted to be with them when they celebrated. That was more important than things, than a place. More important than my business. This was life and family.

Just in case, I would run the deposit to the bank on my lunch break. I wasn't throwing all caution to the wind.

The night before the wedding dinner, Chase showed up at seven, laptop in his scuffed backpack, and took up his usual position in the armchair in the corner. It was crazy, but I'd taken to sneaking over and placing a little *reserved* sign on the seat if it was vacant anytime after five.

Maybe it was bad business, but I didn't care. That was

Chase's seat. He liked to lounge, propping his laptop on his bag, a cup of coffee and a snack at his elbow.

If that's how Chase wanted to work, I was going to make it happen.

Seeing him there, absorbed in whatever was on his screen, absently sipping the Americano I'd put at his elbow, I realized how very much I'd missed him the night before.

I turned my attention back to business and didn't manage more than a wave hello until after I'd locked the door. I took a break, sitting on the couch propping my feet up on the coffee table and looking over at him.

"Project going well?"

He jerked, startled at the sound of my voice. I grinned. I loved the way he threw himself so completely into his work, shutting out everything as his clever brain worked furiously.

Sometimes he sat completely still, staring at the screen, and sometimes his fingers flew over the keyboard until they were a blur.

Knowing he was about to ask I said, "It's eight-ten. Did you eat? Other than that brownie?"

"Humph," he grunted.

"That's not an answer," I said. "You should take better care of yourself."

He flashed me a brilliant grin, his blue eyes bright. "Why bother when you do it for me?"

"Mmm," I said noncommittally. I liked taking care of Chase, mostly because, despite his words, he didn't expect me to.

I leaned closer and caught sight of his hands. His knuckles were bruised, the flesh torn and ragged. I looked from them to his face and back, reaching out to touch.

He snatched his hand and slid it beside his leg, out of sight.

"It's nothing," he said.

I narrowed my eyes in suspicion. That was not *nothing*. I may not have had brothers of my own, but I'd grown up around the Winters and Sinclair boys. I knew what knuckles looked like after a good fistfight.

Jeez, Gage and Aiden alone had had more of those than I could count, especially when they were young teenagers. Sometimes I thought the two of them only communicated with their fists.

It had mystified me how two boys who were so close could be so comfortable beating the hell out of each other. It was a mystery for the ages, and not one I'd figure out in my lifetime.

"Who did you fight with?" I demanded. "Was it one of the Winters? I thought they grew out of that."

Chase shook his head with a grin. "And if I said it was? You going to go over there and yell at them for me?"

"Maybe. It depends. Did you start it?"

Chase laughed, a loose, happy sound. "It wasn't one of the Winters," he said with a grin. "And it's nothing for you to worry about. It's not going to happen again. I was just taking care of a problem."

My suspicions grew. What kind of problem did Chase have that he'd solved it with his fists?

He needed his hands. He couldn't work on his projects if he hurt his hands.

"Who was it? What did you do? I don't want you to get hurt."

"I promise, Annabelle, I won't get hurt. I didn't get hurt. And the person who did get hurt deserved it. This is nothing you have to worry about."

A light flicked on in my head and, for a second, I wondered.

I wondered, but I wasn't going to ask. Before he spoke, I already knew the answer.

Chase leaned forward in the armchair, reaching out with one bruised hand to trace his finger along my cheekbone.

"Trust me. Will you? Will you trust me?"

My heart spoke before my head could get in the way. "I trust you."

The smile that bloomed on his face was so sweet my heart ached. Uncomfortable with the surge of emotion, I stood. "Do you want something to eat before I start cleaning up?"

"I wouldn't turn down a sandwich,"

"Good, because I got some tapenade and I thought I'd make you a Muffuletta."

He'd mentioned how much he liked the Creole sandwich, a delicious meld of Italian charcuterie and spicy olive salad native to New Orleans. When I'd seen the gourmet tapenade on the shelf, I'd tossed it in the cart, already imagining the satisfied look in his eyes as he took his first bite.

I fed Chase, and he helped me close down the café. As I walked him to the back door, I thought about inviting him upstairs, and for the first time in ages, I was embarrassed by my tiny studio.

My bed was a double, barely big enough for two, and it was jammed against the wall.

The whole place was a mess. I hadn't minded much before. I thought about asking him up anyway. Chase wouldn't care. He'd seen the tiny room already and hadn't run screaming.

"Do you—"

He stopped my words with a finger to my lips. A protest rumbled from my throat, somewhere between annoyed and frustrated. With another of those, slow, sweet smiles, Chase melted away my irritation.

His finger slid from my lips and his mouth took its place, feathering across mine with a touch so light I was straining forward for more, reaching up to sink my fingers into his thick hair and haul him closer.

If he wouldn't let me invite him upstairs with words, I'd let him know I wanted him in my bed the only other way I could. I thought he was getting the message.

Chase groaned into my mouth, backing me into the wall, his hands closing around my hips, pulling me closer until the length of his cock pressed exactly where I wanted it.

Where we both wanted it. If only I were wearing a skirt instead of shorts. Dropping my hands to his back, I held on, absorbing the heat of his skin, the flex of his muscles as he moved against me.

I was panting by the time he raised his head, my fingers curled into his T-shirt, gripping the fabric so tightly I thought it might tear.

"I'll be here at six-thirty tomorrow," he promised

"Okay," I whispered, my head reeling. "I can't wait."

CHAPTER TWENTY-SIX
ANNABELLE

I raced upstairs the second Bruce and Marie showed up, just before six. I'd washed my hair early that morning and left it twisted in a bun, knowing I wouldn't have time to deal with it before Chase picked me up.

Jumping in the shower, I washed off the day and slathered on lotion before I took down my bun and hit my still damp hair with a blast from the dryer, pulling the brush through it in quick jerks, feeling the clock tick as every second passed.

This was our first real date. Kind of. The wedding had not been a date. We might have ended up in bed, but we'd gone as friends. I wasn't sorry it had happened, but it hadn't been the plan.

Tonight, Chase was picking me up at my door and he'd invited me in advance. It was a family dinner, true. Not exactly first date territory. And they were his family, not mine, even though I'd known them longer than he had.

All of that aside, in my heart, this was a date, and I had

no intention of meeting Chase at the door with sweaty armpits and limp hair that smelled like coffee grounds. He'd seen me like that enough.

I slapped on some makeup, yanked my dress over my body—still sticky with lotion—and fastened my earrings just in time to hear his voice at the bottom of the stairs calling out my name.

"Just a second."

Shoes. I had shoes here somewhere. I'd even picked them out in advance and set them aside. Ugh, so what were they doing under my bed?

Never mind.

I snagged the pair of high heeled, open-toed sandals I'd bought on a whim and barely worn.

Some women could wear heels all day and look like they were born doing it. I was not that woman. I wore sneakers, and my feet were still killing me by the time I closed up at night. Doing that in heels? No flipping way.

I always marveled at Violet's shoes when she stopped in the café. She strode in on those skyscraper heels and I would have bet she could run a marathon in them if she needed to. That took serious skill.

I clattered down the stairs, spilling through the doorway and almost bumping into Chase before I froze.

I was used to him in jeans and a T-shirt. I loved the way he looked in jeans and a T-shirt. The way his shirts weren't too tight but still hugged his shoulders. How his faded jeans let me ogle every inch of his spectacular ass.

I'd seen him in a suit once, for the wedding, and he'd been so crazy hot he'd made my mouth go dry. Tonight, he wore jeans with a blue button-down that almost exactly matched his eyes.

My mouth watered, and I imagined slipping those

buttons open, one by one, baring his chest so I could trace the lines of his circuit board tattoo with my tongue. I remembered that tattoo.

I remembered every inch of him in vivid detail.

I was so wrapped up in staring at Chase, I didn't notice the look on his face until I reached for his hand and he didn't move.

His eyes wide, he scanned me from head to toe and back again. At the heat in his eyes, I flushed.

"Do you like it? I asked, gesturing down at my dress. It wasn't much; a simple sundress with spaghetti straps, a sweetheart neckline and a full skirt. Simply cut, the style was classic and reminiscent of a forties silhouette.

I didn't have many curves, but the sundress made the most of my narrow waist and small breasts.

Chase reached up to tuck my hair behind my ear. "You look beautiful. Really, really beautiful."

"Thanks," I said, angling my face up to his.

To my disappointment, he didn't kiss me, just took my hand and led me through the back door to his parked car.

He held my hand all the way to Winters House, his thumb rubbing mine absently as he drove.

The whole family was already there, gathered in the formal living room. A small bar had been set up in the entry hall. A uniformed waiter circulated, silver tray in hand.

Waiting for Chase to get us drinks, I hovered at the door to the room, taking in the scene.

Now that they'd all paired off, the assembled Winters family was quite a crowd. The youngest male Winters, Holden and Tate, were there, Holden with his fiancée Jo, and Tate with his wife Emily.

They were both a few years younger than me, and I would have bet they weren't going to settle down until they were at least Aiden's age. They'd spent their twenties working their way through all the willing young things in Atlanta.

All of the Winters were adept at fending off fortune hunters, but Holden and Tate had made an art out of helping themselves to what they wanted and skating away with nary an engagement ring in sight.

I'd never imagined either of them falling in love, to be honest. They were too interested in their company, too focused on working hard and playing harder.

And if they fell, I never would have picked Jo or Emily. Too much substance. Way too much between the ears. I always figured they'd go for empty-headed beauty queens or a nice matching pair of debutantes.

I'd underestimated them. Jo and Emily both had masters degrees in computer science. After much argument and debate, Tate had finally talked Emily into taking a position at Winters Gaming Corp., the company he and Holden ran together.

Holden's fiancée, Josephine, worked on some kind of technology using Bluetooth to help the blind. Honestly, I didn't really understand it.

They'd both met their girls and fallen head over heels in a matter of days, going from confirmed bachelors to settled men in a heartbeat, and they couldn't have been happier about it.

Charlie, the baby of the family, was another one I hadn't seen coming. She stood across the room, laughing, her ocean blue eyes sparkling as she looked up at her husband and sipped a glass of champagne. He held a whiskey and said something that drew a mock scowl from Aiden and another laugh from Charlie.

Only a year ago she'd been utterly miserable and

pretending to be anything but. We'd all known she'd hated her job at Winters, Inc., but she'd refused to leave Aiden as the only Winters at the company.

That was Charlie. Loyalty to family above all else.

She had been so loyal—and so miserable—Aiden had fired her to force her to change. She'd moved into the dump of the house she'd bought in the Highlands, planning to renovate it at some point. When she thought she was going to do that while she worked eighty hour weeks no one knew, especially Charlie.

But suddenly she had nothing but time, and wouldn't you know, she also had a very hot neighbor. Lucas Jackson had fixed up the house next door to Charlie's. They'd bonded over a very expensive bottle of whiskey she'd stolen from Aiden in revenge for her firing. Bonded, kissed, and...

Well, we know where that ended up. Across the room, a child giggled, the first Winters baby since Charlie had been born more than a quarter-century before. Vance held his daughter on his hip, smiling indulgently at her as she tugged at his long hair and blew enthusiastically messy raspberries into his neck.

I could have told you Vance and Maggie were going to end up together. Both of them would have denied it when she first started working for him. Vance had been a mess, Maggie engaged to a loser almost as bad as Tommy, but I'd seen the way Vance looked at her when she wasn't watching. I'd also noticed her looking back.

No one had expected little Rosalie to drop into their lives and turn everything upside down. I never would have guessed Vance would take to fatherhood the way he had. Watching him cuddle his little girl into his chest, letting her climb him like a monkey, I marveled at the way life could change.

Four years ago, he'd been an alcoholic, drinking his life down the drain, blistered with anger and frustration, running from the past straight to the bottom of a bottle. Now he was happily married to Maggie, head over heels in love with his wife and his daughter.

Sophie, tucked into Gage's side, gazed at little Rosie with wistful longing. Her husband, always tuned into all things Sophie, followed her eyes and smiled at his niece, whispering something in Sophie's ear that brought a flush of pink to her cheeks.

I never thought I see this side of Gage again. He'd disappeared from our lives for so long. Only weeks after Hugh and Olivia Winters had been murdered, Gage joined the Army and left home.

We thought he'd come back after a few years, but he'd stayed in, going further and further off the grid until we didn't even know if he was still in the Army. If he was still alive.

Aiden seemed to age a decade the day the Army told him Gage was missing, presumed dead. When he'd finally made it back, he hadn't been the Gage we'd known.

But Sophie, Great-Aunt Amelia's nurse and a source of endless patience, of boundless kindness, had eased what was broken inside him. In return, he loved her with a fierce protectiveness.

Even now, safe among family, he stood beside her, his arm around her waist, tucking her small frame into his much bigger one. He'd almost lost her once, and he wasn't taking any chances.

Chase handed me my beer and took my hand, drawing me further into the room. Lise, my Lise, my best friend since I was a little girl, spotted me. With a wide grin, she practically skipped across the room to pull me into a hug. Riley trailed behind her.

"You came," she said, squeezing me tight.

"I told you I was coming," I said.

"I know you did, but you left the café early. You never leave the café early."

"Well," I shrugged a shoulder a little embarrassed, "I'm turning over a new leaf. I'm experimenting with having a life."

"Yeah?" Lise asked, her eyes popping from me to Chase holding my hand. "How's that working out for you?"

I looked at Chase, feeling a goofy smile stretch across my face at the warmth in his blue eyes.

"So far, I think it's working out pretty well."

Chase started to say something but was interrupted by the sound of clapping. We all turned to see Mrs. W and Abel walking into the room, side-by-side, Abel with a smug, happy smile and Mrs. W her usual restrained self with an added glow of joy.

Aiden led the clapping, but we all joined in a second later, Charlie throwing in an exuberant, "WooHoo!"

Mrs. W lost her composure and blotted a tear from the corner of her eye. She was rescued from the moment when Charlie left Lucas' side to run up and squeeze Mrs. W in a tight hug. Mrs. W cupped the back of her head, gently stroking her tousled auburn curls, and whispered something in her ear that had Charlie's shoulders hitching in a half laugh, half sob.

Though she made a point to say she thought it was entirely inappropriate for the housekeeper and cook to have a catered party in their honor, we all knew Mrs. W was touched. Since their parents had died, she was the closest thing they had to a mother, and none of them would let her marriage pass without celebration.

The night passed too quickly. The food was almost as good as Abel's, and the champagne flowed freely as various Winters got up to tell their stories of growing up with Mrs. W.

Our dessert was individual raspberry shortbread trifles —shortbread because it was Mrs. W's favorite, and Abel made it for her for years. Raspberries because they were his favorite fruit. I happened to know he'd made the desserts himself earlier in the day, and I was going to have to badger him for the recipe.

I sipped my coffee, sorry the evening was already at an end, when Charlie dropped into the chair beside me that Vance had vacated a few minutes before, leaving to check in on Rosalie, sleeping in an empty bedroom.

"Are you ready to move in?" she asked, leaning across me to catch Chase's attention.

"Can I?" Chase's eyes brightened at the thought. He'd adjusted to living in Winters House, maybe even liked it after a few weeks, but I knew he was ready to have his own space again.

"All set," Charlie answered with a wide grin. "Finally. The cleaning crew went through this afternoon and I double checked all the appliances, lights, everything."

"That's the best news I've heard in weeks," Chase said. "Thanks. I know I was a pain in the ass about the delay, but the place looks amazing. Exactly what I wanted."

"You weren't a pain in the ass."

From across the table, Lucas cut in with, "You should have heard her when the lumber yard called about that delivery. Sailors would have blushed."

"I wasn't that bad," Charlie insisted.

All Lucas said was, "Princess."

Charlie's cheeks turned pink and she shrugged a shoulder. "Maybe it was almost that bad. But they deserved it. Sending my oak to the wrong customer. Ridiculous."

A hand came down on Chase's shoulder and I noticed Vance standing behind him, a sleepy Rosie tucked into his arms.

"You good to move in?" Chase nodded. "Need some help? I can call my guy who moves my bigger pieces. Between the two of us, him and his partner and their truck, we can get your stuff over there by lunch."

"That would be great," Chase agreed, "Thanks."

Vance gave him a chin lift. "One sec." He passed Rosie to Maggie and pulled his phone from his pocket. After a conversation so short I could only conclude it was in code, he said, "Good to go. They'll be here at seven thirty in the morning."

Chase said again, "Thanks, man."

Vance only smiled and went to reclaim his daughter. He and Maggie left, Vance saying over his shoulder, "See you tomorrow."

Chase stood, something in him loose, unbound, as if a hidden spring inside him had uncoiled, setting him free. He reached for me, taking my hand and pulling me to my feet.

"Ready?"

"I guess," I answered, not wanting the night to end. I yawned, leaning into Chase and admitted to myself that my four AM wake-up call didn't leave much room for nightlife.

We said our goodbyes and Chase helped me into his car, leaning over to click my seatbelt into place. I batted his hands away, muttering, "I can do it."

"You're about to pass out. I want to make sure you're in the car before we drive away."

"I'm not that tired," I said and then proved myself wrong when my jaw cracked open in a wide, almost painful yawn.

I was exactly that tired. I gave a fleeting thought to the café, wondering if Bruce and Marie had remembered to wipe the inside of the pastry case or put the cups back on the rack so they'd be dry by morning.

Then, for the first time since I'd opened the place, I gave a mental shrug and decided it didn't matter. Whatever was wrong, I'd fix it later. I'd had a brilliant night with my oldest friends and Chase by my side. That was all I cared about.

The next thing I knew, Chase was shaking me awake.

"I fell asleep?" I asked, blinking against the sudden light when Chase opened the car door.

"You were out cold before we cleared the driveway," he said with amusement.

I fumbled in my purse for the keys to the back door, and Chase followed me inside. I was half-asleep, but not so tired I didn't take a quick trip through, checking to make sure everything was as it should be.

To my shock and pleasure, it was. Oh, there were a few things here and there that weren't done the way I would have, but my new hires had done well enough. Better than I'd expected. Maybe if I found one more like them, I could ease off a bit.

Chase closed his hand over my elbow and led me back to the stairs to my studio. Dipping his head, he brushed his mouth across mine.

"Lock the door behind me and go to bed, sleeping beauty."

"Do you want—"

With a low groan in the back of his throat, Chase shook his head. "I do. I really do. But not tonight. Come to my house for dinner tomorrow. A late dinner, after closing."

"Okay," I said, simply. "I'll cook." My sleepy brain was already putting together the menu, heavy on dessert. And chocolate.

"I'll be here to help you finish up," he said, "and we'll walk over together."

"Okay," I said again. One more brush of his mouth over mine and he was gone, saying over his shoulder, "Lock the door and set the alarm, Annabelle."

I did, smiling to myself the whole time. I fell asleep with a smile still on my face, already dreaming of seeing Chase the next day.

CHAPTER TWENTY-SEVEN

ANNABELLE

Chase was early. Instead of working through close, he packed up his things at seven-thirty and headed to the kitchen to start the dishes. I wasn't the only one eager for our date. Fortunately, I'd already cooked dinner and carefully packed it away, out of sight of prying eyes.

I was a little nervous. I'd made Chase sandwich after sandwich, and he loved my baking, but I'd never really cooked for him.

I didn't cook as much as I liked to. It was just me, and I spent so much time in the kitchen baking it didn't seem worth the bother to put a real meal together. I usually grabbed a sandwich on the run, a lot like Chase.

But this was different. This was special.

Thanks to Chase getting a jump on the cleanup and Bruce working a double shift to help close, we were done a full forty-five minutes earlier than usual.

Bruce headed out with a wink and a silent salute. He

didn't talk much, but he was great on the espresso machine and happy to pick up extra shifts here and there.

"Ready to go? I thought we'd walk," Chase said, shifting his weight from one foot to the other.

Was it possible Chase was nervous, too? Ridiculous, considering everything. This wasn't a first date, and we knew each other. That didn't settle the flutter in my stomach.

"One second. Let me grab dinner from the kitchen."

I pulled out my enameled, cast-iron dutch oven with both hands, carefully balancing the heavy weight, the warmth of the metal seeping through the potholders. I set it on two stacked towels, wrapping it securely to hold in the heat and protect our hands.

Between the meal in the dutch oven and dessert, it would take both of us to get dinner to Chase's house. I carried the towel wrapped package out of the kitchen and said in apology, "This is pretty heavy. Maybe we should drive."

Chase took the pot from my arms and moved to unwrap the first layer of towels. I slapped his hand away.

"Nope, no peeking. Let me go get the rest."

"The rest? What did you make?"

The heat of a flush warmed my cheeks. I'd gone a little overboard. A lot overboard. I kept thinking of things Chase would like, and before I knew it the menu had expanded. A lot.

"One second," I said, and dashed back into the kitchen, opening the commercial refrigerator and sorting through café supplies for the three stacked containers I'd placed there earlier in the day.

With Bruce and Marie working that morning I'd been able to spend our slow periods in the kitchen whipping up

246

treats Chase had never seen before. They were a little fussy, and I'd been so exhausted lately I hadn't had it in me to make them on the scale necessary for the café.

For Chase, I found the energy. I couldn't wait to see which one he liked best. I carried the desserts back out and grinned when Chase's eyes went wide.

"You made a feast," he said.

"It's your first dinner in your new house," I said. "That deserves a feast."

We left through the back door and strolled down the block, crossing Highland Avenue and walking down streets overhung by trees and lit by streetlights.

It didn't take long to get to Chase's house, a mere five blocks from the café. I should have seen it by now. I'd been trying to push Chase away, to keep him at a distance.

Going to see his house, so close to the café, would only have reminded me of everything I wanted that I thought I couldn't have.

I hadn't wanted to face reality. Hadn't wanted to imagine myself there, in his home.

Now, my heart beat faster in anticipation.

We turned onto a new street, and I didn't have to wonder which house belonged to Chase. A dumpster sat on the edge of the front yard and the grass was torn up in spots where construction equipment had parked. There wasn't much landscaping to speak of, except for the old-growth trees surrounding the small lot, but the house—the house was a gem.

I wasn't sure what architectural style it was. To me, with its exposed wood beams and shingles, clear paned windows and peaked gables, it looked like a fairytale cottage.

Chase led me to the front door and unlocked it, lifting

one shoulder in a sort of shrug as he asked, "What do you think?"

"It's perfect," I said, stepping through the doorway into the foyer, my eyes drinking in each detail, the house wrapping itself around me, whispering in my ear. *Home.*

But it wasn't the house, it was Chase. He was stamped over every inch of the place. More exposed wood beams, warm and inviting, High ceilings, wide hallways and wood paneling in a deep, rich, smooth-grained oak.

"Absolutely perfect," I repeated in an awed whisper.

The two front rooms—I was guessing formal living room and dining room—didn't have any furniture.

Chase saw my curious glance and said, "We didn't have much of a dining room table in the condo. I got rid of it. Ditto for living room furniture. I'll figure it out later."

"Mmm," I said, my eyes wide as we passed the stairs to the second level and entered the heart of the house.

I stopped and stared. The back of the house was one big room divided into two sections, the far side a wall of windows that looked out onto the tiny yard and the dollhouse of a garage at the back of the property.

On my right was a family room with floor to ceiling stone fireplace, flanked by overstuffed couches angled to catch both the fireplace and the huge flat screen TV opposite the windows.

The left side was taken up by a chef's kitchen and breakfast nook, the space all gleaming stainless steel, gold and brown granite, and warm wood cabinets.

For a guy who said he rarely cooked, Chase had designed a heck of a kitchen. Double ovens with warming drawer, oversized subzero refrigerator, eight burner gas range. Dual wine refrigerators in the island, along with a prep sink and extra dishwasher.

The only thing I could say was, "Wow."

This was... This was a lot more than I expected. In a vague sort of way, I knew Chase did well. He never seemed to be worried about money and his condo had sold so fast I knew he'd gotten more than he'd asked for.

But, while I wasn't a real estate expert like Charlie and Lucas or Jacob, I knew what property cost in the Virginia Highlands. I owned my building and I'd done a lot of research on commercial and residential values before I'd purchased the café.

I had a good idea what a lot like this would cost, not to mention the expense of a fully renovated house with custom woodwork and that kitchen. Chase had spared no expense on what I'd seen so far, leading me to assume the rest of the house, and the garage across the yard, were the same.

My businesswoman's brain was doing the math and coming up with a number that was a hell of a lot more than I'd ever be able to spend on a house. This was all way out of my league.

I had the sense of the floor tilting, knocking me off balance. I'd always thought of Chase and myself as equals. I'd been way off base.

I'd come this far—I wasn't going to start comparing Chase to Tommy again—but I'd been with a guy who had money before and I couldn't help remembering what he'd wanted. What he'd expected. And how those expectations had destroyed everything.

To distract myself, I set the cases holding our desserts on the kitchen counter. I knew my way around an oven, and I turned his on, enjoying the gleam of metal inside. There was nothing quite like a brand-new oven.

Someday it would be banged up and stained on the

inside if anyone used it on a regular basis, but right now it was pristine and gorgeous. Some women got excited over shoes; for me, it was kitchen appliances. I could respect an oven like this. Forget respect, I could drool over an oven like this.

I set it to warm and took the dutch oven from Chase, unwrapping it from the towels and sliding it inside before I turned around and crossed my arms over my chest.

"What's wrong?" Chase asked, reading my face.

"It's nothing," I said, not wanting to admit I might be having second thoughts. I wasn't going to do this. I'd decided—no second thoughts.

I was going to have courage. Be brave. No backing out now. I owed Chase more than that. I owed myself more.

"It's not nothing," Chase said.

He crossed the room, reaching out to close his hands around my upper arms and tugged me closer, pulling me to him until he could slide his arms around my back.

Holding me, surrounding me with his strength, he said gently, "Is it the house? You don't like it?"

"No," I said so quickly he had to know I was telling the truth. "No, I love the house. The house is beautiful. It's like a dream. This kitchen is magnificent."

"I designed the kitchen for you," Chase said, and everything inside me went still.

With numb lips, I murmured, "What do you mean, you designed the kitchen for me?"

That was crazy. He couldn't have. We hadn't known each other long enough.

Chase, always braver than me, laid it all out. "I kept seeing you here. In my house. Every time I imagined what I wanted, how I'd use each room, you were here. When it came time to pick everything for the kitchen I couldn't stop thinking about you. What you'd need. What you'd want."

"Chase," I whispered, my heart aching with love.

He trailed a finger down my cheek, taking in everything he saw in my eyes. "Does that scare you? Am I freaking you out?"

"No," I said, then stopped. "Maybe a little. In a good way. It feels good to know you were thinking of me. I was thinking of you," I admitted.

"Then if it's not the house, what's wrong?" he asked, threading his fingers through my hair.

"You're really rich, aren't you?" I blurted out, then buried my face in his chest to hide my flaming cheeks.

Why couldn't I have found a better way to say that? I was such a dork.

Chase thought so, too, because he started laughing, his chest rumbling beneath my ear. "Pretty much. Why? Is that a problem?"

"Kind of," I admitted.

Chase took a step back but didn't let go of me, running his hands down my arms to close around my wrists.

"I worked my ass off and earned every penny I have. I won't apologize for that."

"You shouldn't. You shouldn't apologize for it. I'm just—"

I knew what I wanted to say, and I didn't know how to say it without sounding bitter and angry. I wasn't either one. Not really, but I was scared. Wanting to be brave didn't erase my fear. Chase watched my thoughts play out across my face and knew exactly what was going through my head.

"You're afraid that I'll want you to quit your job and stay home. That because I make more money, I won't think what you do is important."

"I love what I do. I love my place. I do well now, but I'm never going to make enough to live like this."

I looked around the beautiful great room and stunning kitchen. The nest egg I'd saved for a new house wouldn't buy a tenth of this one. I'd been hoping for a modest condo not too far away. This was an entirely different universe.

Chase shrugged a shoulder. "It's not about how much the café makes, Annabelle. The value is in how much you love it. The value is in your hard work and your customers. What you bring to the community. You're not the only one who loves that place. I'm there almost every day and I can see it. I would never ask you to walk away from that."

"Are you sure? Because—"

He stopped me with a soft kiss to my lips before he pulled back and said, "I'm not Tommy, Annabelle. Anyway, don't you read the news? Do you know how often tech billionaires go broke? Are you going to kick me to the curb if one day we wake up and I'm not rich?"

"Of course not. That's ridiculous."

"Well, then, there you go."

His simple summation of a problem that wasn't a problem left me dumbfounded.

No, he wasn't Tommy. He was nothing like Tommy.

He was Chase, and he was amazing.

"You haven't had dinner yet," I said, needing to do something for him. Needing to show him how much he meant to me. "Let me unpack everything." A sudden realization struck. "Do you have plates? I didn't bring plates."

"I do," he said, dropping his arms to cross the kitchen to open a cabinet, showing me shelves of bowls, plates and glasses.

In explanation, he said, "Vivi didn't have classes today,

so she helped me unpack the kitchen stuff. It's not great, to be honest. Most of it needs to be replaced, but I haven't gotten around to it. It's good enough for now."

He eyed the sealed containers on the counter and said, "What did you make?"

"Dinner is a Gascon-style beef stew in a chocolate and wine sauce with a loaf of crusty bread I baked this morning. I, um, couldn't decide on dessert, so I made three."

"Three desserts?"

"Three desserts," I confirmed, still feeling a little foolish at my excess.

I peeled the lids off the sealed storage containers to show him the contents, explaining as I went. "A flourless chocolate soufflé with a cinnamon-dusted crust. Then a chocolate ganache tart with sea salt and espresso beans. And this is a heaven and hell cake."

Chase's eyes went comically wide at the sight of the shiny chocolate frosting on the last dessert. Almost whispering, he asked, "What's a heaven and hell cake?"

"I don't make them very often. It's really three desserts in one. Layers of angel food cake and devil's food cake with peanut butter mousse in the middle and chocolate ganache on top."

The heaven and hell cake needed to be refrigerated or the peanut butter mousse would get too soft and the layers would sag. I was sliding it into the pristinely empty refrigerator when Chase said under his breath, "You did this for me. You made everything with chocolate, for me. This was a lot of work. And I know you're busy all day..."

His voice faded, and at the befuddled expression in his eyes, I realized that Chase had no idea how I really felt about him. I'd done such a good job of holding him off, of protecting myself, that I'd never taken the one step he needed. That I needed.

I'd never taken the biggest risk. I was done being a coward, done running from my own heart.

I left the other two desserts where they were on the counter and crossed the room back to Chase. I waited until his eyes left the desserts and met mine.

"I love you. I'm in love with you. I love everything about you, especially your weakness for chocolate. And if it makes you happy, I want to give it to you. Every day. All the time."

"Because you love me," he finished for me, his voice dazed, eyes wandering from me to the feast laid out on the island counter.

"Because I love you. I'm sorry I—"

Chase stopped me with a kiss, pressing his lips to mine before he whispered, "No apologies. We got here how we got here."

"Okay," I mumbled. Sliding my hands under his T-shirt, I pulled him closer and kissed him back, my heart set free now that I'd spoken the words aloud.

I loved him.

I don't know when it started, but it had grown every day until I knew he belonged to me. Chase lifted me, setting me on the counter. I wrapped my legs around his waist, pushing up his T-shirt, ready to strip it off right there.

"Can dinner wait?" he asked, his lips moving against my neck, sending shivers through every inch of me.

My brain flitted to the stew warming in the oven. "It can wait all night."

"Good." Chase lifted me again, and I tightened my legs around his hips, giving a squeal of surprise as he carried me out of the kitchen to the wide staircase.

The second floor passed in a blur, but I noticed the bed.

King-sized with crisp white sheets and a navy comforter. I bounced when he tossed me on the bed.

Before I stopped moving he had my jeans and panties down my legs and over my feet. I stripped off my shirt and bra, eating up every inch of his skin with my eyes as he peeled off his own shirt and shucked off his jeans.

His long body pressed me into the mattress, falling between my open legs, his mouth moving against my neck as he whispered into my skin.

Words of love and lust, nonsensical and thick with emotion. Heavy with desire. He hadn't said those three words back. Not before and not when I'd said them only minutes ago.

I didn't need them. Not from Chase. He wasn't telling with words, he was showing me.

He lavished his love on me with his hands and his lips, dropping kisses across my shoulders, stroking my legs, worshiping me until I was dizzy from his touch, begging by the time he pushed inside, filling me with himself.

I held on, my forehead pressed to his neck, his breath hot and ragged, his voice no more than a low hum in my ears. This was all I needed. Chase's arms around me. Chase inside me. Just Chase. Always.

We didn't eat dinner until close to midnight. Actually, we had the stew for breakfast. Dinner was heaven and hell cake with a dessert of chocolate soufflé. We ate side by side, leaning over the kitchen island, stabbing at the sweets with our forks, feeding each other between kisses.

After, hopped up on sugar and chocolate, we tumbled back into bed and had each other all over again.

I woke in the dark, my internal alarm switching on my brain at four o'clock exactly. I blinked into the dim room, lit only by a streetlight beyond the trees, and sat up, my thoughts tumbling slowly.

I was in Chase's bed.

I had to get up.

Had to get to the café.

Chase groaned beside me and hooked an arm around my waist, pulling me back down. Nuzzling his face into the side of my neck, his voice heavy with sleep, he said, "Five more minutes and we'll get up. Promise."

Most mornings I never hit snooze. I couldn't. If I did, I'd do it again, and again, until I ended up serving packaged cookies and grocery store danishes to my customers. That would not go over well.

But for Chase, just this once, I could do five more minutes.

Five minutes turned into fifteen when he pulled me beneath him and kissed me, little feathery kisses across my chin, my ear, down the side of my neck until I was squirming with ticklish lust.

I hooked my feet around his thighs, pulling him to me, urging him inside. It was slow, easy, the orgasm building so gradually, when it hit it took me by surprise, crashing into my brain like a shot of espresso, waking me up and leaving every nerve tingling.

Chase rolled to his back, taking me with him. His lips brushed my ear.

"I love you, Annabelle. I feel like I've loved you forever."

I propped myself up on my elbows, my palms splayed across his chest, and looked down into his eyes, barely able to see his face in the darkness.

I didn't need to see him to feel the truth in his heart.

"I won't give up on you again," I promised. "I love you

too much to do without you now. You're worth the risk. You always were. It just took me a while to figure it out."

Chase proved he meant what he said by rolling out of bed, taking me with him, and leading me to the shower. I didn't have time to appreciate the bathroom, but I caught sight of a claw-footed tub in front of a window and knew I'd be back for that later.

Clean and wearing my clothes from the day before, I prepared to head out. Chase grabbed the pot of stew from the refrigerator and we brought it with us to the café. I started to prep for baking and he heated the meal.

Chocolate and red wine beef stew wasn't the average breakfast, but it was delicious, especially partnered with a slice of chocolate ganache torte juiced with espresso beans.

After breakfast, Chase passed out on the couch in the café, rousing only when the first customers clattered through the door. He left me with a kiss on the cheek and was there at seven fifty-eight on the dot, ready to help me close.

I was going to hire one more person, I resolved. In a few weeks, once Bruce and Marie were solid. Then Chase could work on his project instead of doing dishes and we could start our nights a little earlier.

For the first time in years, I wanted more time.

Time for a life. A life I could spend with Chase.

When I was done with the café, switching off the lights over the counter, he held out a hand.

"Come home with me?"

I slid my fingers into his. "Always."

EPILOGUE
CHASE

It took me over a month to talk Annabelle into moving in. Her tiny closet of a studio played in my favor, as did my proximity to the café.

My girl was still a little gun shy, but after I pointed out that she slept with me every night anyway and she was wasting valuable storage space on the second level, she folded.

It might have been harder to talk her into it if she hadn't been sleeping on a futon crammed in the back of her storage room.

It took two trips to move her out of the café and into my house. Two loads of her things, both of our cars jammed with boxes and storage containers, her clothes still on their hangers draped over the back seat.

Two short trips, and when we were done, my heart settled. With her clothes in my closet, her dishes in the sink, shoes in a jumble by the back door, my new house became my home.

A few weeks after Annabelle moved in, she hired a third

barista. The girl was quiet, had experience, and she showed up on time. After Grover and Penny, those three qualities made her a winner. She also liked working the second shift.

It was a miracle. Every once in a while, Annabelle and I had a whole evening together.

In truth, we had every evening together. For the first few months, I was still at Winters, Inc., working on my app in my spare time, mostly at the café. With a third barista on staff, Annabelle didn't need help closing, and I got an extra hour and a half of work in.

Every night, she locked the door of the café and we walked home, her hand in mine. It was pretty close to heaven.

We spent almost all of our time together. When I finished up at Winters, Inc. and formally left the company, I moved into my office over the garage behind my house. My schedule was all over the place depending on where I was with my project.

Some nights I walked Annabelle home from the café and fell into bed beside her by ten. Some nights I took her to bed, stripping her naked and making love to her, holding her until she fell asleep in my arms before I slipped out to my office and worked until my alarm went off at four.

On those mornings I'd walk her to the café and pass out on the couch until she nudged me awake a few hours later with a strong coffee and breakfast.

The couch wasn't as comfortable as our bed, but it was worth the change in venue for first shot at whatever treat Annabelle had been concocting in the kitchen while I slept.

I'd managed to talk Aiden and Gage out of trying to acquire my app. They always had their eye on business, but family came first. It wasn't that I didn't trust them. I did. I even liked working with them.

But I had plans for the app spinning in my head, and I needed the freedom to make them happen on my own. Working under the mantle of a multinational corporation was suffocating.

I thought they'd have hard feelings, but by the time I had my algorithm ready for the market and could leave Winters, Inc., we'd fallen into the rhythm of family and the company didn't seem to matter anymore.

We had more important things on our minds. Aiden married Vivi just before Christmas, surprising all of us with an impromptu proposal and wedding in Las Vegas.

I gave Vivi away, and I'd been wrong.

It didn't hurt at all.

The joy in her eyes as we walked down the aisle to Aiden was so pure, so strong, it blew away the last lingering bits of reluctance in my heart.

Aiden Winters would take good care of my sister.

I had no doubt.

Maybe it was easier because Annabelle stood by my side, grinning like a fool, her fingers wrapped around mine, squeezing my hand in excitement as we watched Vivi and Aiden take their vows.

So many things had fallen into place in the last six months. Vivi marrying Aiden, Annabelle moving in with me, me leaving Winters, Inc. and starting my own company. Again.

I loved the rush of a start-up. For now, I was content to work out of my garage office, but I'd be hiring coders any day. I was still debating finding office space and bringing on a local team or hiring remote coders and keeping overhead low.

Either way, my project was gaining steam. I didn't know yet if I had a winner, but I had a good feeling about it.

One day, about three months after Annabelle moved in, I left her wiping down the pastry cases as she closed the café and wandered upstairs to the storage room, now taking up the entire level.

There, behind the ten-pound bag of sugar, I found the box of letters from William Davis to Anna Marlow.

I hadn't touched them since the day I'd shown them to Annabelle, sitting beside her on the futon, torn up with anger and sadness. With regret and resentment.

I won't say my feelings about Anna Winters had completely settled, but I'd grown close to my half-siblings and my new cousins.

Close enough to appreciate that however they'd come into my life, they were a gift.

Close enough to know that they still mourned the loss of their mother.

Maybe even close enough to mourn with them.

Tired of wondering, I pulled the box from behind the bag of sugar and brought it to the kitchen counter, now covered in filing boxes filled with god knows what. Annabelle baked like an angel and ran a hell of a café, but her paperwork was all over the place.

Setting the box on the counter, I lifted the heavy lid and pulled out the first letter.

I don't know what I expected. The ravings of a madman. Rage and desperation. Jealousy and hate.

A confession, or a hint of the tragedy to come.

Weirdly, they were boring. Davis had been arrogant enough to believe he would win Anna back. Deluded enough to think that her love for James Winters would pass.

At first, he talked about himself. He wanted her to call. To write him. To tell James to leave her alone.

By the middle of the box, they were getting a little desperate.

When was she coming back? Why would she see James but not him?

There was only one letter that gave a hint at the madness lurking beneath the surface.

June 3, 1981

My Dearest Anna,

I'm at a loss over your silence. You've chosen him over me. Chosen a future with him over the one we should have had together. Your selfishness will have a cost. When it comes due, who will pay?

Always Yours,

William

THE LETTER SENT A CHILL DOWN MY SPINE. THE DATE was a month before my birth. Could Anna have taken the letter as a threat to me?

It was clear enough to be frightening and vague enough that she could have later convinced herself she'd been paranoid.

I didn't have to wonder how I would have reacted if I'd been her. That letter might have pushed her over the edge to adoption instead of keeping me and raising me herself. The more I learned about William Davis, the more I knew she'd done the right thing.

That letter was William's last for a long time.

Four years.

Four years in which Anna and James were married and

had a son. Was the birth of Gage, James' heir, the trigger that had pushed Davis over the edge into obsession? Seeing Anna with a child, knowing his own was lost to him?

We'd never know.

Not long after Gage was born, the letters started again, this time with a layer of formality.

Distance. A note congratulating them on the twins' birth. A polite thank you for a dinner party. Another note when Tate was born. Holiday cards. Birthday cards.

William Davis never again referenced their college love affair. Never gave the slightest hint he pined for Anna or was murderously jealous of James. No hint that he would ultimately be responsible for both of their deaths.

The last letter in the box, sent a few months before they died, was a Christmas card. Simple and prosaic. An embossed tree on the front, a generic message inside, and a short note.

> *December 15, 1994*
> *Happy Holidays to two of my favorite people.*
> *Love always,*
> *William*

THAT WAS IT.

> *Love always,*
> *William.*

I slid the card back in the box and replaced the letters, a hollow ache in my chest. Was it loss? Pain? Frustration at the futility of it all? At the senselessness of their deaths?

Anna had given me away because she thought it was the

best thing for both of us. She'd probably been right. Finally, I was coming to realize that I could be glad I'd had my life, growing up with Vivi, following my own path, and still regret that I'd lost the chance to know her.

I leaned against the kitchen counter, surrounded by disorganized filing boxes, staring at the letters, thoughts tumbling in my head.

The Winters family, my half-siblings and the cousins I'd found through them, were a part of my history, part of where I came from. A good part. One of the best.

This box...this box was a part I'd rather forget. I didn't know what to do with it, with the words of the father I was grateful I'd never known.

I don't know how long I stood there, chest aching, with burning eyes and damp cheeks, wishing the letters didn't exist.

Wishing that, somehow, we could change the past and leave the present intact.

The sounds of the café filtered up through the floor. The murmur of voices. The occasional clank of metal on metal. A door opened and shut. Feet thumped on the stairs.

Annabelle.

She didn't say a thing. She stood beside me, and took the box from my hands, setting it on the floor out of sight. Her fingers tangled with mine as she leaned in, her head on my shoulder.

The familiar sugar cookie scent of her drifted to my nose, filling the hollow space behind my ribs. Her thumb rubbed the back of my hand, and gradually the pain faded away.

When we were ready to go, I put the box back in the corner behind the bag of sugar. I wasn't giving it back to the Winters. They didn't want it. Neither did I.

I couldn't quite bring myself to destroy it, this only link to the father I didn't want, so I put it out of sight and resolved to forget. Surprisingly, it wasn't that hard. My life was too full of good things—my work, family, Annabelle. The good crowded out the bad.

If I'd learned anything in the past few years, it was this: family is what you make it.

Family is the people who stick by you no matter what. It's not blood. It's not genetics. It's shared history. Loyalty. Love.

Vivi and I had been tossed out by the parents who raised us. We hadn't been good enough for them and they'd walked away. I didn't care.

Vivi did, a little. She held on to a thread of hope, and when our parents realized she was connected to the Winters family, to Aiden Winters specifically, they made an attempt to reestablish a relationship.

I was relieved when Aiden put a stop to it.

He'd met them once, and once was enough. He protected Vivi from their attempts to control her, and when Vivi and Aiden didn't invite them to their wedding, Suzanne and Henry Westbrook said a final goodbye.

Good riddance. It hurt Vivi, and for that I was sorry. It always hurts when that last desperate bit of hope is quashed. But, like me, Vivi had so much to fill the empty space. She had it all.

So did I. My baby sister was happily settled, back in school, married to a guy who almost deserved her. I was neck deep in a brand-new start-up, moved into my house, and head over heels in love with Annabelle.

There was only one thing missing. My ring on Annabelle's finger. I'd told her I would take it slow. I had been. Okay, I rushed her into moving in, but she was sleeping in a glorified closet.

I made a deal with myself. If I could get her living under my roof, I'd give her plenty of time before I pushed any further. And I did.

Six long months.

Six months to show her how much I loved her. How good we were together. Six months to show her the life we'd have. Six months for me to learn that she was more perfect than I'd imagined.

I supported her devotion to the café, and she was right there with me, never chiding me for working late and missing sleep. Not getting annoyed when I got so sucked into my project I forgot to show up for dinner.

She was always there, sliding a plate beside my laptop, making sure I ate. Reminding me when I hadn't had enough sleep. Shoving me out the door for a run or rubbing my shoulders when they knotted from leaning over the keyboard.

Taking care of me the way I took care of her.

I went a little overboard on the ring. Nothing too flashy, but it had to be perfect. It had to be Annabelle. I looked for ages, scouring every jewelry store in Atlanta until I found exactly what I wanted.

Annabelle didn't like big diamonds. She wanted something unique. Something that was just right. I found it in a collection of jewelry from an estate sale. A large, cushion-cut blue topaz surrounded by diamonds that sparked like the fire of the sun against the cool blue of the sea. The second I saw it, I knew it was hers. Now, I just had to get it on her finger.

I'd thought about a dozen scenarios—taking her out to

dinner, sneaking the ring in her dessert, a romantic weekend away. Nothing felt right.

Annabelle was wary of grand gestures after her first marriage, and I didn't want to remind her of Tommy.

I wanted this to be about us.

In the end, simple and direct won the day.

I lay beside her in our bed, watching her sleep, her cinnamon hair a shadow in the silvery moonlight. She was turned toward me, her hand on my arm.

She always slept like that, touching me, her fingers warm on my skin.

Gently, careful not to wake her too early, I lifted her hand and slid the ring on her finger. Moments later, the alarm beeped and her eyes fluttered open, dazed with sleep, confused to see me awake.

Usually, if I was awake at four in the morning it was because I hadn't yet gone to sleep. I never opened my eyes before her if we'd gone to bed together.

She watched me, the haze of sleep drifting away as her fingers tightened around mine and her eyes dropped to her hand.

"Chase?" she whispered.

"Do you like it?" I asked, turning her hand until the ring caught the moonlight, stones flashing.

Her eyes flared wide. "It's beautiful. But, what—?"

"I love you, Annabelle. I love you and I want to spend the rest of my life with you. I can't imagine anything else, but you and me. Together."

Annabelle's eyes met mine, tears pooling on her lashes. "You're sure?"

"I've never been more sure of anything in my life. Will you? Will you marry me?"

My heart hitched as her brows drew together. She looked down at the ring on her finger and back to me.

I'd thought I'd given her enough time. Thought she was ready.

I knew I was. I didn't want Annabelle to be my live-in girlfriend.

I wanted her to be my wife.

Annabelle didn't answer. Not in words.

She lifted her hand, the ring bright in the darkness, and stroked her fingers along my cheek, ending at my chin. Holding my face still, she shifted to her side, rolling into me, pressing her mouth to mine.

Her kiss was slow and sweet.

"Is that a yes?" I asked, my lips brushing hers.

"Yes," she said, taking my mouth in another slow, sweet kiss, her tongue tracing my bottom lip before she kissed me again. And again.

"Yes, Chase. Yes. Always yes. Always you and always yes."

That was all I needed to hear. I closed my arms around her, reveling in her shriek of surprise as I flipped her to her back.

Just this once, she was going to be late to work. I'd help her make up the time later.

We had an engagement to celebrate.

Finally, Annabelle in my arms, the last piece of my life slid into place.

UNRAVELED

THE UNTANGLED SERIES, BOOK ONE

CHAPTER ONE

Summer

The knock at the door startled me so badly I almost dropped my curling iron. I wasn't that late, was I? I wasn't supposed to be downstairs for another...

Oh, crap. I *was* that late.

Unplugging the curling iron and giving my lashes a quick swipe of mascara, I rushed to the door, swung it open, and froze.

It wasn't Julie, here to pick me up for a girls' night out.

No, standing in the door was my very own, personal Achilles' heel.

The devil come to tempt me.

Eve with the Apple.

Okay, bad analogy. Evers Sinclair could be a devil, but he was no Eve.

Evers Sinclair was male temptation incarnate, and I had never been able to resist him.

He smiled at me, lips curved into a grin, seasoned with mischief and filled with promise.

That grin always got me, even when I was resolved to resist him.

Especially when I was resolved to resist him.

He leaned in my doorway, one arm braced against the frame, his ice blue eyes doing a slow perusal from my head to my toes, heating as they took in my deliberately-tumbled blonde curls, little black cocktail dress, and mile-high spike heels.

"Going somewhere?"

His voice was all flirtation, but his eyes said something else. Something I couldn't quite read.

Annoyance?

Irritation?

That couldn't be worry, could it?

Giving an internal shrug, I stepped back to let him in. I'd given up on understanding Evers Sinclair. Evers walked in as if he belonged in my apartment, dropping his over-stuffed briefcase on the chair by the front door before heading into the kitchen to help himself to a beer.

Popping the cap off the bottle, he turned and leaned against the counter, taking a long swig.

"I like the dress," he said, lids heavy over those cool blue eyes, gaze smoldering.

Ignoring the heat in my belly at the look in his eyes, I rolled my own. "It's new," I said.

"You didn't answer my question," he said smoothly, his gaze tracing the V-shaped neckline of my dress and the generous display of cleavage framed by black silk. His eyes peeled the dress off my shoulders, stripped me naked. It had been three weeks since I'd seen him, and I felt every day.

The heat growing in my belly kicked up a notch. I

gritted my teeth and pushed it back. I did not have time for this. My body didn't care. It never did where Evers Sinclair was concerned.

He showed up, smoldered at me, and my body was ready to go.

"Which question?" I shot back, always ready to play the game with Evers, even against my better judgment.

Since the moment we'd met, he'd been getting under my skin. As hard as I tried, I couldn't quite work him back out.

"Are you going somewhere? If it's a bad time I can leave."

I stopped, the quick retort frozen on my tongue. I took another look at Evers, seeing past his distinctive eyes, his broad shoulders and sharp cheekbones, past the beauty to the man beneath.

He was tired, I realized with surprise. More than tired, he looked exhausted. His face drawn, lines bracketing his mouth, purple-gray smudges beneath his eyes.

I had no idea what he'd been doing since the last time he'd shown up at my door, but whatever it was, he looked like he needed nothing more than a good meal and a solid night's sleep.

I bit back the sarcastic retort on the tip of my tongue and told him the truth. "I am. I'm sorry, I didn't know you'd be coming by and—"

"Hot date?"

I wasn't imagining the edge in his voice. I debated how to answer.

It wasn't any of his business if I did have a hot date. We had a thing, yeah. A thing neither of us had ever bothered to define. A thing that was definitely not exclusive.

I didn't know who he was with when he wasn't with me. I could never bring myself to ask. That way lay heartbreak.

Evers Sinclair was a player.

He was not a one-woman man, and he never would be.

I'd known from the start I had a choice. Take what he was willing to give or walk away.

It had never occurred to me that he would care if I saw other people, but the way he'd asked *hot date?* didn't sound nonchalant.

Again, I went with the truth.

"Not tonight. You know my friend Julie?" Evers nodded. I'd mentioned Julie before. She and I used to work together and had known each other since college. "She and Frank broke up."

"That was a long time coming," Evers commented.

He'd never met Julie, but he'd heard me bitch about her boyfriend, Frank, more than once. Frank was an asshole who didn't deserve my sweet, funny friend, and she'd finally figured it out. Hallelujah.

"I know. Finally, she saw the light. Caught him flirting with the waitress when they were out to dinner, which would have been bad enough, but when he disappeared to the bathroom for a little too long and she went looking for him—"

"Let me guess, she walked in on them in the back hall with his hand up the waitress' skirt," Evers said dryly.

I shrugged a shoulder. "Close enough. The waitress smacked him — apparently, she had better asshole radar then Julie — and then Julie kicked him in the nuts and walked out."

"Good for her," Evers said.

That was the thing about Evers. He was a player and a flirt, but he was honest about it. He'd never once made me a promise he couldn't keep. Never once implied that he could give me more and let me down.

He was a player, but he wasn't a liar.

That was the only reason I could make this crazy arrangement work. Well, that and the sex.

The sex was amazing.

Fucking fantastic.

Fantastic fucking.

Hell, however you wanted to put it, getting in bed with Evers Sinclair was worth the dangerous game we were playing.

I was going to end up getting hurt eventually. I knew it, but I couldn't seem to stop myself. He was dangerous, but he was Evers.

Just like the second piece of chocolate cake. I kept telling myself *only one more bite* and found myself going back for more.

Over and over.

Eventually, I was going to work up the willpower to give him up completely.

Eventually. But not tonight.

I picked up my purse from the kitchen counter, removing lip gloss, wallet, and emergency cash, transferring them to the small black purse that matched my dress.

"Julie's finally past the sappy movie and ice cream stage and she wants to go out. Get dressed up, you know, have a little fun and discover a new, post-Frank world."

"And you're playing wing-woman?" Evers asked, taking another pull on the beer, his eyes lingering on the short hem of my dress.

"Something like that," I said, the trail of his gaze heating my skin. I found myself wondering if I could bail. I wasn't the only one going out with Julie and—no.

No.

I was not bailing on a girlfriend for Evers.

No way.

This was Julie's night. Ditching her for hot sex, even stupendously, amazingly hot sex, was not cool. I pressed my thighs together, willing my body to stand down.

I swear, one look at Evers and my hormones leapt into overdrive.

He took another pull on the beer and didn't say anything. Something in the line of his neck, the tilt of his jaw made me think he didn't like the idea of me being Julie's wing-woman.

I fought back the urge to make an excuse, to explain that I wasn't going to pick anybody up, I was just there to support a friend.

It wasn't any of his business what I did.

That wasn't what we were.

I didn't know what the hell we were, but I knew it wasn't that. It wasn't explanations and promises.

It was moments of time.

It was the present, not the future.

I knew that. So, why did I find myself saying, "I won't be late. If you want to hang out, I have leftover Chinese in the fridge from last night. Orange beef, your favorite, and some egg rolls. You can eat dinner, watch the game until I get home."

My stomach lurched.

Why did I say that? Evers had never been in my apartment without me. He'd never spent the night. We'd fallen asleep together, too exhausted to move after a marathon of sex, muscles wrung out, nerves fried with pleasure, but in the morning, he was always gone.

So why had I offered him my leftover take-out, my couch, and my TV? And why did he look relieved?

My phone chimed with a text. Julie, downstairs waiting. I didn't have time to figure out the mystery of Evers Sinclair.

"That's Julie. I've got to run. Do you want to stay?"

Evers set his beer on the counter and prowled toward me, cool blue eyes intent on mine. "Come here," he growled, reaching out to pull me into his arms. His mouth landed on my neck just below my ear, sending sparks through every nerve in my body.

Evers could play my body like an instrument, and he did. Moving his lips down the cord of my neck, his strong arms absorbed my shivers, his leg nudging between mine, hand dropping to cup my ass, urging me closer until I ground against him, shuddering under his mouth, the caress of his lips, the heat of his tongue on my skin.

Lifting his mouth, he nipped my earlobe before whispering, his breath hot in my ear, "Have fun. Stay out of trouble. When you get back I'll fuck you until you can't walk."

I thought *promises, promises,* but the words remained unspoken, short-circuiting between my brain and my mouth. All I could do was gasp as his teeth nipped my jaw and his mouth fell on mine.

Evers Sinclair knew how to kiss. Like, he *really* knew how to kiss. I wrapped my arms around his neck and held on for dear life, his lips opening mine, tongue stroking, his hands everywhere.

A heartbeat later I was flushed with heat, hips rolling into his, every inch of me wound tight.

Desperate. For him.

My phone chimed again, the high-pitched sound cutting through the haze. Reluctantly, I eased away, sliding my hips out of his grip, dropping my hands from his neck, breaking the contact between our mouths last.

I had to go.

I had to go, but I didn't want to end that kiss.

I already knew I was a mess, hair all over the place, cheeks flushed, lip gloss smeared across my cheek.

I didn't expect the flags of red on Evers' cheekbones, the tight set of his jaw, the glitter in his eyes. His hands flexed at his sides as if he wanted to reach out. To drag me back.

On shaky legs, I stepped away, hiding the roil of my emotions, lust, and want. Longing.

"I have to go," I said inanely. He already knew I had to go. Why wasn't I leaving?

"Go then. I'll be here when you get back."

His words sounded suspiciously like a promise. They weren't, I told myself as I considered going in for one more kiss, then thought better of it.

If I kissed him again, I'd never leave my apartment and Julie was waiting.

Grabbing my purse, I headed for the door without another word. Standing at the elevator, I lectured myself.

Be sensible.

This is Evers Sinclair.

He might get bored and wander off before you even get home.

Don't count on him being there.

Don't count on him for anything.

I warned myself, but I didn't listen. I never had where Evers was concerned.

I still had no idea what I was doing with him. We were a total mismatch.

From the moment we'd met we hadn't gotten along.

He was bossy, autocratic, arrogant, and an incorrigible flirt. Evers wasn't my type in so many ways. I favored serious guys, usually cute, but not hot. Guys with normal jobs and normal lives.

I sound exciting, don't I? But that's the thing, I'm not exciting. I'm a perfectly normal girl with a normal life. A least I was, until the day Evers swept in and turned my life upside down.

I was at a conference in Houston, kind of bored, kind of having fun, looking forward to the weekend when I was expecting a visit from my best friend, Emma.

Evers had appeared out of nowhere, claiming that Emma was in danger and she needed my help. If I'd heard that line from anyone else I would have laughed him out of town. Especially since he refused to tell me what the trouble was or how she needed my help.

I'd known, the way best friends always know, that Emma was involved in something, but that didn't mean I trusted Evers. Still, I'd gone with him, all the way to Atlanta, bickering the whole way.

I couldn't help myself. He was so high-handed. He strolled in and expected me to do his bidding just because he said so.

It hadn't helped that every time I looked at him, my knees went weak.

Back then he'd worn his hair short, almost military short, and it left every inch of that chiseled face on display, from his dark brows to his ice blue eyes, his sharp cheek-bones and full lower lip.

His face is enough to make a girl swoon. His body kicks the whole package up a notch. I didn't have to see beneath the suits to know that Evers Sinclair was sex on a stick.

So out of my league.

So very much out of my league. We'd bickered and flirted and that had been it.

That had been it until Emma's wedding.

A little too much champagne, an argument over the

wedding cake, and before I knew it I was backed into a wall behind an arrangement of potted plants, Evers' hand on my ass under my bridesmaid's dress.

I could blame the champagne for falling into bed with Evers, but that would be a flat-out lie. It had nothing to do with the champagne and everything to do with Evers Sinclair.

Damn, that man knew how to use his hands. And his mouth. And everything else.

We'd spent Emma's wedding night locked up in my hotel room. And the night after. And the night after that.

Then I'd flown home, he'd left town on a job, and I wrote off Evers Sinclair as a wedding insanity mistake.

Maybe not a mistake.

It's hard to call sex that good a mistake.

And what's wrong with having a fling every once in a while? Every girl should have a fling. I was a serial dater. I didn't fling. One-night stands seemed like too much work for not enough payoff.

With Evers, it was all payoff and no work. When I bumped into him again a year later at a party I'd arranged for a client, my body went on full alert the second my eyes met his.

I'd convinced myself I'd forgotten Evers, but my body had not. Not for one red-hot second.

Evers has his own gravity, a magnetic pull that drew me across the room, demanding my attention even when I was in the middle of a demanding job. At the end of the night, he'd been there, lounging against my car, waiting.

I'd invited him home, we fell into bed, and our non-relationship was born.

He showed up every once in a while, knocking on my door with no notice, and I always let him in. Every once in a while, I'd text and he'd come. I never been to his place, wasn't exactly sure where he lived. Somewhere in Atlanta.

I was in Marietta, northwest of the city. Close enough that we could've seen each other more often, but neither of us offered or asked for more.

I didn't ask because I knew I wouldn't get it, and Evers because he didn't do more. More wasn't his thing.

Julie was waiting in front of my building, the car running, music blaring through the open windows. She was ready to party, but she didn't miss a thing. A grin bloomed on her face when she saw me. I snapped my seatbelt into place as she said, "Your lip gloss is smudged."

"I still have lip gloss?" I lifted a hand to wipe my lips. I'd be shocked if Evers hadn't kissed every speck off my lips. I pressed my knees together at the thought.

Down girl, tonight it's not about you. Not until you get home. If he's still there.

Julie stared at me for just a minute before her eyes flared wide and she glanced at my building. "Is he up there? Did he come by tonight?"

She thought my weird thing with Evers Sinclair was the stuff of daytime soap operas or fairytales. Evers Sinclair of the Atlanta Sinclairs. She imagined he'd fall in love with me and we'd live happily ever after in a little mansion in Buckhead.

I gave a mental snort. Not likely.

I couldn't see Evers settling down, and if he did, it wouldn't be with someone like me. Someone normal. Average.

He'd find some society princess or a former model. An actress. Somebody with flash. With flair. Someone exciting enough to fit into his life.

Evers Sinclair came from a long line of Atlanta Sinclairs

who, a few generations back, had founded the premier security agency in the country.

They protected royalty. Celebrities.

Designed security systems that put Fort Knox to shame.

He was James Bond come to life, from the perfectly tailored suit to the Aston Martin. I wasn't the first to get caught in his orbit and I wouldn't be the last. I was just enjoying the ride while it lasted.

I shook my head at Julie. "He's up there, but don't worry about it. Tonight is about you."

Julie hesitated before putting the car in gear. "Are you sure? I mean, we can go out any night. He hasn't come by in a few weeks, and—"

"I'm sure," I insisted, irritated that even Julie thought the world should stop for Evers Sinclair. "If he wanted to know if I was free, he could have called. He shows up, he takes what he gets. Tonight is for you. He can wait."

Julie leaned over and threw her arms around me in an awkward hug, considering our seatbelts. "You're the best friend, Summer. Most girls would have ditched me for a hottie like Evers Sinclair."

My libido bitched at me when I said, "I'm not most girls, and he'll be there when I get home."

I hoped.

I really, really hoped he'd be there when I got home.

I tried to throw myself into girls' night out. I did. I hadn't lied, tonight was important. Julie needed her friends and some fun.

I did my best. I had a drink. I flirted with a guy down the bar who Julie thought was cute and lured him in so she could give him her shy, sweet smile.

Julie was a catch. Pretty, smart, easy-going, fun. Good job.

She'd settled for Frank, but she hadn't had to. She was going to find a good guy. I knew it. Maybe not tonight, but eventually.

It was closing in on ten, Julie and the other girls diving into a round of shots, when Julie leaned over, nudged me, and said, "Go home."

"No, I'm having fun, I swear, I—"

Julie rolled her eyes. "You're not having fun. You're a sweetheart and I love you for being here, but go home. Somebody should have amazing sex tonight and it's not going to be me."

"You don't know that," I protested. Though, I did know that. We both did. Julie may have been four drinks and two shots into the night, but she'd never picked up a guy in a bar and I didn't think she was going to start now.

"I'm not," she affirmed, "and we both know it. I'm getting get drunk, Steph can drive me home, or we'll get a rideshare and I'll pick-up my car tomorrow. Go home. He might not be back for a few weeks or a month and I'm not going to be responsible for you not getting any. You get cranky when you go without."

She wasn't wrong. "Are you sure? I don't want to bail on you."

"You're not bailing, you idiot. I would have dropped you in a heartbeat if he'd been waiting in my apartment."

"Liar." Julie never would have dropped me for a guy. Friends first. "If you're sure," I mumbled, already pulling up the rideshare app on my phone.

I rode home in an aging sedan, staring blindly out the window, trying not to squirm in my seat as I imagined all the things I wanted to do to Evers when I got there.

He would have stripped off the suit coat. Loosened his tie. I wanted to slip the buttons of his shirt free, one by one.

Push it off his shoulders and down his arms, baring all his smooth skin.

Trace every line of muscle on his chest down to his abs.

Slide his belt from the buckle...

I pressed my knees together, the heat between my legs already out of control.

He always did this to me. So fucking hot.

Half a lifetime passed before I slid my key in the lock and opened my door, so ready to jump him that if he'd been in the foyer, I would have had him on the floor.

Instead, my apartment was quiet but for the murmur of an announcer's voice coming from my living room. The end of the game was on, the volume low, the room dark but for the flicker of the television light.

Evers lay stretched out on the couch, feet propped on the arm, fast asleep. He looked almost boyish with his eyes closed, his hair mussed, his smirk of a smile wiped away.

I reached out to brush his hair from his forehead, a rush of tenderness taking me by surprise. Snatching my hand back, I stared down at him in horror.

I could not feel tenderness towards Evers Sinclair.

Tenderness wasn't lust.

Tenderness was feelings. I could not have feelings for Evers.

I had feelings about *sex* with Evers, sure.

Great feelings.

Amazing feelings.

But that was it. I did not feel tenderness for *him*.

I did not want to lay down on the couch next to him and trace my finger along his lower lip, stroke my hand down his back and cuddle into his warmth.

No, I wanted to wake him up, strip him naked and have sex with him.

That was it. Sex.

Having feelings for Evers was a recipe for a broken heart, and I was keeping mine in one piece.

I turned my back on him, needing to get my bearings. Seeing him so defenseless in sleep had caught me off guard. I couldn't afford to be off guard with Evers.

This thing between us only worked because I followed the rules I'd set up with myself from the beginning.

No making more of it than it was.

No expectations.

No demands.

No feelings.

Quietly making my way to the kitchen, I set my purse on the counter, looking around for my key ring. I'd removed my door key earlier, but if I didn't put it back on the ring, I'd lose it. I finally spotted my jacket on the chair by the front door and remembered I'd tossed there when I'd come home in a rush to get ready.

Evers' briefcase sat on top, the zipper half open. He must have done some work while he was waiting. I picked it up to grab my jacket and the handle slipped through my fingers, the jacket and bag spilling to the floor.

Maybe that last round of drinks had hit me harder than I thought. I felt giddy, not tipsy. Definitely not drunk, but the mess at my feet said different.

I dropped to my knees to put everything back. It wasn't too bad, only a few files, a pen, and a half-eaten bag of sunflower seeds.

I slid the first two folders in the briefcase, barely glancing at them, when the third folder caught my eye. Neatly typed on the label were the words *Smoky W*.

Smoky W.

My heart skipped a beat.

Smoky W. was my father's name.

Why would Evers have a file with my father's name on it?

I sat back on my heels and stared down at the bland manila folder, mind racing. My father's given name was Clive Winters, but everybody called him Smoky.

He and my mom were hard-core hippies, had been forever, and you can probably guess why my dad was called Smoky.

He was a big believer in the spiritual and medicinal benefits of marijuana and partook regularly. He hadn't been the most reliable of parents. Smokey Winters was a man-child—irresponsible, immature, but full of love.

If I'm being honest, I don't know if I could say he was a good dad, but he'd always loved me.

I hadn't seen him as much as usual lately. He and my mom split a few years ago—she wasn't a stoner hippy, she was an energetic activist hippy and she'd grown tired of being the only adult in her marriage.

I love them both to pieces, but I hadn't given my mom a hard time about leaving my dad. I got it. Boy, did I get it. I loved him, too, but I wouldn't want to be his wife either.

Since the divorce, he hadn't been around much, and lately, he'd been... Off. Weird.

Tense.

Smokey Winters was never tense. He was chemically incapable of being tense. He made sure of it.

I'd been meaning to call him, sit down and see what was up, but I had a few new clients, work had been crazy, and I hadn't gotten around to it.

Why did Evers have a folder with my father's name on it?

What the hell was going on?

Feeling absolutely no shame at invading his privacy, I opened the folder and flipped through the pages, my heart turning to ice at what I saw.

Reports on me.

Reports going back all the way to Emma's wedding.

Reports on my father starting six months after the wedding and continuing regularly until a week before. Reports on his movements and activities. Comments on me. What I was doing. Where I'd been. Reports on my clients.

I didn't understand most of it. It was written in code, almost all of the relevant language abbreviated so that it meant nothing to me. Based on the dates I could decipher a few.

1.26.18 Su.W. ctc Sm.W. Cl mt Atl. Su.W. Il 2d. Sm.W. mt B

January 26, 2018. I'd called my Dad on the way to a client meeting in Atlanta before I flew to Illinois for two days to assist another client. I only remembered because I'd had a flat tire on the way to the airport and come close to missing my flight.

Since my client was meeting me there, and she was deathly afraid of flying, the flat tire had caused an avalanche of problems. I'd handled it. I always did. Handling things was what I did best, but the day was etched in my memory as one for the record books. The day from hell.

And Evers had been watching, documenting the whole thing. While I'd been standing on the side of the road, freezing my ass off, splattered by ice as cars flew by, he'd been there. Somewhere. Watching me.

I had no idea what Sm.W. mt B meant. Sm.W. was my father. Based on Su.W. mt Atl, I thought mt stood for meeting. B? No idea. Not that it mattered. My dad's life wasn't my problem.

I flipped through more of the file. Page after page of cryptic notes. Me, my father. A few on my mother, spanning over two years.

The ice in my heart turned to nausea. I remembered Emma and how she met her husband, Evers' brother Axel. Emma had been a job. Axel was investigating her on behalf of a client for suspected embezzlement. She'd been innocent, but that wasn't the point.

She'd been a job.

Just like me.

I was a job. My mouth watered and, abruptly, I realized that I was going to vomit. Moving as if trapped in molasses, I set the folder on the floor and rose, walking deliberately to the bathroom, then racing as my mouth flooded and my stomach hitched.

I hit my knees in front of the toilet and threw up a night's worth of frothy drinks and shots, everything inside me turned upside down, inside out, body heaving as my head spun.

I sat there for what felt like a year, my clammy forehead braced on my arm, leaning over the toilet, my mouth sour, breath shallow, heart racing.

I couldn't get my bearings.

I should have known. I should have known it was a lie.

I'd had the good sense to keep my distance from him. I thought it was because he was a player. A flirt. I didn't want to fall for him and get my heart broken.

The stab in my chest told me I'd fucked it all up.

I hadn't kept myself safe at all because my heart was breaking anyway.

I hadn't even known it could. Not over Evers.

I'd tried so hard to keep him at a distance. I thought I could keep my heart safe if it was only sex. I thought I was protecting myself. He couldn't break me if I didn't let him. Wrong. I was an idiot and he was a liar.

I thought I knew him. I thought I was in control.

Seeing the last two years in black and white, I'd been so blind. He'd been watching me, chronicling my every move and reporting it to... Who? Why? Why was he investigating me and my father? None of this made any sense.

I hadn't done anything. I couldn't imagine my father had, either. He didn't have enough motivation to do anything. There was nothing in my life that justified this kind of invasion.

I worked, had fun with my friends, and for a while I had an affair with Evers.

He was the most exciting thing to happen to me in years. And he was a lie. He was a fucking lie. He wasn't here for me. He was here for a job.

Not anymore.

Not for another second.

Mechanically, I stood, leaned over the sink and turned on the water to brush my teeth. When I was done, I set my toothbrush back in its holder. Flushed the toilet. Washed my hands. Replaced my father's file back in the briefcase beside the others. Zipped it closed.

I left it on the floor and went to wake Evers.

Every step to the living room fell like lead. I stood over Evers, fists clenched at my side, staring down at him. His eyes flashed open and warmed, a sleepy grin spreading across his face.

It halted abruptly as he took in my expression.

"Hey, babe, what's wrong?"

"Get. Out." I couldn't bring myself to say any more than that. Couldn't trust myself not to choke on the words, was desperately afraid the tears prickling the back of my eyes would spill down my cheeks.

I would not cry in front of Evers. No fucking way. He'd lied to me. He'd used me. Fine, that was done. I'd been a fool, but I didn't have to let him see me cry. He already knew he'd lied to me. He didn't need to know he'd hurt me.

Evers rolled to his feet, instantly in command of his body, of the room, of everything.

I stepped back and repeated myself.

"Get. Out."

"Summer, babe, what's wrong? Did something happen?"

I wasn't playing this game anymore. Flirty, mischievous Evers wasn't going to cajole me out of my mood to get what he wanted. Forget that.

"I saw my father's file in your bag. I know you've been watching me this whole time. I don't know what you want. I don't know why you're here. But get out. Do your job somewhere else."

His face went utterly blank. Most people would jump straight to defensiveness, making excuses or accusing me of snooping.

Not Evers. A wall went down behind his eyes, his jaw set, and he straightened his shoulders.

"Summer, if you give me a minute, I can explain."

The flirtation was gone, the glint in his eye extinguished.

This wasn't charming Evers, this was Evers on the job. Hard. Cool. Detached. This was what he hid beneath the smooth veneer. What he hid from me.

"Can you?" I demanded. "Can you explain lying to me for a year? Watching me? Taking notes on everything I do? Is there anything you can say that makes that okay?"

We locked eyes, Evers' ice blue assessing, analyzing. He

was flirty and sexy, but behind that façade, he was a cold-blooded machine. I knew it. I'd always known it.

I'd fooled myself into thinking he left the machine at the door when he was with me. I'd been wrong.

"Summer," he started, "it's complicated."

"Just tell me one thing, Evers. At Emma's wedding, was that premeditated?"

"No. Absolutely not."

That was something. I would have bet anything our first hook up had been an accident. A collision of lust and champagne resulting in two spectacular days in his hotel room.

I already knew the answer to my next question. "And last year? At my client's party?"

A muscle flickered in the side of Evers' jaw before he admitted, "I knew you'd be there."

"So it was a setup. This whole thing is a setup."

The muscle flickered again. He nodded.

My heart squeezed, and I blinked hard. Tears pressed the back of my eyes. My nose tickled. I had about a minute before I lost it.

I felt it coming, the wave of anger and pain rising too fast for me to hold it back.

I couldn't talk to him anymore. I wouldn't. There was nothing he could say to justify this.

He wasn't my boyfriend. This wasn't real.

It was convenient sex, and it was over. Turning my back on him, I walked a few steps down the hall to his briefcase, still on the floor where I'd left it. Scooping it up with one hand, I turned for the door.

Evers' hand closed over my elbow, stopping me in my tracks. With a jerk, I pulled free, reaching the door with him a pace behind. I swung it open and tossed his briefcase into the hall.

"Get. Out. I don't care what you have to say. Leave. This is over. Get your information some other way."

"Summer, at least let me explain."

"What is there to say? Are you going to tell me why you're investigating me? Are you going to tell me whose job this is? Why you're really here?"

Evers stared me down, his silence my answer.

"That's what I thought. Don't come back."

I watched him leave, briefcase in hand, his long, smooth stride carrying him to the elevator without a hitch.

If I'd known how soon he'd be back, I wouldn't have thrown him out the door.

I would have shoved him out the window.

Click Here for more of Unraveled

ALSO BY IVY LAYNE

Don't Miss Out on New Releases, Exclusive Giveaways, and More!!

Join Ivy's Readers Group @ ivylayne.com/readers-group

THE UNTANGLED SERIES

Unraveled (October 2018)

Undone (Winter 2019)

Uncovered (Spring 2019)

SCANDALS OF THE BAD BOY BILLIONAIRES

The Billionaire's Secret Heart (Novella)

The Billionaire's Secret Love (Novella)

The Billionaire's Pet

The Billionaire's Promise

The Rebel Billionaire

The Billionaire's Secret Kiss (Novella)

The Billionaire's Angel

Engaging the Billionaire

Compromising the Billionaire

The Counterfeit Billionaire

Series Extras: ivylayne.com/extras

THE ALPHA BILLIONAIRE CLUB

The Wedding Rescue

The Courtship Maneuver

The Temptation Trap

ABOUT IVY LAYNE

Ivy Layne has had her nose stuck in a book since she first learned to decipher the English language. Sometime in her early teens, she stumbled across her first Romance, and the die was cast. Though she pretended to pay attention to her creative writing professors, she dreamed of writing steamy romance instead of literary fiction. These days, she's neck deep in alpha heroes and the smart, sexy women who love them.

Married to her very own alpha hero (who rubs her back after a long day of typing, but also leaves his socks on the floor). Ivy lives in the mountains of North Carolina where she and her other half are having a blast raising two energetic little boys. Aside from her family, Ivy's greatest loves are coffee and chocolate, preferably together.

VISIT IVY
Facebook.com/AuthorIvyLayne
Instagram.com/authorivylayne/
www.ivylayne.com
books@ivylayne.com

Made in the USA
Monee, IL
28 April 2022

95585086R00167